I0780658

A Dream in Tonopah

G.K. Montilla

A Dream in Tonopah

G.K. Montilla

Table of Contents

Dedication

To those who have endured violence within the walls that
should have sheltered them—
May your pain find release, your wounds find healing, and
your spirit find strength.
Though the world has shown you cruelty, may you discover
deep kindness, a greater resilience, and the courage to rise
beyond what was done to you. But most of all, I pray you
find love. Love that heals, love that cleanses, love that
nurtures you, a love that will guide you.
This book is for you, a reminder that even in brokenness,
there is hope, even in suffering, there is power to persevere
and become whole again.
You are wonderful, you are amazing, you are precious…

Chapter 1: Hidden Talents

A gentle breeze blows the sheer curtains of an open living room window, knocking a plastic cup off the antique dinner table. The cup falls off the table, spilling drops of grape juice onto an old, tattered rug below as it lands. The breeze comes in again, pushing the curtains all the way up to the ceiling, and revealing a beautiful Sonoran landscape outside. A postcard of Saguaro cacti, desert flowers, palo verde trees, red mountains in the distance, and a bright blue sky above. Birds can be heard chirping nearby. One of them lands on the windowsill, chirps as it looks around, then flies away.

The green living room is decorated with very old furniture, hand-me-downs from grandparents, possibly; they have too much detail and dust to be appreciated today. Pictures on the wall depict a beautiful and happy interracial family of three: mother, father, and a beautiful baby girl. The pictures show the family together on a journey from the birth of the baby until she is about ten years old; from then on, the pictures only show the girl and her father.

From the other room, we hear a teen's voice; she's talking on the phone with someone, she's in the kitchen.

"Ok, ok…I understand. Mrs. Walter. Yes, I will let him know!" Says Chloe.

Chloe Borgia, now grown up, sits at the kitchen table in front of a laptop computer. The kitchen is pretty small, with yellow flowered wallpaper on the walls, white linoleum floors, light brown cabinets, and an open window above a sink filled with dirty dishes. Mountains can be seen in the distance, and a large open sky above.

Chloe is beautiful, she has caramel skin and very long curly brown hair with light brown eyes. She navigates a website on her laptop with one hand while talking on the phone with the other. She has schoolbooks and textbooks on the table, right beside some small makeshift model homes.

> "Don't worry about it, Mrs. Walter, I'll tell my dad to head over to your house right away…Yeah, I sure will… he's at Mr. Sander's right now, and you're next!" Says Chloe

Chloe looks at her phone and hangs up the call. She looks at her computer screen, then begins to type. A light breeze enters the room through the window, and she hears chirping. Chloe turns and sees a desert finch sitting on top of the dirty dishes, looking at her.

> "There you are…" Says Chloe.

She picks up a box of crackers from the table, takes one out, and crumbles it in her hand. Looking and smiling at the little bird, she stands and places the crumbs on the other end of the table and quickly sits back down. The little finch flies over to the table and begins to peck at the crumbs. Chloe smiles, picks up her phone, and dials. Chloe's dad answers the phone on the other side.

"Dad? Ok, so after you're done at Mr. Sanchez's, you need to head over to Mrs. Walter's place. Well, she said her water heater is not working again. It's an electric one. I don't know… I hope it's plugged in. I didn't ask, I guess you'll find out when you get there. Hold on a sec…"

Chloe hangs up and looks over at the bird, who is already looking at her, chirping, having finished the cracker. Chloe stands up, gets another cracker, and crumbles it in her hand as she walks to the back door in the kitchen. She opens the back door and holds her hand out to the bird. The finch flies and rests on her thumb as it begins to eat the crumbs. Chloe pets it as she steps out to her backyard.

Chloe walks to her patio area, a bird in one hand and a phone in the other. Behind her, the small home is dwarfed by the large open Sonoran Desert and the mountains behind it. Chloe looks up at the bright blue sky and smiles as she puts the phone back up to her ear and says.

"Yeah, I was looking at the University website just a few minutes ago. No, I haven't applied yet, but I will… I promise, I still have time. And Dad, we seriously need to do something about your website. People should be able to place appointments on it, and give us their address, and… No, it's not ok, it sucks, dad!! Ha, ha, it's over twenty years old. Yeah, I can help you with it. Okay, don't forget Mrs. Walter's water heater…love you, bye."

Chloe hangs up the phone with one hand as she continues to watch the bird feed from the other. A gentle breeze comes through again, and it slightly picks her hair up. She closes her eyes and enjoys the moment.

Meanwhile, on the other side of that phone call, her dad, Anthony Borgia, is still trying to put his cell phone away in the holder. He finally gives up and drops it in his back pocket. Anthony is a medium-built guy, almost six feet tall, fair-skinned with dark brown hair and hazel eyes. Standing in the front yard of Jose's house, covered in sweat, he has opened a pipe that leads to the main sewage line. He looks around, then calls out to Jose,

"Jose! Jose, come out here, man!" Says Anthony.

Anthony looks at his handiwork, the large trench he dug up, and the open pipe before him. He sees that everything is ready for him to explain to his client.

"Jose! C'mon, man!" Anthony yells.

The side door of the house slowly opens and out comes Jose. Holding a beer in one hand and puffing on a cigar with the other, he slowly makes his way down the driveway of the one-story home. As he walks past his large blue truck, he blows a kiss at it and smiles. Anthony shakes his head as Jose finally makes his way toward him and stands beside him.

"Wssup amigo…you fix it yet?" Asks Jose

Anthony gestures for Jose to come closer to the pipe he's opened up and says,

"I'm about to, I wanted to show you the problem real quick."

Jose slowly walks closer, stops, and takes a sip of his beer.

"C'mon, man, I gotta hurry this up, I've got Mrs. Walter next, problem with the water heater." Says Anthony.

Jose gets closer, takes a puff from his cigar, and says,

"Mrs. Walter's water heater…"

Anthony jumps into the trench, reaches into the open pipe, and says,

"Look what I found in your main, you know the single drain that goes out to the city…"

Jose looks intently and nods with anticipation. Anthony reaches in deeper and pulls out a handful of used condoms. He throws them in the front yard, reaches in and gets another handful, and another and another.

"Wha…what the fu…" says Jose with a trembling voice.

"Look it's ok man…ha, ha, ha. I'm not saying stop making love to your wife, but after I clean this up, put the rubbers in the garbage, ok. 'Cause there's A…LOT more in there for me to dig out."

Jose's countenance changes to shock and stoicism, his eyes are glazed over, and he has turned pale.

"Hey, man! It's ok, you don't have to be embarrassed! It's not gonna be that much to fix, you're my friend and I'll give you a break, ok?" Says Anthony.

Jose does not respond, but his lower jaw begins to slightly move as a long line of saliva begins to fall from his lip as he looks at the rubbers.

"Hey, you're freaking me out, man. It's just a learning moment for you…" says Anthony.

Jose slowly looks up at Anthony and says,

"I just got back from a two-week run…I never wear rubbers…"

Anthony looks over at Jose and says,

"Oh no…"

In the meantime, back at the Borgia house, Chloe sits on a chair from their old patio set in the backyard, rocking back and forth while she continues to pet the little bird perched on her hand. The patio set sits on a large piece of artificial turf in the middle of the large backyard, made up of desert landscaping surrounded by chain-link fencing. She looks up to the sky and sees large cumulus clouds coming from behind the mountain tops. She hears a rattle on the chain-linked fence, and when she looks, she sees a cat that hit the fence coming from the large shed at the end of the property. The cat begins to make its way to Chloe, and the little bird in her hand flies away. The cat sees the bird and sits down on the turf. Chloe talks to the cat,

"See what you did…"

The two look at each other for a moment. Chloe looks down at her feet and takes her sandals off. She wiggles her toes, and the cat immediately goes into hunting mode, crouching down. The cat slowly approaches the wiggling toes, then attacks! He grabs her left foot, bites her large toe, and begins to kick her heel with his hind legs. Chloe laughs, leans forward, and picks up the cat and puts it on her lap.

"Come here, you crazy cat!" She says.

Chloe tickles and plays with the cat

"Chloe! Chloe!" Mrs. June calls out to her.

Chloe turns and looks over to the large prefabricated home sitting on the lot beside her home. Mrs. June, an elderly black lady, stands in front of it holding her right hand up, waving at her. Mrs. June is retired, lives alone, with only her cat Gilbert to keep her company. She's well respected and active in her community and the Christian Church she attends.

Chloe sees Mrs. June and smiles at her, then quickly holds up the cat over her head.

"Here he is!" Says Chloe.

Mrs. June smiles with relief and places her hands on her heart. Chloe gets up and walks over to the chain-linked fence dividing their properties. Mrs. June stands there smiling, a bit overdressed for the Sonoran Desert, wearing a beautiful long blue dress with white flowers, and a fake white rose in her hair. Mrs. June's home seems small compared to the size of her property, all of it desert landscape. She reaches over the fence, and Chloe gives her the cat.

"Here you go. You know, you have five times the amount of land that we do, but he just loves to go behind our shed for some reason, ha, ha." Says Chloe.

"Thank you, honey… I know, he's probably hunting for bugs back there…" says Mrs. June.

Chloe looks at Mrs. June, she takes a good up and down look, and says,

"Now, Mrs. June…I've never seen you in that dress before! It's beautiful!!

Mrs. June smiles and slightly spins from one side to the other, showing off the dress as she smiles.

"One of these mornings, ya'll gonna come looking for me and guess what?" Asks Mrs. June.

"What?" Asks Chloe.

"I'll be gone! Home with the Lord!" Says Mrs. June.

"Mrs. June, stop talking like that!" Says Chloe.

"It's true! And when you do find my body, I'll be ready for burial." Says Mrs. June.

Chloe chuckles and shakes her head. Mrs. June smiles and humors Chloe for a few seconds. Then she becomes serious, the smile wiped from her face, she leans over to Chloe, and Chloe leans in as well, expecting her to say something.

"What?" Asks Chloe.

"Honey, go ahead and apply, you're getting in."
Says Mrs. June.

"Wha…" asks Chloe, but Mrs. June quickly says,

"University! Stop straddling the fence and apply already!"

"How could you possibly know that!" Asks Chloe.

"Just promise me you'll put that application in, baby, you're supposed to become an architect, I just know it!" Say, Mrs. June.

"That's the dream, Mrs. June…" says Chloe.

Mrs. June takes Chloe's hand and touches the tip of her nose with the other and says,

"No baby…That's your future."

Chloe smiles, reaches over, and pets Gilbert.

"Who's gonna take care of my dad? How's he gonna manage his business alone?" Chloe asks.

"He'll be fine, he managed before, and he will manage again." Says Mrs. June.

Chloe takes a deep breath and slightly shakes her head, looks down, and says,

"Yeah…I know."

Mrs. June lifts Chloe's head with her index finger and says,

"Do it."

Chloe nods and says,

"I will…promise."

Mrs. June nods in approval and smiles. Chloe pats her on the shoulder and says,

"Ok, Mrs. June, let me get in the house and log in to my school site. I gotta take some finals today."

"Ok, honey, go on now." Says Mrs. June.

Chloe begins to walk back to her house, then she looks back and asks,

"Let me know if you need anything, ok?"

Mrs. June waves and says,

"I won't bother you; you go on."

Chloe reaches the back door of her house, turns around, smiles at Mrs. June, and goes inside.

Later in the day, Anthony and Jose sit in the back corner booth of the local taqueria, sitting on the same lot as the local truck stop. Anthony's back is against the window, giving him a full view of the whole restaurant. The gas station outside is very busy, with trucks coming in and out of the station right outside. The restaurant inside is packed with people waiting to be seated by the front doors and waitresses running from one place to the other, taking orders and bringing out large plates of food from the kitchen.

Jose holds his head with both of his hands, elbows on the table, and has not touched his food. Anthony eats his tacos, but his eyes are transfixed on something in the restaurant.

"I can't believe it…so many rubbers, how many men had my wife man? It must have been hundreds…hundreds!" Says Jose.

"Could just be, ahh… one man," Anthony says, then takes another bite of the taco in his hand.

Jose looks up at Anthony and says,

"It doesn't make it any better, man!"

Anthony takes a sip from his beer and says,

"Actually, there is a difference."

Perplexed, Jose puts his hands down on his lap and stares at Anthony with puppy eyes.

"Let me explain…" Says Anthony as he puts the taco down, and readies himself to elaborate his point of view.

"So if your wife is having sex with all different types of men, we can maybe assume one of two things. A, that she's a nymphomaniac and you're not enough to satisfy her. Or B, she's prostituting on the side." Says Anthony

Jose starts hitting his head in frustration and says,

"No, man. Noooo, it can't be!"

"Well, we don't know anything at this point, we're just speculating, right? I personally don't think she's prostituting."

Jose puts his hands on the table and erratically moves his fingers.

"Is there another option?" Jose asks.

Anthony raises his eyebrows and takes another bite of his taco, as Jose anxiously watches him. Anthony finishes, takes a sip of his beer, and says,

"Well, option C is a worst-case scenario…"

Jose balls his hands into fists and says,

"What could be worse than hundreds of sausages in my wife's man!"

Anthony points to Jose's quesadilla, and Jose nods. Anthony picks one off Jose's plate and says,

"It could be that she's in love with someone else."

"What!" Says Jose as he watches Anthony take a bite of his quesadilla.

Anthony swallows his food and says,

"She could be madly in love with another man."

"Oh god!" Says Jose.

"You know, she invites him over to the house when you're not home and brings her presents. They make fun of you, laugh and make passionate love afterwards." Says Anthony.

Jose puts his hands down on the table, looks at Anthony intensely, and says,

"I saw her wearing some new clothes the other day, and she had a diamond bracelet. I don't remember giving that to her."

Anthony reaches for another quesadilla on Jose's plate and says,

"They cuddle and drink liquor after sex, and they probably do it multiple times per visit."

"I came back yesterday and saw that all my tequila was gone…I had two bottles before I left for my two-week delivery run!" Says Jose.

Anthony nods in affirmation as he chews. He holds his index finger up, takes another sip of his beer, and says,

"There's also option D, and this one is bad."

Jose, clearly distressed, takes the glass of water in front of him and violently drinks it all.

"It could be a minor." Says Anthony.

"Oh…hell no!" Says Jose

"One of those punk ass skateboarder kids around the trailer park!" Says Anthony.

"I'll kill 'em…I'll kill 'em, Anthony!" Says Jose

Anthony takes a sip of his beer, wipes his mouth, and says,

"But maybe, just…maybe…"
Jose grabs the fork and knife in front of him and squeezes until his knuckles turn white and says,

"Stop it…stop it"

"Maybe it's a trans girl, you know, the ones that have a penis." Says Anthony.

Jose shakes his head and says,

"Noooooo! Why?"

"Well, she can go under the radar a lot easier that way. They go shopping together, have lunch together, hang out…everyone thinks they're friends. Until they get to your bedroom, and she parks the bus in your wife's garage, if you know what I mean." Says Anthony.

Jose grabs his head and begins to rock back and forth as he pulls on his hair. Anthony reaches out and puts his hand on Jose's shoulder to try and keep him from rocking back and forth. Anthony says,

"She obviously has a bigger bus than you, those rubbers were definitely magnums…"

Jose claws his face and cries out,

"Aaaaaaaaaagh!!"

Anthony reaches over and pulls Jose's hands away from his face and says,

"But you can't come to any conclusions yet."

"After everything you just said!" Says Jose.

Anthony places Jose's hands flat on the table and says,

"You need to talk to her and find out what's really going on."

"How…" says Jose.

"Just ask her about the rubbers," Anthony says.

"I don't know if I can." Says Jose.

"It's not optional at this point…" says Anthony.

Anthony looks over Jose's shoulder and into the restaurant, and his eyes suddenly widen. He sees something he likes. Jose notices, turns around, and sees a very large waitress approaching their table. Anthony is taken aback by her and blushes. Jose turns around and notices, then looks back at the mountain of a woman coming towards them.

The waitress stops in front of their table and smiles. She stands just a few inches below the ceiling lamps, the face of a supermodel, but very muscular with long blonde hair tied up in a ponytail and bright green eyes. The tight yellow t-shirt shows off her broad shoulders and bulging biceps; the blue apron she wears is dwarfed by the thickness of her muscular thighs, exposed by her jean shorts. Anthony, completely captivated, looks her up and down, smiling. She notices and smiles.

"Hey guys, my name is Tatyana, your waitress just quit, so I'll be taking care of you for the rest of your stay." Says Tatyana.

Both men nod without saying a word.

"So, is there anything I can get you?" Asks Tatyana.

Jose points to what remains of his quesadilla. And says,

"I'm not gonna finish this, can I get a box or something?"

"Sure, I'll bring out a box for you, and you?" Asks Tatyana as she looks over to Anthony, who is still mystified by her.

Tatyana points to his empty beer bottle and asks,

"Can I bring you another beer?"

Anthony, as if in a trance, continues to look at this beautifully built woman. Jose and Tatyana look at him as he smiles and takes her in with his eyes.

"Sweetheart…need another drink?" Asks Tatyana again as she slightly stoops to get his attention. Finally, Anthony reacts. He looks down at his empty beer bottle, then he looks into her eyes and says,

"Yes…yes, please. I'm sorry, ha"

"Be right back, fellas!" Says Tatyana with a big smile, loving the attention.

Tatyana slowly walks away, checking on the other tables as she passes them. She gets to the kitchen door, ducks down to enter, and disappears as she enters the kitchen.

Jose excitedly jumps up and down in his seat. Anthony continues to look at the door through which Tatyana disappeared through. Jose taps on the table to get Anthony's attention, but Anthony does not budge until Jose finally says,

"Hey!"

Anthony turns and looks at Jose, who is smiling with excitement.

"I know her! I know her, Anthony!" Says Jose.

"You know her?" Asks Anthony.

Jose smiles wider and says,

"Yes!" Says Jose.

"Who is she?" Asks Anthony.

Jose raises his hands and gestures as if showcasing a name in lights, and says in the voice of an announcer,

"That's 'La Muerte Rusa!'"

Anthony does not understand and asks,

"La what?"

Jose puts his hands down in disbelief and says,

"La Muerte Rusa! She was a wrestler…Back in the day, Lucha Libre was my thing, man! You, you never heard of her?"

"No." Says Anthony.

"Well, I saw her a lot when I lived in Texas. She was up and coming back then; she was one of the bad guys in the ring, or bad girl, I guess, ha, ha.

Man, I loved to see her wrestle! There was a lucha libre circuit; they traveled all over the southwest and into Mexico. They went town to town, hitting bars, fairs, all types of events, all kinda places! My cousins and I would go see the matches all the time! I loved it…I still love it!" Said Jose.

Anthony looks back at the kitchen door and says,

"Wrestler, really?"

"Yeah! She was a badass. She would even wrestle some of the guys sometimes, and kick their asses too, he, he, he."

The kitchen door swings open, and Anthony immediately looks up to see Tatyana. Jose looks directly at Anthony, smiling, watching his eyes. Tatyana walks into the dining area with a styrofoam container and a cold beer bottle. Anthony gets a really good look at her now, her broad shoulders, muscular arms bulging, and thunder thighs as they tighten and release with every step she takes towards him. She looks at Anthony, intrigued by the way he's looking at her. She gets to the table and is about to place the beer in front of Anthony as she smiles at him.

"I know you!" Says Jose with excitement.

Tatyana quickly turns to Jose and asks,

"Do you now?"

"La Muerte Rusa!" Jose yells out, causing Tatyana to knock the beer bottle over, spilling beer everywhere.

Tatyana quickly grabs a small towel from her apron and begins to clean the spill.

> "I'm so sorry! I'll bring you out another one right away!" Says Tatyana as she wipes the table.

Anthony looks at her muscular arms as she quickly cleans up the spill, transfixed, watching as the muscles contract.

> "I just hadn't heard that name in such a long time." Says Tatyana as she finishes up and looks at Jose. Then says to him,

> "How do you know me? I haven't done anything under that name in almost fifteen years!"

Jose's eyes lit up like a little kid, and he said,

> "I'm a big fan! I loved watching you body slam those other wrestlers. The way you threw the men around the ring like little dolls was awesome! You were a badass! A badass, man! La Muerte Rusa! Right in front of me! I can't believe it, it's like a dream!"

Tatyana smiles ear to ear now, takes a seat right beside Jose, and puts her gigantic arm around him. Anthony and Jose look like children sitting with an adult as Tatyana sits a foot and a half taller than they, her back wider than the two of them up together.

> "So you're a fan, really?" Asks Tatyana.

> "I'm your biggest fan! Wow…you look exactly the same, actually, you look more muscular now! I got all your t-shirts, the towel, the white sunglasses…I

even have the sweatshirt with the skull and the blade thing, you know that blade." Says Jose.

"The skull and sickle, yeah, yeah, ha, ha, ha!" Says Tatyana.

Anthony is amused, smiling as he listens. Tatyana looks over at him and winks; there's an obvious chemistry developing between them.

"I always wondered what happened to you…" Says Jose as he realizes she's not paying attention to him anymore, but locking eyes with Anthony.

Jose taps her on her shoulder for a few seconds, and she snaps out of it, looking back at him as she wipes the sweat from her forehead.

"Why did you stop?" Asks Jose.

Tatyana pats Jose's head and says,

"I got pregnant, the father didn't want to help me with anything really, he just disappeared. So, I had to take time off to take care of my baby. One month turned into a year, and it was hard to get back into it. I needed something steady where I didn't have to travel. I've done a lot of personal training, security work, even construction, but I never did go back to wrestling, though I've thought about it many, many times."

Tatyana then flexes her free arm, showing her enormous bulging bicep, and says,

"Still work out though, almost every day."

The guys smile and nod at Tatyana, impressed really by her musculature.

"Damn, man!" Says Jose.

Anthony can't help himself; he reaches out to touch her arm with both hands. Tatyana loves it and flexes even more as he cups her bicep. Anthony looks over at Jose, who is staring at him wide-eyed, realizes what he is doing, and pulls his hands away quickly. Tatyana is amused; she can tell by the way Anthony looks at her that he really likes her.

"So yeah…I've been keeping busy at least," Says Tatyana.

"And, ah, what brings you around these parts?" Asks Anthony.

Tatyana points to the mountains clearly visible through the windows and says,

> "I fell in love with Arizona back during my wrestling days. We would come to Phoenix for a few nights, then pass through these parts on our way to California. After moving a few times in the past few years, I decided to come out here for good, you know?"

> "We haven't seen you before, so you probably just got here. You got a place to stay?" Asks Jose.

Tatyana points to the kitchen and says,

> "Well, I've been here for a few days, and Jimmy, the owner of this place is letting me and my son rent one of the rooms in the back for now. But I'm

looking for something better, maybe a bit bigger, you know?"

Jose points to Anthony and says,

"Anthony has a nice place for rent!"

"Wha…" says Anthony, in complete shock as he looks over at Tatyana, staring at him with a pleasant smile.

"Really? Can you tell me a bit more?" Asks Tatyana.

Anthony, nervous now, swallows before saying,

"Well…. It's actually a large RV garage that I renovated and set up as a rental apartment. It's a one-bedroom, but it's got its own living room and dining space, decent-sized kitchen, and a new A/C unit."

"Hey, that sounds pretty good!" Says Tatyana.

Suddenly, the kitchen door slams open, and this little old greaseball of a man comes out. No more than five feet tall, the little white man with slicked black hair and a white t-shirt stuck to his body from sweat, quickly looks around the dining area until he sees Tatyana. He raises his hands and yells,

"Tatyana! Tatyana! Some people need to be seated, sweetheart! What are you doing, baby?"

Tatyana turns around and looks at the old man and quickly stands up. She fixes her apron and says,

"I'm sorry, boys, this was nice, but I gotta get back to work. That's Jimmy, so I gotta go. But hey, if you're interested in renting, let me know because I really am looking for a new place!"

Jimmy looks, smiles at the customers by the door, then he turns to Tatyana and loudly says,

"Are you spoon-feeding them? C'mon, I need your help over here!"

Tatyana pats Anthony on the chest and smiles, puts their bill down, and walks away.

"I'm coming, Jimmy, I'm coming for crying out loud!" Tatyana says.

Jose and Anthony both watch as Tatyana walks away from them, reaches the front door, and begins to usher the new guests into the restaurant. They both look at each other and smile.

"That is a big girl!" Says Anthony.

"I know you liked her," Says Jose.

Anthony smiles, then asks,

"Hey, what was I supposed to be doing?

"Mrs. Walter's water heater." Says Jose

"Yes…Mrs. Walter's water heater." Replies Anthony.

CHAPTER 2: A DREAM WITHIN A DREAM

The Night After Meeting Tatyana

Warmly lit bedroom with soft pink walls holding white shelves filled with books, stuffed animals, and a few model homes. A large wooden desk sits in the corner, loaded with model-making materials and a few house models that are partially built. The night sky is clearly visible through the open windows facing the back yard, and a warm breeze pushes the drapes onto the bed where Chloe lies. Wearing an oversized t-shirt and pajama pants, Chloe moves from one side of the bed to the other as she works on her laptop. Hip-Hop blasting from the large earphones she wears, she is completely focused on what she's doing. She then smiles, picks up her head, looks over at her bedroom door, and yells,

> "I know you're there, Dad!"

Anthony pokes his head out from the hallway and into Chloe's bedroom. Chloe takes the earphones off and smiles.

> "How could you possibly know I was here? You couldn't have heard me with that music blasting in your ears!" Anthony says.

> "I felt you coming in the house a few minutes ago…" Says Chloe.

Chloe gets up and starts to walk towards her dad.

"I told you to stop wearing those earphones when you're alone in this house." Says Anthony.

Chloe reaches the doorway and hugs her father. Anthony picks her up and walks into her bedroom, puts her down, gives her a kiss on the cheek, and smiles. Chloe pats his cheek, runs over to the other side of the bed, and jumps on her bed.

"You… forgot about Mrs. Walters' dad!"

Anthony sits in the chair by her desk and says,

"I know, I know. Jose got some pretty bad news, and I felt bad for him. I didn't want to leave him alone because he was so messed up, and I completely lost track of time."

"Yeah, she called like three times, her garage flooded, I could hear her parakeet laughing at her in the background, she was crying, and I couldn't get a hold of you." Says Chloe.

Anthony takes a deep breath and says,

"I took care of her, I replaced the water heater, helped her clean up the water on the floor, gave her a nice discount, and everything."

"And the talking bird?" Asks Chloe.

"He sang 'Beat It' by MJ the whole time I was there." Says Anthony.

"Well, she must have been happy with you because she gave you a great review online!" Says Chloe as she picks up her laptop off the bed and brings it closer to her.

Chloe smiles at her dad, and he smiles back, then nods at her laptop.

"What are you working on?" Asks Anthony.

Chloe opens the laptop, turns it around, and shows Anthony a 3D rendering of a house blueprint. Anthony is surprised and says,

"That looks awesome! WOW! So I have to ask you now…did you apply?"

Chloe takes the laptop, closes it, and throws it on the bed. She lies down on the bed and folds her arms.

"Dad, if I go to College, you'll be completely alone here. Who's gonna help you?" Asks Chloe.

Anthony grabs Chloe's foot and softly moves it back and forth while he smiles and looks at her.

"I will be just fine, baby doll… why are you worrying about me?"

Chloe slams he arms on the bed and says,

"Who's going to help you with the business? Who's going to take your calls? You were supposed to build your own shop, and if I go, you'll be way behind schedule!"

Anthony grabs her foot again to get her attention and says,

"Chloe, you want to be an architect, and the only way you will ever be one is by going to school. Plus, I'm expecting you to make the blueprints for my dream office, so you have to go to college!"

Chloe looks at her dad dead in the eyes and softly smiles. Anthony smiles back at her and says,

"I'll be fine…"

Chloe jumps up and gives her father a big hug; he hugs her back. Chloe then sits back on the other side of the bed, picks up her laptop, and continues to work. Anthony stands up, walks over to the door, and looks back at Chloe, concentrating on her work. She looks up at him and says,

"You have three appointments in Phoenix tomorrow. Check your phone, I already sent you the information. I love you dad, Good night!"

"Thank you, good night, baby doll." Says Anthony and walks out, Chloe puts her headphones back on.

Early next morning, Chloe moves about in the kitchen, she places the last of the clean plates on a drain mat, and heads over to the table. Anthony walks into the kitchen and plants a kiss on Chloe's head. He heads over to the coffee machine and starts loading it with coffee grinds.

"You want some coffee?" Asks Anthony.

A rooster is heard crowing in the distance, and a few rays of sunshine begin to pierce through the top of the mountains in the distance and through the open kitchen window.

"I would loooove some coffee. I put your lunch in your cooler and packed you an extra water bottle. It's gonna be hot, so make sure you drink it!" Says Chloe

Anthony turns around and looks at the cooler sitting at the end of the table.

"Well, thank you. Hey, do you want some pancakes? I was going to make some pancakes this morning." Says Anthony.

"There's a breakfast sandwich in the microwave I already heated up for you."

Anthony goes to the microwave under one of the kitchen cabinets, opens it, and takes the sandwich out. He picks up his cooler from the table.

"Thank you, honey, you have class today? Asks Anthony as he points to her laptop.

"Yeah, just getting ready for a History exam later today." Says Chloe.

"Okay, I won't bother you, have a good day!" Says Anthony as he kisses Chloe on the top of her head, and she pats him on the back.

Anthony exits through the kitchen door, and as soon as he closes the door, Chloe looks back at the coffee pot being filled with coffee.

"You forgot your coffee…" she whispers, then turns around and hits play on a history video on her laptop.

Chloe watches the video for a few minutes, then pauses. Something is troubling her, and she can't concentrate; she looks at the window on top of the kitchen sink. Concerned, she stands up and walks over to the window to look outside. It's a beautiful morning out there, the sun is coming up over the mountains, creating a beautiful sunrise of pinks and yellows as its light hits the clouds above. Desert birds sing and fly from one tree to another, one of them flies right over Anthony as he heads up the driveway towards his truck at the end of it. She then sees Mrs. June walking really fast behind him, trying to catch up to him. Mrs. June sees Chloe at the window, quickly waves, then continues after Anthony.

Outside on the driveway, Mrs. June calls out to Anthony.

"Anthony! Anthony!" Says Mrs. June.

Anthony turns around and sees Mrs. June coming up to him, very disturbed by something. He glances over to the window and sees Chloe looking at them from inside.

"Anthony, I had a very disturbing dream, and I really believe it's a warning!" Says Mrs. June."

"Mrs. June! Hi…what are you talking about?" Asks Anthony.

Mrs. June grabs Anthony's arm and says,

"Let me tell you, you have to pay attention." Says Mrs. June.

"Dad, Listen!" Yells Chloe from inside as she leans out the window.

Mrs. June turns to look at Chloe, nods, then looks intensely at Anthony.

"What is it, Mrs. June?" Says Anthony.

Mrs. June grabs Anthony by the arms and says,

> "I had a dream last night… I saw a beautiful meadow, green grass, beautiful trees; it was a beautiful sunny day, and you were standing on a mound. Then, slowly, a beautiful white horse came up to you out of nowhere. You were surprised, but glad to see the horse, and you began to pet the horse. You loved that horse, and that horse loved you. Then you jumped on top of it and began to ride the horse through the fields. You and the horse were happy together."

"That's not that bad," says Anthony, but Mrs. June shakes her head and continues.

> "But without you knowing, the heart of the horse became spoiled with greed, deceit, and the lust for power. And the horse transformed into a gigantic lion, or lioness, it had no mane. The wild cat began to devour everything in sight: the trees, the pond, the hills, everything! You tried to appease it, but you couldn't. You chased the lioness and tried to find something of the relationship you had with it, but its hunger for something more could not be quenched, then he came." Says Mrs. June.

"Who came?" Asks Anthony.

"The man dressed in black, a very evil man, it could have been the devil himself. He showed up at a moment when you were not looking. He showed the lioness a magic mirror made of gold and jewels, and a reflection of a promise of fame and glory. The lioness' heart filled with pride, and she ate the mirror and again transformed. But this time, she transformed into a gigantic red dragon. Everything around the dragon turned to fire, and then it devoured you. It killed you, Anthony, and destroyed everything you love!" Said Mrs. June

Anthony and Chloe looked on, speechless; they just stared at Mrs. June in silence for a minute. The awkward silence is broken by the sound of a pick-up truck stopping at the end of the driveway. A white Ford pick-up truck parks right in front of the house, and everyone looks, including Chloe, who opens up the curtains to see better. Anthony then turns to Mrs. June and says,

"I...I don't know what to say, Mrs. June, that sounds like a crazy dream to me..."

Anthony pats Mrs. June on her arm and begins to walk away as he says,

"I have to get going, but you have a good day, Mrs. June."

Mrs. June waves at Anthony as he walks down the driveway and says,

"You be careful, Anthony!"

Mrs. June turns to Chloe, she looks very distraught about the way Anthony brushed her off. She blows Chloe a kiss and walks away, back to her home. Chloe continues to watch her father as he walks down the driveway and is curious as to who is in the truck that just arrived.

The truck's door swings open and out comes Tatyana, standing almost two feet taller than the roof of the truck. She turns, smiles at Anthony, and closes her truck door. She walks around the front of the truck and onto the front yard. Wearing a long white see-through sundress, she waves and smiles at Anthony as he walks up the driveway towards her. Tatyana brushes her long, wavy blonde hair from her face as a light breeze comes through and slightly picks her dress up. Her one-strap sundress reveals large, muscular shoulders that glisten in the morning sunlight.

Anthony waves back, surprised by the visit, and makes his way quickly towards her and shakes her hand.

Chloe leans way out the window to see who it is, and her jaw drops when she sees Tatyana and what she's wearing.

"Who is this Amazon with the one-inch nipples?" She whispers to herself.

Tatyana straightens out her dress and says,

"Hi"

Anthony tries to muster some words, but is stunned by the see-through dress and the fact that she's not wearing a bra.

"I, I hope you don't mind, I came to see the place you're renting." Says Tatyana.

"How…" says Anthony.

"Oh, your friend left me your information on the receipt yesterday…at the diner? I hope. You don't mind." Says Tatyana.

Anthony looks a bit bewildered, Tatyana asks,

"I'm sorry, is this a good time?"

"Ugh, yeah…sorry, yeah, now is a good time, of course! C'mon back, it's the RV garage back there, let me show it to you." Says Anthony as he catches himself and politely smiles, pointing to the RV garage in the back of his property.

"Ok, good," Says Tatyana as she smiles widely, charming Anthony with her glance.

Anthony gestures with his hand for Tatyana to walk in front of him. Tatyana smiles and proceeds to walk towards the back of the property. She passes Chloe, who is staring at her through the window. Tatyana waves and smiles at her. Chloe smiles and nods. Walking behind her, Anthony gets a really good look at her large, muscular back, and his eyes widen. He looks over at Chloe, who is looking at him through the window. She mouths 'Who is that', Anthony shrugs his shoulders and points to the RV garage.

Tatyana reaches the RV door, turns around, and smiles. As she does, Anthony gets a strong scent of her perfume; she smells like strawberries and flowers.

"This is a really nice place you have here, Anthony, so much open land all around. And this RV garage is huge, what is this two stories high?" She says.

Anthony walks up to the door to unlock it, but Tatyana does not move out of the way. Anthony has to brush up against her to insert the key, he says,

"Yeah, it's pretty big, so people can fit their large motor homes…you know"

Tatyana looks at Anthony in the eyes and says,

"Of course.."

Anthony leans back as he struggles with the door and touches her breast with his shoulder.

"Sorry." Says Anthony.

"That's okay, I'm a big girl, I know." Says Tatyana as she pats his shoulder.

"Nothing wrong with big." Says Anthony as he looks at Tatyana while fidgeting with the keys.

Tatyana looks him in the eyes and smiles warmly. Anthony's eyes are locked into hers. He finally unlocks the door, and it slams open into the garage.
Tatyana enters the garage first, her head almost touching the top of the door frame as she ducks down to get through. Anthony looks at the top of the door frame, enters, and closes the door. He turns the lights on to reveal a very large two-story RV garage transformed into a really nice apartment with a loft upstairs, turned into a bedroom, and a kitchen and living room downstairs. Everything looks new, clean, and up-to-date. Tatyana walks into the kitchen, reaches up to touch the ceiling, and says,

"This is bigger than I thought… this is nice!"

Anthony nods in approval and begins to talk about the apartment. He says,

> "The bathroom is through that door over there. Everything is new, I just remodeled it. The appliances are new as well. The thermostat is in the living room, and the unit has its own air conditioner around the back. The large couch over there comes with it, but I can remove it if you don't want it."

"No, leave the couch, I love it." Says Tatyana.

Tatyana walks around the apartment, opening cabinet doors, touching the countertop, she opens the fridge door, looks over at Anthony, and gives him a big smile.

> "Everything looks new. Has anyone ever lived here?" Says Tatyana as she walks over to the living room.

> "No, you would be the first; everything is brand new." Says Anthony.

Tatyana walks over to the large black leather couch in the middle of the living room and sits down. She extends her arms out and is able to reach both ends of the couch. She sits with her legs open, the dress drapes between her legs. Anthony's eyes are locked into hers as he says,

> "The…there's satellite TV, included in the rent."

> "How much do you want a month?" Asks Tatyana.

Anthony pauses for a second as he stares at the giantess sitting on the couch in front of him. He is terrified and excited at the same time.

"Twelve hundred a month…There's a one-month deposit as well, just to cover damages." He says.

"I have a fourteen-year-old son, is that ok?" Asks Tatyana.

"Yeah…yeah, that'll be fine. The bedroom upstairs is big enough to fit two beds, or this couch opens up and turns into a bed, so…" Says Anthony as a bead of sweat falls from his brow.

Tatyana smiles widely and says,

"Excellent!"

Suddenly, Chloe enters the room and surprises the two. Anthony straightens up, and Tatyana crosses her legs and folds her hands on her lap. Chloe looks at the two for a second and says,

"Hello."

Anthony turns to Chloe and says,

"Hi, honey."

Tatyana stands, walks over to Chloe, shakes her hand, and says,

"Hi, I'm Tatyana."

"Chloe." Says Chloe.

Tatyana takes Chloe in with her eyes, the long curly hair, the mocha-colored skin, the light brown eyes, and says,

"Well, hello Chloe, you sure are a beautiful girl."

Chloe smiles, and Anthony goes and stands next to her.

"This is my daughter," Anthony says.

Tatyana looks at Chloe and says,

"Your mom must be very proud."

"She's dead." Says Chloe

Tatyana is taken aback for a second, Anthony looks a Chloe, not believing how she just said that.

"Sorry about that…. yeah, she passed away some years ago," Says Anthony.

"I'm sorry to hear that." Says Tatyana.

Anthony nods and watches as Chloe walks right beside Tatyana and looks up at her.

"How tall are you?" Chloe asks.

"Chloe, that's not polite!" Says Anthony.

 Tatyana is amused, looks at Anthony, and says,

"That's ok, I get it all the time, I'm seven feet tall."

Chloe moves Tatyana's light blonde hair and places it behind her shoulder, exposing more of her face and jawline, and says,

"Wow…And you're really pretty. Some of those tall chicks are really manly looking, their faces look like a train wreck, but you…But you have the face of an angel."

Tatyana covers her mouth and says,

"That is so nice of you to say, honey! You're making me blush over here!"

Chloe puts both of her hands around one of Tatyana's biceps, and she can't get both hands around it; her arms are so big.

"Look at these arms! You're like a Greek Goddess, an Amazon from the old world!" Says Chloe as she rubs Tatyana's arm.

Tatyana loves the attention; she smiles and flexes her bicep, then her tricep, as Chloe is mesmerized by the movement of her muscles.

"Ah, ok, Chloe, come on, that's enough," Says Anthony.

But Chloe does not listen; she moves over to Tatyana's back and begins to glide her hands along her trapezoids. Tatyana moves her hair so Chloe can get a better feel.

"You are glorious, you have more muscles than a racehorse…Are you on steroids?" Asks Chloe.

Anthony gets embarrassed and quickly grabs Chloe and pulls her back to him.

"I'm sorry, I'm so sorry about that. I don't know what's gotten into this girl." Says Anthony as he looks at Chloe with anger and continues to say,

"What is wrong with you? She's here on business!"

Tatyana steps forward and interrupts Anthony by putting her hand on his shoulder. She looks over at Chloe and says,

"It's ok if you want to know…Yes, I do take them, along with other supplements. It's not like the old days; steroids are not taboo like they used to be. I would never be this big without them, ha, ha."

Tatyana caresses Chloe's cheek and winks. Chloe smiles. Anthony watches the interaction between them as he walks over to the fridge and gets three water bottles. He watches closely, and the girls continue to look at each other as he brings the water bottles back to them. Tatyana takes a bottle, and so does Chloe.

"Thank you." Says Tatyana.

Anthony takes a sip of his water, then asks,

"So what do you think? Did you want to look upstairs?"

Tatyana looks around for a few seconds, then says,

"No need, I love it!"

"Really?" Asks Anthony.

"Yeah! I need a new place, and I need it now. This is perfect." Says Tatyana.

Anthony claps his hands with excitement and says,

> "Great! If you give me an email address, I'll send you the lease agreement today. You can give me a check, or electronic PayPal, or whatever you're comfortable with…"

> "Sounds good."Says Tatyana, and quickly pulls her cell phone from her dress pocket, and begins to type, and says,

> "All right, I'm texting it to you now, and I'll bring cash by later today."

Tatyana finishes typing and looks over at Anthony, who is a bit confused. Tatyana smiles and says,

> "Your friend Jose wrote your phone number down on the receipt as well."

> "Ah, Jose…" Says Anthony.

DING!

Anthony looks down at his phone and says,

> "Got it."

Tatyana takes a last look at the place, then looks at Anthony, who has his hand out to her. She quickly takes his hand and shakes it.

> "Thank you, " Says Tatyana. Anthony nods.

Tatyana looks over at Chloe and says,

> "By sweetie."

"Bye..." Says Chloe.

Anthony and Chloe watch as Tatyana walks over to the door, her dress like a wedding train flowing behind her. Tatyana opens the door, looks back at Anthony and Chloe, and asks,

"I forgot to mention, my son is gay, is that going to be a problem?"

Anthony and Chloe shake their heads at the same time.

"No..." says Anthony,

"Of course not..." Says Chloe.

Tatyana smiles and exits, slowly closing the door behind her. Anthony and Chloe look at the shut door for a moment, then look at each other.

"What do you think?" Asks Anthony.

"She seems nice...Aaaaand I saw the way you were looking at her! There was definitely something going on between you two!" Says Chloe as she laughs.

Anthony blushes, he smiles, and says,

"Stop it."

Chloe jokingly pushes Anthony and says,

"I can tell she likes you...but she'll break you in half, Dad!"

"I can handle myself." Says Anthony.

Chloe points to the door, shakes her head, and says,

"Not with that…ok!"

The two walk out of the apartment and step out to their backyard, both of them laughing up a storm. As they walk towards the driveway, they both notice Mrs. June sitting on her patio chair, looking at them with a somber face as she pets her cat. Chloe and Anthony walk up to the fence dividing their properties. They are going to greet their neighbor, but before they could say anything, Mrs. June spoke,

"Anthony, you've been warned."

Antony smiles and shakes his head, not really getting what Mrs. June is saying.

"What?" Says Chloe.

Chloe, a bit confused, realizes she missed something and looks over to her dad, then to Mrs. June, trying to understand what's going on. Mrs. June picks up her cup of coffee, takes a sip, points the cup at Anthony, and says,

"You've been warned, Anthony…"

Anthony smiles, grabs the fence, and leans into Mrs. June's yard, saying,

"I hear you, Mrs. June, and thank you for sharing your dream with me… have a good day, I have to go to work now. Chloe, I'll call you later, ok?"

Anthony smiles and walks away, heading to the driveway, whispering to himself,

"White horse, a lion, and a dragon…really?"

As Anthony turns the outside corner of the house and heads down the driveway, Mrs. June realizes that he is not taking the warning seriously. She walks up to the fence and stands right up against it, and puts her hand on Chloe's shoulder.

"Lord have mercy…" Says Mrs. June

Chloe looks over at Mrs. June, concerned because Mrs. June has been a good friend of the family, and Chloe values her word.

"What's going on, Mrs. June?" Asks Chloe.

Mrs. June walks over to her chair and sits down.

"Did you hear me telling your father the dream God gave me?"

Chloe walks to the gate a few feet away and enters Mrs. June's yard. She goes and sits right next to her and says,

"Well, I heard most of it."

Mrs. June takes a sip of her coffee, then says,

"Dreams can mean a lot of things sometimes; they may have multiple interpretations. But not this one, I know the dream I had was a warning for your father. But Anthony is not listening. That woman may seem harmless now, but she's deadly…"

"Really? Mrs. June, she's just a bodybuilder looking for a place to live with her son." Chloe says.

Mrs. June turns and looks Chloe in the eyes and says,

"Not what's on the outside, that's the problem, it's what's in her heart. If your father gets entangled with her, he'll regret it."

Chloe looks at Mrs. June, concerned about her father's welfare, and says,

"Then I'm gonna have to convince him not to let her move in, Mrs. June…and that's it!"

Chapter 3: The Mare

A Week After Mrs. June's Dream

It's a beautiful sunny morning, the sun is high in the sky, and there's not a cloud to be seen. A warm desert breeze passes through, making the trees slightly sway. There's a lot going on in the Borgia household this morning. Tatyana's truck is parked at the end of the driveway, filled with boxes, plastic containers, and all sorts of luggage. Wearing high white shorts, a white bikini top, and flip flops, Tatyana squats down to pick up a large box sitting on the driveway by her truck. Her large, muscular thighs seem to explode as her muscles flex when she stands up with the box. She begins to carry the box up the driveway, hair tied up in a ponytail, wearing sunglasses and a large smile, and she chews on a piece of bubblegum.

As she reaches the backyard, Chloe comes out of her house, runs up to Tatyana, and asks,

"Need some help?"

Tatyana blows a bubble with her chewing gum, collapses it, and says,

"No, we're ok gorgeous…"

Chloe nods, then turns to look at Tatyana's truck. Someone is moving around in there.

"That's my son Daniel." Says Tatyana.

Tatyana turns to face her truck and yells out,

"Daniel!"

A boy looks up from the backseat of her truck and waves.

"Daniel! Come here, son!" Yells Tatyana.

The teen jumps out of the truck, smiling, and he runs towards the girls wearing a red bikini top and jean shorts. Daniel trips over his sandals as he runs, recovers, then stands next to Tatyana as if nothing happened. He puts his hand on his mom's lower back and stares at Chloe. He's a good-looking boy, with blond hair, deep green eyes, and thick, heavy eyebrows. Tatyana looks at him and asks,

"Is that my bikini top?"

Daniel smiles and poses for her.

"Ask me next time, I don't mind sharing…just ask." Says Tatyana

Daniel nods, adjusts his pose, and smiles.

"Give me a kiss, princess." Says Tatyana to Daniel. She puckers her lips to him, Daniel gives his mom a quick kiss on the lips and says,

"Love ya!"

Tatyana looks over at Chloe with a big smile and says,

"Chloe, this is Daniel. Daniel, please say hello to Chloe."

The two teens look at each other and smile.

"Hi Chloe." Says Daniel.

"Hi, Daniel." Says Chloe.

Tatyana hands the box she's holding to her son and says,

"Take this into the house, Danny."

Daniel nods and walks away with the box. Chloe and Tatyana watch as Daniel enters the apartment. He closes the door, and they look at each other at the same time.

"You sure I can't help with anything?" Asks Chloe.

Tatyana puts her hand on Chloe's cheek, squeezes it, and says,

"We're good, honey. I'm sure you have other things to do. Aren't you supposed to be in school right now?"

"I go to high school online, I'm finished for today though." Replies Chloe.

Tatyana puts her hands on her hips, looks into Chloe's eyes, almost as if she were looking for something in them.

"It's a different world today…" Tatyana says as she continues to search in Chloe's eyes.

Tatyana adjusts her bikini top and sees that Chloe is paying close attention.

"Well, I'm planning to go to college in the fall, and I definitely want to actually go there, I mean, to the building, stay in a dorm, you know, not online.” Says Chloe.

Tatyana reaches into the front of her pants and adjusts her crotch, and sees Chloe blushing. That’s exactly the reaction Tatyana was looking for; she quickly takes her hand out and puts it on her hip.

“I get it, where are you going? Asks Tatyana.

Chloe swallows and looks up at Tatyana, who is smiling warmly at her.

“I’ve been thinking ASU, but I haven’t applied yet…” Says Chloe.

“Why, why haven’t you applied?” Asks Tatyana.

“I don’t know, just afraid of rejection, I guess.” Replies Chloe.

Tatyana shakes her head, smiles, and puts her hand on Chloe’s shoulder.

“I have some contacts at the admissions office at ASU.” Says Tatyana.

Chloe’s eyes widen with excitement.

“Go ahead and apply, and then I’ll make some phone calls for you. At the very least, it will get some eyes on your application.” Says Tatyana.

Chloe jumps up and down with excitement, hugs Tatyana, gives her a kiss on the cheek, and runs into her house.

"Thank you, thank you, thank you!" Says Chloe as she runs away.

Tatyana smiles as she watches Chloe run with joy, and does not see Daniel coming up behind her. He snaps his mother's bikini strap and says,

"Don't mess with her…she's nice."

Tatyana lightly taps Daniel in the groin, and he bends over forward as if in pain. Tatyana pushes him and says as she walks back towards her truck,

"Stop it, I hardly touched it…" Says Tatyana, then begins to walk away.

Daniel stands up straight, looks at his mother as she walks away from him, and flips his mother off. Tatyana, now a ways down the driveway, raises her hand, then her middle finger back at him without looking back. Daniel is stunned; he whispers.

"How…how did she know?"

Daniel watches his mom as she walks all the way down the driveway to her truck, shakes his head, and gets back to work.

A Month after Tatyana Moves In

Tatyana and her son are getting settled into their new home. Anthony has decided to throw a party to welcome Tatyana to their neighborhood and introduce her to some of his friends. It' a Saturday evening and the sun is setting in the distance behind a beautiful purple mountain range. Purple, red, and pink clouds cover the sky as the last rays of light hit them from below. On the opposite side of the sky, the stars are beginning to shine through.

Anthony's backyard is loaded with people. String lights run from the house to the RV and to the trees in the backyard. There is a big sign on the RV garage with large letters saying 'Welcome La Muerte Rusa!' Foldable chairs and tables are set up and sporadically placed throughout the backyard. There are portable coolers and large garbage cans filled with ice and drinks against Anthony's house wall. At the end of the yard is a small makeshift stage with large speakers and a karaoke setup. A drunk middle-aged red-headed woman sings as a large group of rowdy people sing along with her, everyone with a drink in their hand.

Anthony stands in front of his deluxe six-foot stainless steel grill flipping burgers as he talks to Jose.

Chloe comes out of the house holding a few bottles of soda pop. She's struggling as she tries to hug the bottles and not drop them while coming down the back staircase. Daniel comes out from within the crowd of people standing around, runs up to her, and eases her load as he takes a few bottles off her hands. Chloe warmly smiles and says,

"Thank you, sir!"

"You are most welcome." Says Daniel as he accompanies her to the coolers.

The teens excitedly put all the drinks into the ice-filled coolers by the house, turn around, and take in the party as they bop to the music. They see people walking around with drinks, people laughing, others sitting in groups at tables talking, and everyone is having a great time. Through the large crowd, Chloe catches a glimpse of Mrs. June on the other side of the fence. Chloe begins to make her way over to her, Daniel sees her leaving, and follows her as she weaves in and out of the crowd. When they get to the chain link fence, they stand right up against it and look at Mrs. June, as she is sitting on a rocking chair rocking back and forth, looking up at the sky as she pets her cat.

> "Mrs. June, Mrs. June! I didn't know you were back! How was your trip?" Asks Chloe as she crosses through the gate dividing the two yards, runs to Mrs June, and gives her a big hug.

Mrs. June hugs her back, smiles, and says,

> "It was so nice seeing my grandchildren, family, and such. Sometimes one month is not enough, ha, ha. But I'm glad to be back here with you."

> "Well, come on over and get something to eat!" Says Chloe.

Mrs. June looks over to the kids and smiles, then looks back up at the sky and says,

"Ain't it beautiful!! Just look at God's handy work…"

Chloe and Daniel look up and gaze at the sky; an innumerable number of stars can now be seen up in the sky, with traces of the Milky Way in the distance.

"Yes, it is…" Says Chloe.

"WOW…It sure is beautiful, never seen it like this!" Says Daniel.

The teens look back down and see that Mrs.June is smiling at them.

"Your daddy already brought me a hamburger, honey. Thank you." Says Mrs. June.

'Why don't you come over?" Asks Chloe.

"Baby, I'm right here, I can see all of you, hear all of you, I got some delicious food, and I get to hear bad singing, ha, ha, ha!"

The teens laugh right alongside Mrs. June as she playfully waves them away with her hands.

"Don't worry about me, I'll be just fine."

"Alright then, Mrs. June, if you need anything, you just let me know, ok? You can even call me, you got my number." Says Chloe as she holds her cell phone up and shows it to Mrs. June, who is shaking her head and smiling.

"You can call me, too, Mrs. June. I'd be glad to help you!" Says Daniel

Chloe realizes she has not introduced the two, slapping her forehead, she says,

> "I'm so sorry, Mrs. June… this is Daniel, he's
> Tatyana's son, they moved in a few weeks ago. And
> Daniel, this is Mrs. June, she's our neighbor, but
> more like our mother, and a really close friend of
> the family."

> "Hi Daniel, what a beautiful soul you are." Says
> Mrs. June.

Mrs. June gives Daniel an endearing smile. Daniel is touched by the gesture and smiles back. He gets a warm feeling inside from Mrs. June's words; they feel genuine to him, and his immediate desire is to go and give her a hug. Something inside him tells him that she is a loving person, and love is something Daniel has had very little of; his soul yearns for it.

Across the backyard, Tatyana opens the door to her apartment and comes out wearing tight red shorts, a little black tank top, high pumps, and blood red lipstick; her long blonde hair is rolled up into hair horns. The first thing she sees as she steps out of her threshold is Chloe and Daniel all the way on the other side of the yard, as they talk and laugh with Mrs. June. Tatiana looks stoic as she sees her son laughing and carrying on something about that does not sit well with her.

> "La Muerte Rusa!! Ladies and gentlemen!" Screams
> Jose as he gestures towards Tatyana as if he were an
> announcer.

Tatyana quickly turns to look, and her demeanor immediately changes as she smiles and sees Jose and Anthony by the grill with wide open smiles. Jose gestures for her to come over. She approaches them as if she were on a fashion runway, moving seductively with every step, the guys stare with their mouths open. When Tatyana finally reaches them and stands right next to them, she puts her hands on her hips.

"Well, I'm ready to have some fun!" Says Tatyana in a heavy Russian accent.

"Yes! Yes! Ha, ha, ha!" Jose burst into clapping and screaming, and Tatyana laughs.

Jose holds his hands out to Anthony, as if framing a picture, and says,

> "That was the walk, man! That was the walk! She would come out of the bleachers wearing a red Russian cape, you know, the hook and the hammer thing."

"Hammer and sickle," Says Tatyana.

> "Yeah, yeah… then she walks down to the ring, just like that, while they played the Russian music. Says Jose.

> "The old soviet national anthem." Says Tatyana, correcting him.

> "Ta, ta, tada ta, tada ta….ha, ha, ha, ha." Jose sings the melody.

Tatyana puts her hand on Jose's shoulder and says,

"It's amazing you remember all of that!"

She looks over at Anthony and winks at him. He blushes and smiles.

"Yeah, man! How could I forget! And then, and then you just got in that ring and beat the crap out of anyone that walked into it."

The grill suddenly flares up, flames lashing upwards, startling everyone. Jose and Anthony step backwards, but Tatyana quickly grabs the beers in their hands and puts the fire out. With the fire extinguished, Tatyana puts her thick arms around the guy's neck and smiles.

"Aren't you glad I came along?" She asks, and the guys quickly nod.

Tatyana gently squeezes Anthony's pectoral muscle, then slowly removes her arms from the guy's. She turns to look at Anthony, and he is staring at her. She can see his desire for her all over his face. Tatyana lustfully looks back at him, clearly letting him know her intentions in a single glance. They stare at each other for a few seconds, eyes locked in.

But her attention is suddenly diverted to the other side of the yard, where she sees Chloe and Daniel still by the fence, still talking to Mrs. June.

Chloe and Daniel let go of the fence and walk back towards the coolers. Chloe feels her phone vibrate, takes it out of her back pocket, and quickly begins to read. Her face lights up as she reads something on her phone, her eyes widen, and tears begin to fall.

"What's the matter?" Asks Daniel.

Chloe looks up at Daniel with her mouth open.

"Everything ok?" Asks Daniel

"AAAAAAAAAAHHHHHHH!" Screams Chloe, getting everyone's attention.

"This is AWESOME!!" Yells Chloe.

"What! What!" Asks Daniel.

Chloe gives Daniel a huge smile, grabs him by the shoulder, and tells him,

"Come with me!"

Chloe and Daniel run over to Anthony, Jose, and Tatyana.

"Dad! Dad!" Chloe yells

Tatyana is already watching them, but Anthony and Jose turn around to see what's happening.

"What's the matter, baby?" Asks Anthony.

Chloe runs into Anthony's arms and embraces him while Jose, Daniel, and Tatyana watch with anticipation. Chloe holds up her phone to her dad's face and says,

"Look, Dad! Look!"

Anthony tries to see what she's pointing to on the phone, but can hardly make it out, he says,

"I can't read this, the wording is too small, what is it? What is it?"

Chloe puts the phone closer to his face and says,

> "I got an email from a recruiter at ASU, she pulled up my application and wants to meet with meeee, Yeeeeeeees!"

Jose, Anthony, Daniel, and Tatyana clap and congratulate her as she hugs her dad again.

> "Congratulations, baby!" Says Anthony as he hugs her back.

> "Linda Shultz?" Asks Tatyana.

Chloe looks down at her phone and reads for a few seconds, then looks up at Tatyana, completely surprised.

> "How did you know?" Asks Chloe.

Tatyana smiles, then puts her index finger up to her lips and looks up as if she were completely innocent, like the kids do.

> "Did you do this, Tatyana? Did you call them for me?" Exclaims Chloe with excitement as she jumps up and down.

Tatyana nods in approval.

> "I told you I would, girlfriend...."Says Tatyana with a big smile on her face.

Tatyana holds her arms open wide, and Chloe runs into them and hugs her, saying,

> "Thank you, Tatyana! Thank you soooo much! That is so nice of you!"

Tatyana hugs Chloe back and says,

> "You guys don't have to keep calling me Tatyana, call me 'T', all my friends call me 'T'. It was my pleasure to do this for you. And you know what, it was nice catching up with Linda anyway, it's been a while since we talked."

> "Well, thank you, T, this means so much to me!" Says Chloe as she slowly pulls away.

Tatyana puts her right hand on Chloe's Cheek, warmly smiles at her, and says,

> "I told you I would try…"

> "You don't know how much I appreciate this, thank you, really." Says Anthony.

Chloe smiles, and Jose says,

> "That's real nice, T, real nice…"

Tatyana puts her hands on the guys' shoulders and says,

> "Let me get you guys new drinks."

> "Thank you." Says Jose.

> "Thank you, Tatya… I mean, thank you, T." says Anthony.

Tatyana slightly chuckles at Anthony, leaves the group, and walks over to the drink coolers by the house. It's noisy, the music, the people singing and talking, and Tatyana is loving every minute of it. She grabs two beers, and as she is shaking the ice and water from the bottles, she turns and sees Mrs. June looking straight at her. Mrs. June smiles and waves at her. Tatyana's countenance changes: she stops smiling and becomes inquisitive as to who this woman is. She slowly approaches the fence and stands right in front of Mrs. June. In an animated voice, Tatyana says,

"Hi sweetie, I don't think I've met you before."

Mrs. June rocks back and forth on her chair, continues to pet her cat, and stares at Tatyana for a few moments without saying a word as they both look at each other in the eyes. Mrs. June finally says,

"Hello there…my name is June."

Tatyana stoically looks at Mrs. June and says,

"I'm Tatyana."

Mrs. June smiles and says,

"Pleased to make your acquaintance, Tatyana."

Tatyana is taken aback by the comment, saying,

"Please to make your acquaintance… A little too proper for today's times, don't you think?"

Mrs. June smiles without saying a word.

"My son and I moved into Anthony's apartment, the RV garage back there." Says Tatyana.

Tatyana can tell that Mrs. June is seeing right through her, and it makes her uneasy. She looks at her for a few seconds, and the tension in her eyes grows; she becomes disgusted by Mrs. June. Tatyana stands up straight, tightens her shoulders, and pushes her pecs out as she continues to look at Mrs. June.

"You sure are a big girl." Says Mrs. June.

Tatyana is overwhelmed with pride and says,

"I'm an athlete."

"You look strong, built like a horse for sure." Says Mrs. June.

Tatyana smirks and flexes her biceps, then out of the blue, Mrs. June says,

"God loves you, you know."

Tatyana's smile disappears, she quickly puts her arms down, and says,

"Why did you say that?"

Mrs. June stops petting her cat, takes it off her lap, and gently places it on the ground.

"Because it's true, and I really believe you need to hear it." Mrs. June says.

Tatyana looks dead into Mrs. June's eyes, her disgust for Mrs. June kindled like a fire now, crawls up from her heart, to her throat, and comes out of her mouth saying,

"You one of them Bible people?"

Mrs. June reaches for the large glass of iced tea next to her, takes a sip, looks at Tatyana, and says,

"Well, I do love the Bible."

Tatyana's disgust is now clearly evident on her face as she slightly snarls and says,

"Yeah, you're one of 'em."

"Bad experience?" Asks Mrs. June.

"You people are not to be trusted." Says Tatyana.

"But you don't even know me yet, honey?" Says Mrs. June.

"I know your type, and I don't like your type." Responds Tatyana.

Mrs. June stands up and, with a somber face, approaches Tatyana and stands right in front of her. She says with a soft, kind voice,

"That's ok. You don't have to like me. People will always fail you in one way or another, but God will never fail you; He will always do right by you."

Tatyana shakes her head, then her shoulders and arms, as if shaking off a feeling.

"OOOOOOKAAAAAYYY, that's enough for me! B-bye!" Tatyana proclaims as she puts a hand in front of Mrs. June to stop her from talking.

Tatyana turns around and walks back to the party, shaking her head, saying,

"What… the hell… was that!"

She makes her way back to Anthony and Jose, gives them their beers, and just stands there looking at the grill.

"You okay?" Asks Anthony, but she does not respond.

"Superstar, what's the matter?" Asks Jose.

"Hugh?" Says Tatyana as emotions of pain and anger run through her heart.

"You out there somewhere…" Says Jose.

"Something's up," Says Anthony.

Tatyana puts her hand on her forehead, trying to play it off, saying,

"I'm good, man! Just had a little flashback, that's all, ha, ha."

"Flashback of the duplex you gave to 'El Galancito' on that Summer Madness event?" Jose says as he smiles, waiting for a response from her.

Tatyana turns and looks at Jose, completely surprised, and says,

"You remember that?"

"Who can forget!" Jose says as he takes a few steps back and begins to set the scene,

"It was the last event of the night, 'El Galancito' was fighting 'El Sovieta', and it was a brutal match, I mean bad! Jumping off ropes and elbowing in the face, kicking each other in the nuts, it was crazy.

Anyway, towards the end of the fight, 'El Galancito' had 'El Sovieta' on the mat, and everyone thought it was over. The ref started counting down,

One…Two… But before he got to number three." Jose explains as Tatyana smiles widely because she knows what's coming.

"Out of nowhere!" Jose holds his hands out as if he were presenting Tatyana and says,

"La Muerte Rusa!!" Anthony and Tatyana clap and chuckle. Jose continues to say,

"She comes out of nowhere, jumps into the ring, and begins to hit 'El Galancito' in the head with her elbows, then her fists. He tries to get away, but he can't; she's too quick. He tries to hit her back, but she deflects every blow. La Muerte grabs him by the nuts and by his neck, high above her head and body slams him, not once, not twice, but three times! Then she gets him up, sets him up for a suplex, and BAM!

He is done, I tell you, I mean dooooone. Ha, ha, ha" Tatyana raises her hands in victory, and Jose and Anthony clap.

"You remember all of that? Asks Tatyana.

"I told you I was a fan!" Says Jose.

Tatyana grabs Jose and gives him a bear hug, rocking him side to side as he laughs. She puts him down and pats his shoulder, saying,

"Wow, you brought back some memories for me!"

"You ever think about getting back in the ring?" Ask Anthony.

Jose nudges Tatyana and says,

"Yeah, you need to get back in there!"

"To wrestling?" Asks Tatyana,

"Yeah!" Yells Jose as his eyes widen with excitement.

Tatyana begins to shake her head as she says,

"I lost touch with every…" but she is cut off by Jose.

"My cousin Raul!" Jose screams out.

"Raul, the lawyer?" Asks Anthony.

"Yeah, I think he knows a guy!" Says Jose.

"A guy…" says Tatyana.

"Raul! Yeah! He knows a guy that may be able to help you get back in that ring, man!" Screams Jose.

"It would be pretty cool to see you wrestle." Says Anthony.

"I honestly have not thought of it for a while. I was looking to continue my personal training thing, you know…but it's always been in the back of my mind." Says Tatyana.

"Let me talk to Raul, yeah, let me talk to him, he owes me a favor, ha!!" Says Jose.

Tatyana nods in agreement. Chloe suddenly runs up to Tatyana, points to the mini stage, and says,

"You're up!"

Tatyana smiles and tells everyone around her,

"You guys better take your phones out, it's my turn at the mic!" She turns to Chloe and says, "You're coming with me!"

Tatyana and Chloe run up to the mic and start singing the song "Maniac" from the movie Flashdance. The whole backyard joins in and starts jumping and singing with them. Jose and Anthony find a table and sit down as they watch the girls onstage.

"Where's the wife?" Asks Anthony.

"Home," Jose says, looking at Anthony side-eyed, he knows where this is headed.

"Did you talk to her?" Asks Anthony.

"Right before I came here, I told her you found the rubbers." Answers Jose.

Anthony puts his head down for a second, then picks it up and says,

"I'm sorry, man."

Jose puts his beer down, looks at Anthony dead in the eyes, and says,

"It wasn't good…"

"What did she say?" Asks Anthony.

Jose looks away and takes a sip of his beer.

"I understand, man." Says Anthony.

"Not like that." Says Jose.

"What?" Asks Anthony.

Jose turns to Anthony and says,

"I told her you found the condoms, and then I asked her who she was cheating on me with. She began to laugh! I brought out the large kitchen garbage bag with all the rubbers, and she kept laughing."

"What?" Says Anthony.

"Yup…she laughed right in my face. And could not say a word because she couldn't stop laughing." Says Jose

"So what did you do?" Asked Anthony.

"Maaaaaan…. I got so angry I screamed at her, and I never scream at my wife. But today I screamed at her to stop laughing at me." Says Jose.

"And?" Asked Anthony.

"She laughed harder and farted at the same time, farted so hard she soiled herself…." Says Jose.

"WHAT!" Says Anthony.

"Yeah, she farted and laughed, laughed and farted all the way to the front door. She was following me, trying to say something as I was walking out. And I just couldn't take it, so I left and came to the party." Says Jose.

Anthony burst out in laughter, almost spilling his beer. Jose shakes his head, turns around, and continues to watch Tatyana as she sings and dances on the little stage; she's got the whole backyard singing along. Mrs. June, on her side of the fence, watches everything. She rocks back and forth as she pets her black and white cat.

Chapter 4: Back in the Fight

Two Weeks After the Party

Sunny skies, birds chirp in the distance, and a morning breeze pushes a lost paper cup from the party into the driveway of the Borgia house. The cup travels towards the back, and it ends up in front of the RV garage apartment. The door opens, and Daniel runs out with his school bag, leaving the door open, kicking the paper cup down the driveway as he runs. Tatyana walks out of the apartment wearing her waitress uniform, tucking in her shirt as she keeps her eyes on Daniel. Tatyana yells,

"Daniel! Stop playing around and get in the truck! You're going to be late for school!"

Tatyana struggles to keep her shirt tucked in as she looks for the keys in her purse to lock the door. She turns to look at Daniel again, but her shirt rips at the shoulder seam because she is so big. She looks at it and whispers,

"Well, I don't have time to change now."

She looks down the driveway and sees Daniel getting in the truck.

"Good girl," she whispers.

She finally finds the keys, and as she's about to lock the door, Mrs. Junes' cat rubs up against her legs. Tatyana looks down at the cat that's looking up at her and purring, then she quickly looks around to see if anyone is watching her. She looks down at the cat and says,

"Well, hello there... You're the old lady's cat, aren't you?"

Tatyana looks around one more time, opens the door again, and pushes the cat inside with her leg. She enters the apartment again and closes the door. Tatyana quickly picks up the cat and, with a single twist of her wrist, she breaks its neck. She takes several garbage bags from underneath the kitchen sink, wraps the cat in a towel sitting on the countertop, then puts the cat in the bags, ties them, and puts the cat in her freezer.

A few minutes later, the door opens wide, and Tatyana rushes out. She looks all around and sees that there's no one around. Adjusting her shirt, she quickly makes her way down the driveway; she sees Daniel egging her to hurry from inside the truck.

Tatyana looks around again and sees Mrs. June coming out of her house on the other side of the property. Mrs. June waves at Tatyana, but Tatyana stares her down in disdain as she makes her way down the driveway. Finally reaching her truck, Tatyana pauses and hears

Mrs. June calling for her cat in the distance. She smiles and gets into the truck.

"Well, you took your sweet time!" Says Daniel.

Tatyana smiles, starts the truck, and says,

"Hey, you've been hanging out with Chloe a lot lately..."

"Yeah, she's pretty cool." Says Daniel as he opens his backpack and looks through his books.

Tatyana accelerates, pulls off from the front of the house, and begins to drive down the street. She looks in the rear-view mirror at Daniel as his hair moves with the wind coming in from the open window and says.

"Chloe's pretty." Says Tatyana.

Daniel looks up and stares back at her through the rear-view mirror. He knows where she is headed in this conversation.

"She's got those pretty eyes." Says Tatyana.

"Stop!" Says Daniel

"Those perky little titties," Tatyana says as she chuckles.

"STOOOOOP!" Says Daniel.

"You're both young, you should be all over that. I mean, if I were your age, I would be all over that!" Says Tatyana.

"MOM! You know I'm not that way!" Says Daniel.

"I'm not saying stop being with boys, give her some love too!" Says Tatyana.

"Okay... Stop talking! We're friends, that's it!" Says Daniel.

"Fine, fine.... Jeeeez." Says Tatyana.

Tatyana turns the corner and stops the car at the front of Daniel's school. She turns around, looks at Daniel, and says,

"You're beautiful, you're my baby, and I love you. All I'm saying is... someday, I want some grandkids. You don't have to marry the girl...just put a baby in her."

Daniel reaches over and kisses his mom on the cheek and says,

"I love you, Mom."

Tatyana smiles at Daniel, who gets out of the truck and comes over to her door.

"I love you more." Says Tatyana, Daniel smiles and walks towards the school building.

Jose and Anthony enter Manuel's Taqueria looking for Tatyana. The place is packed with people. Every table is full, loud talking, loud Mexican music playing, kids crying, and a small crowd waiting to be seated by the front door. Waitresses quickly move from one part of the restaurant to the other like busy bees in a beehive. The guys move through the small crowd at the door, and as they get to the front desk, Anthony tries to get the attention of one of the waitresses passing by with a tray loaded with food.

"Excuse me…" Says Anthony, but the young lady keeps walking.

Anthony looks over at Jose. Jose smiles and says,

"Let me try."

Jose steps forward as he sees another waitress coming his way with a large tray filled with food. He steps right in front of the waitress and asks,

"Señorita! Done hesta Tatyana?" (Young lady, where is Tatyana?)

The waitress stops in her tracks and looks at Jose, a bit confused. She asks,

"Quine es Tatyana?" (Who is Tatyana?)

"La montaña blanca, tú saves, la musculosa!" Says Jose.

(The white mountain, you know... the muscle woman)

"A si, nosotros la yamamos Titi, la acabo de ver en la cocina." Says the waitress.

(Oh yeah, we call her Titi. I just saw her in the kitchen.)

"La podemos ver por favor?" Asks Jose.

(Can we see her, please?)

"Valla pues." Says the waitress as she walks around Jose and goes on her way.

(Go ahead.)

Jose turns to Anthony and says,

"C'mon, she's in the kitchen!"

The guys begin to walk toward the kitchen door behind the bar, and Anthony asks,

"What did you ask her?"

"I asked her where the muscle mountain was, ha, ha." Says Jose.

"That works." Says Anthony.

Anthony and Jose make their way through the dining room. Jose looks over at the waitress who helped him. She's at a table serving some guests, unloading all the heavy plates of food. Jose nods and smiles at her, and she nods back and keeps working. The guys get to the door and enter the kitchen.

They walk into what looks like a circus act. Waitresses running to and fro in the kitchen getting things they need, the cooks lined up against the wall with towers of fires in front of them, the dishwasher moving large crates of dishes from one side of the dishwasher to the other, as the busboys continue to bring more dishes. In the center of it all, at the prep table, stands Tatyana with her massive back to the door.

Jose and Anthony walk up to either side of her as she cuts Mexican limes into a large steel bowl. Tatyana sees them, smiles, and says,

"Hey guys! What are you doing here?"

"We got a surprise for you," Says Anthony.

Tatyana looks Anthony up and down and says,

"Oh, Yeah?"

Jose puts his hand on Tatyana's shoulder and says,

"Big one"

"You guys sound excited about this!" Says Tatyana.

Tatyana puts the knife and the lime down and puts her hands on her hips.

"I'm overdue for a break. What are you guys up to?" She says.

Anthony takes the apron off of Tatyana, and they lead her out of the kitchen as she smiles at them. She begins to chuckle as the guys begin to walk her backwards out the door, each one with an arm under each armpit.

"Enrique! Enrique!" Tatyana yells out.

A big Mexican man pokes his head out of a back office, holding a bundle of money.

"Hey! Hey, where are you going?" Enrique yells.

Tatyana waves goodbye as the guys continue to make their way to the door with her.

"I'm taking my break and lunch, be back in 90!" Yells Tatyana.

"C'mon, man! We're busy right now!" Says Enrique.

Tatyana turns around and walks out with the guys and says,

"We're always busy, Enrique!"

They make their way outside to the busy parking lot, as trucks move in and out of the gas station a few feet away. Jose unlocks his black SUV, and they all get in: Tatyana in the back seat, Jose drives, and Anthony on the front passenger seat. Jose pulls out of the parking lot and gets on the highway. Tatyana looks at the large mountain range on the side of the highway, somewhat blocked by large factories and warehouses. After a little while, she says,

> "So… are you guys going to tell me where we're going? You're not trying to kidnap me, are you?"

> "I don't think we could even if we wanted to, ha, ha!" Says Jose as he exits the highway into an industrial complex.

Anthony turns around and says,

> "I think you're going to love it! By the way, you're making me hungry, you smell like tamales!"

> "Man, I wasn't gonna say nothin, Ha, ha, but yeah!" Says Jose.

Tatyana sits up, puts her hand on Anthony's hair, and says,

> "So I'm making you hungry? You like to eat tamales?"

Anthony smiles and blushes as Tatyana caresses his hair.

"We're here!" Jose yells out as he stops in front of a large building.

Tatyana continues to look into Anthony's eyes for a few more seconds, then breaks away and quickly gets out of the vehicle, leaving Anthony alone in there for a minute as he stares at the back seat. She looks up at the large building before her, looks around at the whole industrial complex, then begins to read the large letters on the side of the place.

"Blood...bath...Arena. Is this the big surprise? We're watching a fight or something?"

"No, no, no! Let's go inside!" Says Jose as he quickly opens one of the large glass doors to the building and ushers them in.

They walk into a partially lit stadium. It's huge, with hundreds of chairs surrounding a wrestling ring in the middle where most of the light is coming from. The three slowly walk down to the ring. There are repair crews working on the right side of the entrance they came from, and another crew further down, painting the walls leading to what could be locker rooms.

At ringside, there is a film crew with cameras, microphones, and lighting equipment, capturing two wrestlers fighting. A few dozen more wrestlers wearing their costumes, sparkled masks, and painted faces are sitting down in the first few rows, watching the fight as a member of the production crew gives them instructions. Jose, Anthony, and Tatyana make their way down to the production crew.

Tatyana looks around the whole stadium and says,

"This is definitely a surprise, guys..."

"The best part is coming." Says Anthony.

"Yeah! I can't wait for you to see what this is all about! I see Raul from here!" Says Jose.

The three make it down to ringside. One of the members of the production crew, a young girl with purple and pink hair, looks up at the three of them and taps the man speaking to the wrestlers on the shoulder. The tall and skinny Hispanic man turns and smiles when he sees the three standing there. He yells out,

"Jose! There you are! Ha, ha, ha!"

Jose raises his hands up in the air, runs down to Raul, and hugs him.

"It's been too long, Raul!" Says Jose.

"I know, I know, I've been so busy man! But thank you for calling me!" Says Raul.

They both turn around and look straight at Tatyana.

"And there she is..." Says Jose.

"The Russian mountain!" Says Raul.

Jose slowly turns to look at Raul in disgust and slaps him hard on the shoulder, saying,

"La Muerte Rusa! La Muerte Rusa! Get it right man!"

Raul walks up to Tatyana and slowly begins to walk around her, looking her up and down.

"What's your name, beautiful?" Asks Raul.

"Name's Tatyana, so what's this about?" Asks Tatyana.

"So what's your backstory? You like a Russian killer that works in an American diner as cover?" Asks Raul as he continues to take her in.

"What?" Says Tatyana.

Raul looks over at Jose and asks,

"Jose, what's with the waitress costume?"

"It's not a costume! I really am a waitress, in a restaurant, currently on my lunch break...Anyone here going to tell me what's going on?"

Raul looks over at Jose, a bit concerned.

"Surprise!! This is the surprise," Says Jose.

"It's a reality show, baby!!" Says Raul.

"Surprise! You're gonna be the biggest star!" Says Anthony.

"What?" Says Tatyana is not really understanding it all yet.

"Yeah, yeah, let me get the director, hold on." Says Raul.

Raul looks over to the girl with the bi-colored hair, talking to the cameraman, and says,

"Jessica! Jessica, come here, please?"

Jessica smiles, walks over to Raul, and shakes Tatyana's hand, saying,

"It's a pleasure to meet you, La...Muerte...Rusa!" She says in a low Russian accent.

Jose hits Raul on the shoulder again and says,

"Somebody did their research!"

Jessica points to the ring and says,

"We're doing a documentary, slash reality show on the underground world of wrestling. I want to tell the stories of people who have been trying to make it for a while, those who are just getting in, and, of course, your story. I think it fits in perfectly. I mean... after Raul told me about you, I did a little digging and looked into your wrestling career, and you were amazing!"

Tatyana blushes a little, holds her hands up to her mouth, and says,

"Thank you..."

"Look, I want you to come back to the ring, and I want to be the one to tell your story." Says Jessica.

"Well damn, I don't know..." says Tatyana

Anthony gets closer to Tatyana, reassures her by putting his hand on her massive shoulder, and says,

"T, I looked at some of your old videos. You look better now than back then!"

Tatyana looks at Anthony and smiles, then Jessica proceeds to say,

"You do, you look amazing. You got more muscle than any girl here, more than some of these guys, actually. Anyways, the whole thing is, we want the ones that love the sport, the showmanship, the way the crowd loves their hero...and sometimes roots for the villain and loves them more sometimes. That's why I want you."

Tatyana smiles widely and asks,

"So you want me to be in your show?"

"Heck yeah! We're doing auditions right now. All you've got to do is get in that ring and show us your stuff. What do you say?" Asks Jessica.

Tatyana grabs Jessica by the arms and picks her up, saying,

"I could kiss you!"

"Maybe later, just, just put me down for now, ha, ha," says Jessica

Tatyana puts Jessica down; Jessica smiles and turns around. She yells at one of her helpers standing by the wrestlers,

"Debbie! Get the guys out of the ring and put the shark woman up there!"

A skinny woman dressed in black and white leotards, sitting amongst the other wrestlers, stands up and says,

"Hey! I'm Killer Orca!"

Jessica smiles and shakes her head, saying,

"Right, right, sorry about that."

"No, keep the guys up there." Says Tatyana.

Jessica slowly turns around with a sparkle in her eyes and says,

"Really?"

"You want a show, I'll give you a show!" Says Tatyana.

Raul steps in and says,

"Wait a minute, you can't just enter the ring like that, we gotta get you some spandex or something. Unless you want to be called the flying waitress or something."

"Ah, no." Says Tatyana.

"Yeah, he's right, let me get someone from wardrobe..." Jessica says.

Tatyana pulls her t-shirt off and says,

"No need, I got this!"

She takes her shorts off, hands her clothes to Anthony with a smile as she winks and says,

"La Murte Rusa only wears red!"

Tatyana makes her way up to the ring wearing a tiny red bra, a red thong, and white sneakers. Jessica and the guys immediately follow after Tatyana. Jessica jumps up on a chair and starts giving directions to the crew. Anthony and Jose stand ringside, anxiously watching as Tatyana enters the ring and begins to warm up.

The two wrestlers look at Tatyana without saying a word. One of them, a tall, hairy man, wearing a green mask and green shorts, exits the ring and stands outside the opposite corner, holding on to the post. The other, a short, muscled guy, wearing a full grey bodysuit, stands in the middle of the ring and continues to stare at Tatyana as she jumps from one side of the ring to the other, doing a warm-up routine. Jessica holds her hands up in the air and yells,

"Alright, people! Let's go! Camera one, I want you getting wide shots only, camera two, you're following the action, and camera three, you're all over Tatyana! Wrestlers show me what you can do, and no one gets hurt, at least not seriously!"

Tatyana and the wrestler in gray spandex get closer to each other at the center of the ring and face off. They circle the ring and begin to grasp at each other. Tatyana stands about a foot taller than the muscled man. She easily grabs him by the neck with her long arms and brings his face close to hers; they are forehead to forehead in an arm lock.

"So what's your ring name?" Asks Tatyana.

"I'm the elephant man..." he says.

"You're kidding, right?" Asks Tatyana.

"No, I'm not, and you?" Asks the elephant man.

"La Muerte Rusa." Says Tatyana

"Well, I'm gonna fuck you up, Muele Sushi!" Says the elephant man.

Without saying a word, Tatyana reaches down and grabs his leg. She picks him up onto her shoulders, then up above her head, and violently body slams him onto the mat. The elephant man is stunned. Tatyana runs to the ropes, bounces and comes back, leaps into the air, and falls with an elbow to his face. She gets up, quickly picks him up off the mat, and lifts him over her head again, this time his legs straight up in the air; he's completely upside down.

SLAM!

She slams him down again! The other wrestler with the green mask comes into the ring. Tatyana sees him and runs towards him. She jumps and kicks him right in the chest with both legs; he falls backwards onto his butt.

The elephant man is on his feet. He comes up behind Tatyana as she tries to get up and places her in a chokehold. The green mask quickly gets up, takes advantage that Tatyana is on her knees and restrained, and begins to punch her in the face.

Green mask runs back to the ropes, bounces, runs back to Tatyana, jumps up, and lands a hard elbow right on her nose. Blood erupts from her nose, down her mouth, and onto her chest; she is covered in it.

Tatyana blows out the blood in her mouth, and it hits the green masked man in the eyes. As he tries to wipe it off, she jumps to her feet and kicks the green mask in the balls. He falls on his knees. She jumps up and puts all her weight onto her left heel as she steps on Elephant Man's foot, making him loosen his hold. She then flips Elephant Man forward, over her shoulder, and lands on top of him.

Tatyana spits out more blood, and her nose continues to bleed; she looks like a wild beast as her hair is frazzled and her whole face is blood red from the smeared blood. She reaches down, picks up the elephant man over her head with ease, and violently body slams him again!

SLAM!

His body bounces off the mat. Tatyana wipes her face with her forearms, turning them red. She looks over to the green masked wrestler, and he's on his feet, looking at her. She begins to walk over to him, and he runs towards her and throws a kick, but Tatyana deflects the kick and punches him hard right in the chest, knocking is wind out. She grabs him by his torso, picks him up, turns him upside down, and positions him for a suplex.

BAM!!

They hit the mat hard. Tatyana quickly gets up and sees that the wrestlers are not getting up; they are moaning and crawling to the edges of the ring. Tatyana walks over to the elephant man, grabs him by the left foot, and drags him back to the center of the ring.

"Okay! That's enough! That's perfect, thank you everyone!" Says Jessica.

Tatyana turns to look at Jessica and drops the elephant man's foot; he sighs with relief. She looks over to the green masked wrestler, who's reached the edge of the ring and drops off the edge onto the floor.

"That's it? Was that good?" Asks Tatyana.

Jessica runs into the ring as all the wrestlers begin to stand up, cheer, and clap. Jessica walks up to Tatyana, clapping and smiling. She hands her a towel for her nose and says,

"That...was...awesome!"

Jessica hugs Tatyana tightly around her waist, and it takes Tatyana by surprise. Tatyana slowly hugs Jessica back. She looks up into the stands and sees everyone cheering her on, not just the wrestlers, but the production team, arena staff, and even the repair crews working throughout the arena. She looks down at ringside and sees Jose, Raul, and Anthony clapping with big smiles on their faces. Tatyana begins to tear up; she becomes emotionally moved by the love, and the tears begin to create streaks down her bloody face.

Jessica pulls away from Tatyana, they both look eye to eye, and Jessica says,

"You're a fucking star!"

CHAPTER 5: RIDING DANGEROUSLY

The sun sets behind beautiful purple mountains in the distance, its last rays light up the sky and clouds above in shades of pink, orange, and yellow. Flocks of birds go from tree to tree as they do their last dance before nightfall. Their singing is loud, and it fills the air. Jose pulls up to Anthony's house and parks right up against the front yard. Anthony and Tatyana step out and stand at either side of the car, looking at Jose, but he's not getting out with them.

> "Jose, what are you doing? C'mon, let's go inside and have a celebratory drink!" Says Anthony as he stands in front of the passenger side door.

Tatyana stands right next to Jose's door and says,

> "Come on, Jose, a drink sounds great right about

now."

Jose puts both of his hands on the steering wheel and says,

> "I can't, guys…I got to go home."

Tatyana puts her hands together as if she were praying and asks,

> "Just for a little while?"

Jose laughs and slams his hands against the steering wheel, saying,

"You were amazing today, Rusa! It was awesome to see you back in that ring! But I can't, you guys, have one for me, ok?"

"None of this would have happened without you guys, especially you, Jose. Thank you." Says Tatyana.

"Jose put it all together. I just helped bring you along, ha, ha. But you're welcome." Says Anthony, as he watches Tatyana's hair blow away with a warm breeze that passes by.

Tatyana looks back at Anthony as he watches her closely, her eyes glistening with the light of the sunset. He's captivated, and she knows it.

"You're welcome, Rusa! It was my pleasure to help you!" Jose yells out as he starts his SUV.

Tatyana and Anthony take a step back, Jose waves and slowly takes off and drives away. Tatyana and Anthony wave at Jose, then as they bring their hands down, they look at each other and smile.

"So, did you want to have that drink?" Asks Anthony.

Tatyana looks down at herself and says,

"I need to go and get out of these clothes! That's what I need to do, ha, ha, ha. Maybe another time on that drink?" Tatyana says.

Anthony nods, walks up to her, and extends his elbow up to her, saying,

"Of course, c'mon, I'll walk you home."

Tatyana puts her arm through his, and they begin to walk up the driveway together.

"Thanks, it's such a perilous journey home, ha, ha." Says Tatyana, and it makes Anthony chuckle.

The two walk up the driveway laughing. They walk through the backyard and stand in front of Tatyana's door, looking at each other. Suddenly, Mrs. June slams the door to her house open and comes out to her backyard yelling,

"Gilbert! Gilbert! Where are you, honey!"

Mrs. June sees Anthony and Tatyana over in his yard, and she says,

"Anthony! Anthony!"

Anthony and Tatyana look at Mrs. June as she waves at them. Tatyana shakes her head, puts her hand on Anthony's shoulder, and says,

"I'm going inside."

"Okay, have a good night. I'll see what's going on with Mrs. June." Says Anthony.

Tatyana enters her house, and Anthony makes his way to Mrs. June. He walks up to the fence and says,

"Hey, Mrs. June, is everything ok?"

Mrs. June puts her hand on her forehead and walks up to Anthony and stands on her side of the fence.

"I can't find Gilbert!" She says.

"Your cat?" Asks Anthony.

Mrs. June continues to look around her yard, then starts looking over at Anthony's yard and says,

"He's never been gone this long; something is not right…"

Anthony looks in the direction she's facing and says,

"I'm sure he's ok, Mrs. June…"

Just as Anthony is about to say something else, Mrs. June interrupts him.

"No, Anthony, I can feel it, something bad has happened to poor Gilbert, I just know it." She says.

Anthony looks at Ms. June and feels sorry for her. It's dark now, a little chilly, and she's out here looking for her cat in her nightgown and slippers.

"Mrs. June, it's getting late. Why don't you go inside, and I will look for Gilbert, ok?" Says Anthony.

Mrs. June turns to him with a relieved smile and says,

"Will you?"

"Yes, of course I will." Replies Anthony.

Anthony opens the gate, enters Mrs. June's yard, and helps her to her door. Mrs. June pats his back as they walk.

"Thank you, Anthony." Mrs. June says as she enters her home and looks back at Anthony.

“Have a good night.” Says Anthony as he smiles.

Suddenly, Mrs. June’s countenance changes, as if all of a sudden a knowing had dropped on her heart, or someone had whispered something into her ear.

“Don’t bother looking for Gilbert, he’s not coming back, Anthony.” Says Mrs. June with a somber look.

“We’ll find him, Mrs. June, don’t you worry.” Says Anthony.

Mrs. June looks at Anthony dead in the eyes and says,

“No…we won’t. But thank you, Anthony, for being so kind. Have a good night, son.”

Mrs. June closes the door, and Anthony lingers, wondering why she suddenly changed her attitude like that. He turns away from the door, walks down the steps, crosses over to his yard, and looks back at her door, still wondering about her behavior. Anthony looks up at the sky, now filled with stars, and the very last rays of sunlight disappear behind the mountains as he looks. His cell phone rings, and it startles him. He tries to get it, but it is stuck in his back pocket. After struggling for a few seconds, he digs the phone out of his back pocket and looks to see who is calling… It's Tatiana.

Anthony looks over to her apartment and answers.

“Hello? Everything ok?” Anthony asks.

There is heavy breathing coming from the line, but no one is responding. Anthony looks up and sees that the door to her apartment is slightly ajar, and a soft pink light is emanating out of the small opening from inside. Anthony slowly walks towards the door, looking around to see if anyone is watching, but there is no one else out there. Anthony opens the door slightly and looks into the apartment.

"Hello?" Says Anthony, but there is no response.

He looks into the apartment, and he sees no one in the kitchen.

"Tatyana, is everything ok?" Anthony asks as he leans over to take a look into the living room.

Tatyana walks into the living room from the back, looking straight at him, still wearing her work clothes. She had been waiting for him to come through the door. The soft pink light coming from the ceiling fan bulb fills the room, and it slowly changes to shades of violet, red, and back to pink. Anthony stares at her with anticipation and drops the phone from his hand as his heartbeat accelerates.

They stare at each other for a few moments, a gust of wind pushes the door wide open, and Anthony slowly enters the apartment. Mystified by what is unfolding before him, he watches as Tatyana points her phone at a large set of speakers on the table, and the song 'Sweetest Taboo' begins to play. She slowly runs her hands from her neck down her legs. When she gets to her feet, she takes her sneakers off, then her socks, revealing large, round calf muscles and shapely feet. She slowly stands up straight, her eyes locked into Anthony's as she throws her cell phone on the couch.

Anthony slowly makes his way from the door to the living room as he watches intensely. Tatyana takes her shirt off, and then her shorts, standing before Anthony in her skimpy underwear, she flexes her tremendously large upper body, then shows off her large, muscular legs. Her bulging pecs, shoulders, and leg muscles ripple as she begins to dance to the soft music. Anthony is completely entranced by her as he watches her muscles flex and contract while she dances underneath the soft pink glow, her body and allure of her delicate movements and strength call to him, something he's never seen before.

Tatyana reaches to the side table by the couch, takes a small bottle of baby oil, pours it onto her chest and massive shoulders, and begins to cover herself in it. Anthony cannot contain himself, filled now with desire, he quickly walks over to the door and shuts it.

Mrs. June sits on her chair in her yard looking up at the stars, under the cover of darkness, and happens to see Anthony enter Tatyana's house, then close the door a few moments later. With a disappointed look on her face, she whispers a bible verse to herself,

"He goes after her, like an ox to the slaughter…"

The night passes, moonlight turns to sunlight as the morning quickly comes. The birds are chirping, a soft breeze sways the branches of the desert trees from side to side, and the morning sun seems to brighten up every inch of the backyard. Tatyana's door opens, and Anthony steps out. He looks down at the ground and sees his phone and picks it up, he looks like he was hit by a freight train. He looks at his phone, puts it in his back pocket, and slowly makes his way to the back of the apartment, pulls out two large garbage cans by the back fence, and says to himself,

"Almost forgot it's garbage day…"

He pulls the cans out and begins to drag them into the back yard. As he gets to the front of the apartment, Chloe opens up the back door to his house, runs out with two large garbage bags, and makes her way to him.

"Dad! Dad!" She says.

Anthony looks up and stops right as he reaches the edge of the driveway. He sees Chloe coming and lifts the lid off one of the cans, and Chloe throws the bags in.

"Dad, you won't believe what happened!" Says Chloe with excitement.

"What baby, what's going on?" Asks Anthony as he tries unsuccessfully to pat down his messy hair.

Chloe jumps up and down as she grabs his arm and says,

"Just got an email from ASU, I have a meeting with one of their recruiters. They have a scholarship they want to talk to me about!! AAAHHHH!"

Chloe's excitement is infectious. Anthony smiles, throws his hands up, and reaches to hug her as he says,

"What! What! That is wonderful, honey!"

At that moment, Tatyana walks out of her apartment barefoot; she's wearing only a large t-shirt barely covering her nakedness. She holds a small frozen garbage bag in one hand, smiles as she sees Chloe jumping up and down, and says,

"Someone's happy! Ha, ha, ha!"

Chloe runs up to Tatyana and gives her a big hug. Tatyana hugs her back and asks,

"What's this for?"

Chloe looks up at her as she hugs her and says,

"I know it was you, T! I've tried so hard to get a scholarship to get into the program! You don't know!"

Tatyana rubs the back of Chloe's head and pats her on her back, saying,

"I can't believe they notified you already! That was quick!"

"I got the email this morning!" Says Chloe as she slowly pulls away from Tatyana.

"Awesome! Well, all I did was make a phone call to an old friend, your grades did the rest, honey!" Says Tatyana as she lifts the garbage bag in her hand to Anthony and asks,

"Can I throw this in there?"

Anthony lifts the can lid up again and asks,

"Sure, what is that?"

"Spoiled meat, I had to freeze it so that I wouldn't have to smell it." Says Tatyana as she throws the bag with the cat in it into the trash can.

Chloe watches as the bag goes into the can, then turns to Tatyana and says,

"Thank you again for helping me, for making the call…really."

Anthony reaches over to Tatyana, gives her a small kiss on the cheek, and says,

"Thank you, T."

Tatyana looks at Anthony for a few seconds, then grabs him by his waist and easily pulls him in close to her. She plants a big kiss right on his mouth and begins to stroke his hair. Chloe's mouth drops as she watches, and as they continue to kiss passionately, she says,

"Hey! What's going on here!"

Tatyana pulls away, looks over at Chloe, smiling, and says,

"You need to ask your daddy, he wants to be modest and kiss me on the cheek, but I'm being honest about it. Anyway, I'd better get going."

"Wha…" says Chloe with her mouth open.

Tatyana pats Anthony on his butt and walks away, saying,

"Bye y'all!! See you later, Anthony!"

Chloe and Anthony watch as Tatyana walks away, opens her door, and enters her apartment. When the door closes, Chloe at once looks at her dad and asks,

> "Well?"

Anthony blushes and says,

> "Well, I think you already know."

> "Did you have sex with her?!" Asks Chloe.

Before he could answer, Daniel walked up to them and surprised them both, saying,

> "Yeah! They went at it all night. I hardly got any sleep; it sounded like a rodeo downstairs. First time I heard my mom sound like a horse though… so, that was new."

Anthony looks back at the apartment, then looks back at Daniel and says,

> "You… you were in there the whole time?"

Daniel smiles and says,

> "Ugh…I live here! Anyways, I'm going to school, I'm sure I'll catch a good nap in History class…Byeeeeee!

Daniel walks down the driveway as if he were walking down a fashion runway, spins, waves at them, and keeps walking towards his mom's truck.

Anthony looks at Chloe, they are both shocked. She slaps her dad on the shoulder.

"Dad!" She says.

Hours later

Anthony stands at Jose's front door, ringing the doorbell. Impatient, Anthony looks over to one of the front windows. He quickly walks up to the window, looks inside the house as he knocks on the glass repeatedly, saying,

"Jose! Jose, where are you?"

Anthony goes back to ringing the doorbell until he finally hears movement coming from inside the house. He puts his ear to the door and begins to knock. He hears things falling over, then it sounds like someone tripped and fell.

"I'm coming, damn it!" Says Jose from inside.

More things fall, and we hear steps coming to the door, then a big bang!

"Aaaahh! What was that!" Says Jose from inside the house, Anthony keeps knocking on the door.

The lock moves, the door slightly opens, and Jose opens the door, wearing rubber shorts and a robe. He holds his right foot in his hand, having obviously gotten hurt on the way to the door. Anthony barges into the house saying,

"Where's my twenty-inch straight hex wrench, sir?"

"What?" Asks Jose as he slightly jumps in place, holding his foot.

Anthony looks around the living room, searching for the wrench.

"My wrench, man! The one you borrowed! I need it for a job, like, right now!" Says Anthony as he demonstrates the size of the wrench with his hands.

"Oh! That wrench, yeah, hold on." Says Jose, and limps into the kitchen, ultimately out of Anthony's sight.

We hear a cabinet door open in the kitchen, then it slams shut. Another opens, and we hear Jose moving pots around, then a glass shatters on the floor.

"She's gonna kill me for that."Says Jose from the kitchen.

Jose limps back to the living room and hands the wrench over to Anthony.

"Thanks, man. I'm sorry to bother you like this. I completely forgot you had it until I went to use it on a job across town. Hey, you ok?" Asks Anthony.

"Yeah, I'm good." Says Jose.

Then suddenly, coming from the back bedroom of the home, we hear Yolanda, Jose's wife, call out to him.

"Jose! C'mon, baby!" Yolanda says.

Anthony smiles when he hears Jose's wife and says,

"Sounds like you guys are doing ok…"

"Yeah, yeah, the rubber thing, it was a big misunderstanding." Says Jose as he begins to push Anthony towards the front door.

Anthony hears high heels coming down the hallway.

"Baby, it's almost time for the show!" Says Yolanda from the hallway.

Jose really tries to push Anthony towards the door now, but Anthony starts to resist, looks at Jose, and asks,

"The show?"

Jose keeps trying to push Anthony towards the door and says,

"Yeah, I can't really talk about it right now… You gotta go!"

Jose is about to reach for the door when suddenly, Yolanda steps into the living room. She's a beautiful, short, voluptuous Latina. Long dark brown hair to her waist, light brown eyes with long eyelashes, long manicured nails, and copper skin. Anthony raises his eyebrows when he sees her come in wearing lingerie, an open see see-through silk robe, high heels, and a whip.

"Amor, we're on in five minutes, we've got almost one hundred viewers already in the room! What are you doing?" Yolanda asks.

Yolanda sees Anthony, she smiles, waves, and says,

"Sorry, Anthony, didn't know you were here… How are you doing, honey?"

"Good," says Anthony, not knowing how else to respond.

Jose turns around, embarrassed, and faces his wife.

"Yoli! Don't be putting our business out for everyone to see! What are YOU doing?" Asks Jose.

"Anthony is family! What are you trying to say!" Says Yolanda as she waves at Anthony again. He smiles and waves back.

"Anthony, you want something? Maybe some water or juice?" Asks Yolanda.

Anthony looks down at the whip in her hand, then quickly looks back up at her.

"No, I'm good, actually. Got my wrench," He says as he holds up his wrench.

Yolanda points to the kitchen and says,

"I made some chocolate chip cookies….Jose! give him some chocolate chip cookies! Don't be rude!"

"He doesn't want nothing! Just give me one minute to say goodbye. One minute, okay?" Jose asks.

"You tryin to say Anthony's not family?" Yolanda asks.

"No, baby, not at all. Just go back to the bedroom, and I'll be right there, promise!" Says Jose.

Yolanda puts her hands around her waist and says,

"I'm trying to be nice, cordial to our guest, Jose!"

Yolanda smiles and winks at Anthony. He nods and smiles back. Yolanda then looks over at Jose and says,

"Fine! But hurry up, Jose! And bring the cucumbers from the kitchen table!"

Yolanda turns around and walks away; her footsteps resonate from the hallway. Jose looks at Anthony and smiles nervously.

"Bye, Anthony! It was good seeing you!" Says Yolanda as she snaps the whip.

"Bye!" Says Anthony.

The bedroom door slams shut, and Jose looks at Anthony and says,

"I can explain!"

"I don't want to know," Says Anthony.

"Yolanda's got this online account and…" Says Jose

"I don't want to hear it." Says Anthony.

"She was using the rubbers with fruit." Says Jose

"What?" Asks Anthony.

"Yeah, part of the act, you know." Says Jose

Anthony does not respond, but raises his eyebrows.

"Okay, okay. Remember how she got fired from her office job a few months ago?" Asks Jose.

"Yeah," Anthony responds.

"Well, she didn't know what to do, so she made an adult account thing to see if she could make some money, you know, until she got another job. But she never told me! Anyway, when I confronted her about the rubbers, that's when she told me what she had been doing.

And then she showed me how much she's been making…I was blown away, man! She's been putting rubbers on all kinds of fruit, and then playing with 'em, people love it and give her money."

Anthony stares at Jose; he does not know what to say.

"Make a long story short, I'm part of the show now and we're doing some kinky stuff online…"

Anthony shakes his head slightly and says,

"Hey man, looks like it's working out for you, so…"

"She made more money in the last five months than I made last year!"

Anthony smiles, holds up his wrench, and says,

"Okay, I need to get going. I got a customer waiting."

"Alright then… and ugh…about the cucumbers…" says Jose

"I'm not gonna ask about the cucumbers." Says Anthony

"Good, you probably shouldn't." Says Jose

Anthony makes his way to the door. He grabs the door handle, and just as he is about to open the door, Jose grabs him by the shoulder and stops him. Anthony turns around, and Jose says,

"I almost forgot to tell you. I found out why Tatyana stopped wrestling years ago."

"Why?" Anthony asks, intrigued.

"She was in jail for beating up her boyfriend and another dude," Jose replies.

"What?" Asks Anthony.

"From what my cousin told me, it was pretty bad, man." Says Jose.

"Which cousin told you, Raul?" Asks Anthony.

"No, Jasinto." Says Jose.

"Who's Jasinto?" Asks Anthony.

"The detective you never met." Says Jose.

"Okay…so…" Says Anthony.

"So, she was pregnant with her boy, what's his name, Daniel?" Asks Jose.

"Yeah." Says Anthony.

"She came home early from a doctor's appointment, and when she got to the bedroom, she caught her boyfriend playing hide the pickle with another guy, in the act. She went completely ballistic and beat the crap out of them both. I mean, she broke her boyfriend's jaw, his clavicle bones, some ribs, and cracked his hip bone." Says Jose.

"And the other guy?" Asks Anthony.

"Over thirty-five broken bones, internal bleeding, fractured skull, I mean…bad!" Says Jose.

"Oh my gooosh!" Says Anthony.

"The guy with the fractured skull, she used his head as a ram repeatedly and put holes in the wall, screaming, 'Penetrate this! Penetrate this!' It was the next-door neighbors who called the cops. It took twelve of them to get her subdued; they tased her six times, man!"

Anthony, in complete shock, looks at Jose in dismay, at a loss for words.

"The only reason I'm telling you is because she lives in your backyard, bro!" Says Jose.

The bedroom door slams open, and it hits the hallway wall.

"ONE MINUTE JOSE!" yells Yolanda from the bedroom.

Anthony slowly opens the door and steps outside, saying,

"Yeah, yeah, thanks."

"So don't get too close, ok?" Says Jose.

Anthony nods, still in shock from the news. He quickly makes his way to the truck as Jose watches him.

"That's weird." Says Jose.

"Thirty seconds!" Yells Yolanda.

"Coming, my love!" Says Jose, as he closes and locks the front door.

Later that day, at the Borgia Household, Chloe is taking a little break from her school work and is walking up the driveway, bringing back the two large empty garbage cans from the curve. It's a beautiful afternoon, a nice bright day without a cloud in the sky. As she brings up the cans, she looks over at Mrs. June's house, but she's not out and about like she usually is. All of a sudden, the sky roars with the sound of jet fighters. Chloe looks up and sees a group of F-35s flying above her house.

She continues to watch them as she walks the cans back, the sound of the plane engines slowly begins to subside, and she begins to hear what sounds like 70's disco music. She looks around and, as she walks out from the driveway and into her yard with the cans, she realizes that the music is coming from inside Tatyana's apartment. She continues to drag the cans and decides to look into the apartment window.

Surprised, she drops the cans. Through the window, she sees Daniel wearing a flashy gold skirt, a matching bra, and high heels. He's dancing to the music in front of a large mirror. Chloe looks in amazement as Daniel takes off the bra and continues to dance like a stripper. As Daniel is about to take the skirt off, in the mirror, he catches a glimpse of Chloe looking in. Chloe quickly looks away and continues to walk towards the back of the building. She drops the cans off by the back wall and hears the door to the apartment open.

“Chloe!” Daniel says.

Chloe comes out of the back of the building, and as she walks into her back yard, she sees Daniel looking for her, now dressed in a t-shirt and gym shorts. Daniel runs up to her and says,

“Chloe! Hey, I hope I didn’t freak you out or anything.” Daniel asks, truly concerned with how Chloe perceives him.

“No, you didn’t, I’m sorry, I was being nosy,” Says Chloe.

Daniel grabs her hand and continues to say,

“This is something that I keep private right now. Please don’t tell anyone yet.”

Chloe hugs him and says,

“Daniel, I would never tell… I mean, that’s very personal, I’m sorry, I should not have been peaking in the first place. It was the music, it drew me to your window because it was catchy…”

“I like being watched. If you want to watch, I would not mind,” Says Daniel.

"What?" Asks Chloe.

"Never mind. I'm just not ready to show the world that part of me yet, that's all," Says Daniel.

"Does your mom know?" Asks Chloe.

"She's the one who started me up in dresses and skirts when I was a kid." Says Anthony.

Chloe nods, removes a leaf from Daniel's hair, pats him on the cheek, and says,

"Ok, well, I'm your friend, no one will ever find out, until you want them to, I promise."

"Find out what?" Mrs. June asks from across the yard as she comes out of her house holding a large glass of lemonade.

Daniel and Chloe look over at Mrs. June, shocked because they thought they were alone and no one was listening. Mrs. June looks at them and says,

"That Daniel here likes to sissy dance in front of the mirror while he masturbates, and that you, Chloe, have been enjoying the show?"

Daniel shakes his head and says,

"How… what?"

He begins to pace back and forth, shaking his hands rapidly, saying,

"This is just not the right time, I, I wasn't ready for anyone else to know yet!"

Chloe runs over to Daniel and tries to calm him down, saying,

"It's ok! Mrs. June would never tell on you; she's not like that."

Chloe looks over at Mrs. June, who is observing the whole thing.

"Right, Mrs. June? You're not saying anything to anyone, right?" Asks Chloe in desperation.

Mrs. June looks on without saying a word. She sits on her patio chair and takes another sip of her lemonade as Daniel's pacing becomes more agitated.

"I'm not ready yet! No! This is not the right time!" Says Daniel as he shakes his head.

"Calm down! It's ok, Daniel!" says Chloe

SLAP!

Mrs. June slaps her hands together loudly to get their attention, and it works; Chloe and Daniel stop what they're doing and stare at her.

"Both of you, come here…let me talk to you for a minute." Says Mrs. June.

Chloe and Daniel make their way across the gate of the chain link fence, over to Mrs. June's yard, and stand in front of her like little children.

"Honey, that's not the first time I've seen you dancing like that." Says Mrs. June.

"What!" Says Daniel as he begins to tear up.

"Let me finish now…Like I was saying, not the first time. But every time I seen you start, I close my blinds to give you privacy. Not my business, y'see." Mrs. June says, then takes another sip of her lemonade before continuing,

"What is my business, is what's God's business… and that's your soul, baby." Says Mrs. June.

Daniel wipes his face and says,

"God hates gays…Is that what you're going to say?"

Chloe puts her hand on Daniel's shoulder and says,

"That's not true…"

Mrs. June puts her drink down on her little side table and says,

"No, it's not true. God loves people, he made us, He made me, and He made you. If God were to start judging, like we truly deserve, no one would be left standing, not even me!"

Mrs. June pauses for a second, then continues to say,

"God don't hate gays! That's like saying God hates fornicators and they will have no chance at Heaven. Or… or saying something like God hates the drug addicts, they're all going to hell. No, no, no God loves people, he hates sin, whatever sin that may be."

"So what are you really saying?" Asks Daniel.

As Mrs. June looks at Daniel, her complete countenance changes, and she looks at Daniel with tenderness. She says,

"God loves you tremendously, Daniel. He made you, He knows you, and wants you to come to Him."

"Mrs. June, I don't think…" Says Chloe, but Mrs. June quickly interrupts and continues to say,

"Daniel, God is holding His hands out to you, come to Jesus baby, He's got all the love you need."

Daniel, captivated by Mrs. June's words, just stares at her for a few seconds, then says,

"Mrs. June, I'm not religious at all."

"I'm not offering religion, or church, or anything like that. I'm offering Jesus." Says Mrs. June.

Daniel looks a bit puzzled.

"What are you saying? All I hear these bible people talk about is that God hates gays, and we're all going to hell." Says Daniel.

"We're all born in sin, into a sinful world. But that's why Jesus came so that we, if we believe in Him, can have a way out. The God who created you wants you to come to Him. Believe that He loves

you and just wants to spend time with you.
Just…believe." Says Mrs. June.

"Just believe?" Asks Daniel.

"That's simple." Says Mrs. June.

"And then?" Asks Daniel.

Mrs. June smiles and says,

"Walk through the door first, Daniel, then you'll see
what's on the other side."

Mrs. June gets up from her chair, walks up to Daniel, and
hugs him tenderly. Daniel looks amazed, shocked even at
what he's feeling. She hugs him for a few more seconds,
pulls away from him, and pats him on his shoulder.

"There's millions of heterosexual people in Hell
right now, and that's because any sin will take you
there. A true Christian will show you love and also
tell you the truth." Says Mrs. June.

Daniel looks at Mrs. June intensely as she goes back to her
chair and sits down.

"No one has ever hugged me…like that." He says.

"What do you mean? Your mom never hugged
you?" Asked Chloe.

"No…not like that. It… it felt good," Says Daniel.

"WOW, well, that's what love feels like." Says
Chloe.

"God loves you…He loves your soul. Remember, the only way to Heaven is through Jesus." Says Mrs. June.

Daniel nods his head and stands there looking stoic for a few seconds. He slowly walks out of Mrs. June's yard, and Chloe follows him as she waves goodbye to Mrs. June. As Daniel walks into Chloe's yard, he turns around and says,

"Mrs. June!"

Mrs. June looks up at him.

"Thank you!" Says Daniel.

Mrs. June looks at him with kindness and nods. Daniel and Chloe walk back to the apartment door. Chloe begins to say,

"Hey, I'm sorry about Mrs. June, she…" but is cut off by Daniel,

"It did not bother me, actually; what she said made a lot of sense to me." Said Daniel.

"What?" Asks Chloe.

"All these nasty church people out here, and none of them that I met ever told me that they love me, let alone show me any kindness!"

Daniel turns around and faces Mrs. June's yard, very emotional now as a tear falls down his cheek.

"I know that woman meant it…that, that was real." Says Daniel.

"I know, I…" Chloe begins to say.

"It's real." Says Daniel.

Chloe puts her hand on Daniel's shoulder and says,

"Awe…it's ok, don't cry."

"You don't understand that's the first time anyone…" Says Daniel

"One thing I know about Mrs. June is that if she says she loves you, she means it." Says Chloe.

Daniel nods as another tear falls down his cheek.

"I'm your friend, and I also love you. You can be yourself around me, you don't have to hide." Says Chloe.

They reach the apartment door, Chloe's hand still on Daniel's shoulder. Daniel opens the door, and Chloe asks,

"You gonna be ok?"

Daniel puts his hand over Chloe's hand, sitting on his shoulder, and says,

"Thank you, Chloe, I… I just need to be alone right now."

Chloe smiles and nods as Daniel enters the apartment.

"You understand, right?" Daniel asks.

"Of course, is it ok if I check on you later?" Asks Chloe.

"See you later." Says Daniel as he nods and closes the door behind him.

Chloe takes a deep breath and looks back over to Mrs. June's place, and begins to walk back to her yard as she looks back up to the clear blue sky.

Chapter 6: Things Open Up

A week after Daniel's Dirty Dancing

Anthony walks down a long corridor inside the Bloodbath arena. He enters a small gymnasium holding a large bag of Mexican food. The place is very old, with old gym equipment filling almost every spot in the place. Free weights are scattered all over the rubber floor. Green faded peeling paint on the walls, with framed pictures of wrestlers from years past. Heavy metal music is blasting from a large Bluetooth speaker hanging from one of the benches.

Anthony stands at the threshold as he stares at Tatyana on the other side of the gym. Tatyana squats over five hundred pounds on an Olympic bar with a large muscle man standing behind her as he spots her on the way down. A cameraman captures every moment as he places the camera right up close to the action. The Mic man holds the boom microphone over their heads as Jessica directs everything up close; they all look like they're in a huddle.

"Aaaaaaahhhh!" Tatyana screams as she pushes up the weight and stands.

"That's four! One more! One more!" Says the muscle man named Clarence.

"You got me Clearance?" Asks Tatyana

"I got you, go!" Says Clarence.

Tatyana squats down again, the muscle man grabs onto the back of her thighs, standing closely behind her so close he could be her shadow. The cameraman follows them down as he captures the shot from the side, then quickly moves to the front, where he can capture her from below.

"Yeaaaaaaahhhh!!" Tatyana screams as she pushes up again.

Every vein on her neck and forehead is protruding and pounding, as sweat drops down her face and flies off her upper lip, her spotter helping her towards the end as he puts his hands on her butt and helps her push the weight upwards.

"Push! Push!" Yells Clarence.

Tatyana fully stands, the man takes a few steps back, and Tatyana drops the weights.

BOOM!

"Hell Yeah!" Says Clarence as he slaps her butt.

He holds his hands up and Tatyana gives him a double high five, then they chest bump.

"You're a monster! That was awesome!" Says Clarence.

As Tatyana laughs, she sees Anthony looking at her from the threshold of the room. She waves at him, and he waves back. Tatyana turns to Jessica, the director, and says,

"Hey, can you give me a sec?"

Jessica nods, taps the cameraman on the shoulder, and says,

> "Alright, people, it's lunch time. Everyone take an hour. When you come back, let's meet in the parking lot. We need to take some shots of the wrestlers going home!"

Jessica turns to Tatyana and extends her fist; Tatyana fist bumps her.

> "That was awesome, darling, you were made for this!" Says Jessica.

> "Thank you, honey!" Says Tatyana

The crew begins to power down their equipment and exit the gym. Clarence taps Tatyana on the shoulder and asks,

> "Hey, I'm gonna go grab some Chinese food, you want anything?"

Tatyana begins to walk towards Anthony with a smile and says,

> "No, I'm good! I got lunch right here!"

Tatyana picks Anthony up, gives him a big hug, kisses him on the lips, and puts him down. They look at each other for a few seconds, their eyes lock into each other in a pregnant pause. She suddenly picks him up again, grabs Anthony's legs, and wraps them around her waist. She passionately kisses him again, and again, taking him completely by surprise as she holds him up like a child. Tatyana walks him over to the nearest wall and leans him up against it, making her way down his neck. She continues to kiss him passionately. Anthony then says,

"Wait…wait…baby."

And then something snaps in her mind, she comes to her senses, and she is suddenly unplugged from the heat of the moment. Realizing what she was doing, she put him back down gently, takes a few deep breaths, and says,

> "Sorry, I'm so sorry, I'm so sweaty… but I just couldn't help myself, you're so sexy, baby!"

> "Don't be sorry, I…I don't mind!" Says Anthony, smiling.

Tatyana bites her lower lip as she looks Anthony up and down and says,

> "I want you so bad…." Then she looks at the bag he's holding and asks, "Whatcha got there?"

Anthony holds up the large bag in his hand and says,

> "I stopped by the taqueria to have lunch with you, and they told me you were here. So I brought us some lunch."

Tatyana grabs Anthony in a bear hug and twirls him around as she plants kisses all over his face.

> "Thank you, honey! That is sooooo sweeeet," Says Tatyana.

Clarence walks by them and asks,

> "So, you sure you don't want anything?"

Tatyana looks at him, enraged now, and slowly puts Anthony down. She gathers herself for a second, takes a deep breath, and in a deep voice says,

"I said no, stupid!"

Clarence quickly turns away and hurriedly walks out of the gym. Tatyana's countenance quickly changes, and she smiles brightly, turns to Anthony, and says,

"Where were we?"

Anthony reaches up to Tatyana and slowly brings her down to his face. They are about to kiss when they are suddenly interrupted by Clarence, who has come back and now stands in the doorway.

"Hey, can I ask you something real quick? Clarence asks.

Without moving away from Anthony or breaking eye contact with him, she loudly barks at Clarence,

"IF YOU DON'T GET THE HELL OUT OF HERE, I WILL GRAB YOU BY YOUR TONGUE AND SWING YOU INTO A MIRROR!!"

Clarence runs away, they hear the footsteps quickly darting down the hallway, and they smile, then softly kiss. Tatyana takes the bag from Anthony, and they both sit down on opposite workout benches.

"Who was that guy? asks Anthony

Tatyana chuckles as she reaches into the bag.

"Remember audition day? She asks,

"Yeah." Says Anthony.

"The guy dressed in green?" She asks.

Tatyana opens a container with guacamole, dips her finger in it, and licks it.

"Thank you for bringing lunch," Tatyana says as she licks her lips.

"Yeah, I remember that guy," Anthony says.

"That's him, he calls himself the caterpillar, HA!" Says Tatyana as she gives Anthony a burrito.

Tatyana takes a bite from her burrito and slowly chews as she closes her eyes.

"Mmmmmmmmm, thif ith thooooo guuuuuud," she says.

Anthony smiles, she swallows, and leans over and plants a kiss on his lips as he chews.

"So does this mean I'm your girl?" She asks.

Anthony looks at her intensely, as he chews and smiles, he opens his mouth to answer, when suddenly a member of the production team bursts into the room, it's Jessica's assistant. She runs in, drops her phone on the floor, trips over it as she reaches to get it, and hits her head on a dumbbell, making a loud noise. Tatyana and Anthony quickly turn to look. The girl tries to stand up, trips again, and knocks a camera stand down. She tries to pick it up, but falls in front of it.

"What the hell is wrong with you! Don't you see we're busy here! Get out!" Says Tatyana.

The girl looks at Tatyana with fear as she repeatedly tries to get up. She finally does and says,

"I'm so sorry, sorry to interrupt, I forgot my wallet in my bag here." The girl says as she goes through a purse hanging from a barbell.

Tatyana and Anthony watch as she finally gets her wallet, then starts heading out the door. The girl goes to say something, but Tatyana squints her eyes, and the girl runs out. Tatyana shakes her head, then takes another bite of her burrito and looks over at Anthony.

"You ok today?" Asks Anthony.

Tatyana swallows her food and says,

"It's the steroids, I get a little jumpy at the beginning of an on-cycle."

Anthony's mouth drops.

"You taking steroids? Isn't that dangerous?" Asks Anthony.

Tatyana puts her hand on his knee to reassure him and says,

"No, baby! Don't believe all that stuff they say. You just have to know what you're doing. My voice gets a little bit deeper, and they make me a little bit jumpy at first, but after a few days, I'm fine. I gotta work through some unnecessary anger sometimes, that's all."

"Unnecessary anger?" Asks Anthony.

Tatyana puts her burrito down, looks Anthony in the eyes, and says,

"I would never get angry with you, or do anything to hurt you…You're my man now."

Anthony smiles and takes another bite of his burrito. Tatyana looks around, puts her right hand on his knee, and says,

"There are some other hidden benefits of these supplements," Says Tatyana.

Anthony looks around, then looks back at her and says,

"Oh yeah?"

Tatyana smiles and says,

"I'm always in the mood, if you know what I mean."

Anthony puts his Burrito down and swallows his food.

"I haven't been able to stop thinking about you since the other night." Says Tatyana as she reaches for him.

"What are you doing! Anyone can just walk in!" Says Anthony.

"Then you better hurry up!" Says Tatyana as she grabs him and pulls him into her.

Daniel is hanging out with Chloe in her bedroom. Chloe sits on her bed barefoot as she works on her laptop and looks out the window at the afternoon sunlight coming into her room. Her walls are covered in posters of pop stars and anime characters, shelves loaded with books and stuffed animals. Her computer speakers are blasting dance music, and Daniel is on the floor playing a game on his phone. Chloe looks up from her laptop at Daniel and says,

> "I hope you don't mind me asking, but did your mom buy you dresses or just allow you to put her clothes on?"

Daniel picks up his head and looks at her. Chloe thinks she may have touched on a sore point and says,

> "Sorry, that may not have been appropriate."

Daniel smiles and says,

> "No, that's cool." He looks up at the ceiling and continues, "I mean, my mom, as long as I can remember, has allowed me to wear her clothes, but she has bought me some things down through the years."

> "Oh yeah?" Says Chloe.

> "Yeah, a few summer dresses, a skirt, some blouses. She loves putting make-up on me, honestly, I really believe it turns her on more than it does me, ha, ha."

Says Daniel as Chloe chuckles as she reads something on her laptop.

"Did your mom ever talk about why she stopped wrestling?" Asked Chloe.

Daniel puts his phone down and says,

"She told me she got pregnant with me, and my dad disappeared, so she had to raise me alone."

Chloe points to her laptop and says,

"Well, not exactly. It looks like she was locked up for beating up her boyfriend and another guy. You never did any research on your mom?"

Daniel opens his mouth in surprise and jumps on the bed next to Chloe to look.

"What! I never saw that she was arrested!" Says Daniel.

"Look at this old article from a local newspaper. It says here she was sentenced to five years for assaulting David Newman and Michael Johnson. Look at this picture of her being brought into prison," Says Chloe.

"She was pregnant!" Says Daniel.

Chloe nods in agreement.

"That's me!" Daniel shouts.

Chloe and Daniel look at each other.

"I was born in jail!" Says Daniel.

“She never told you?” Asks Chloe.

Daniel gets up from the bed and begins to pace back and forth in the room nervously.

“No! She never mentioned any of this! What else did you find? Asks Daniel.

“What’s the earliest memory you have?” Asks Chloe.

Daniel jumps back on the bed and says,

“I remember my grandmother more than my mom… I spent most of my time with grandma when I was very young.”

“So what is your first memory of your mom?” Asks Chloe.

Daniel looks up, puts his hand on his chin, and thinks for a moment, then says,

“Well, I remember my grandma and I taking trips to see my mom at work, or at least they told me she was away at work. The place was big, we always met in the playground…” Daniel puts his hand up to his forehead as he realizes the truth, then says, “…and that was prison, wasn’t it? They actually took me to prison to see her and told me she was working… damn.”

“You were just a little kid, you didn’t know!” Says Chloe.

"I… I remember living with my grandmother the most. I must have been around nine when my mom started coming to visit me. I guess she was out by then. But it was a few years later that she took me to live with her." Says Daniel

"That makes sense, your granny took care of you while she was in prison, then she came and got you." Says Chloe.

"If she was in for five years, why did she wait so long to come get me?" Asks Daniel.

Chloe points at something on the laptop and says,

"Well, look, it says here in this article that they added three years to her sentence when she was inside, due to bad behavior."

"What?" Asks Daniel.

"Looks like she beat the crap out of a few inmates when she was three years in, so she got some added time for that. Then, a year after that, she got into it with a guard and beat him up really badly, so she got time added for that. Then she went silent. She served a total of eight years, a bit more than that." Explained Chloe.

"WOW…" Says Daniel.

"So you remember her coming around when you were nine. When did you start living with her?" Asked Chloe.

"She took me away from my grandma when I was about eleven. This is so messed up! How come I never put it together?"

Chloe puts her hand on Daniel's shoulder and says,

"Daniel, I'm sorry, I was just curious and started digging."

"How could I have not known, or realized… she lied to me my whole life!" Says Daniel.

"Daniel…"Says Chloe

Daniel begins to pace around the room.

"She told me she was working, all those phone calls, Birthdays, Christmases!" Says Daniel.

"But she's here now, Daniel, she did come and get you when she could." Says Chloe.

"I wish she had left me at my grandmother's house, honestly."

Chloe puts her laptop aside, gets up, and asks,

"Why? What happened?

Daniel looks at her, and his eyes begin to tear up. Chloe approaches him and asks,

"What?"

Daniel does not respond.

"Please, Daniel… what did she do to you? What happened to you?" Asks Chloe.

Daniel shakes his head and says,

> "You're the first person that I am going to tell this to."

> "It's that bad?" Asks Chloe.

> "You have no idea." Says Daniel as tears flow down his face.

> "I'm sorry." Says Chloe.

Daniel wipes his eyes and says,

> "Soon after my mom got me from my grandmother's house, we moved to Texas. Everything was new, and it was a little weird to be with her rather than my grandmother because I really had no solid relationship with my mom. Mom did promise me that everything would be fine, that she would make things work. But it was hard for her to find steady work, money started drying up, and it got to a point where I would see her less and less when I got home from school. It seemed like I did not fit in her world. She came home late one night with some guy from a bar, and they were both drunk. I was in my room asleep, but they were making so much noise that they woke me up. I got up, walked to the living room, and walked in on them…"

> "She got mad?" Asks Chloe.

Daniel looks at her, wipes his eyes again, and says,

"She beat me so bad, I couldn't walk for days. She kept me home from school until I got better and told the teachers I was sick."

"Oh my gosh!" Says Chloe.

"As soon as I could walk, I ran away from home. I wanted to go back to my grandmother's, but I had no phone number for her, I didn't know her address, I wandered the streets for a few days, living with the homeless people. They treated me surprisingly good."

"What happened? Did anyone come looking for you?" Asks Chloe.

"No. Eventually, and out of hunger, I made my way back to my mom's apartment. I rang the bell and she let me in without saying a word, as if nothing had happened, as if I had only been away for a few hours. It was… so bizarre. She microwaved a TV dinner for me, bathed me, and put one of her blouses on me."

"Wow, that is weird." Says Chloe.

"I broke the awkward silence when I told her I liked the blouse. Without saying a word, she went to her room and got one of her skirts; she put it on me. For some reason, my dressing up in women's clothing became like a bonding thing between me and her. It went from that to make up to bathing with her, and so forth; that's how we started to form a relationship. She treated me like a little girl, and I guess I liked it, I liked the attention, I liked the fact that she did not hit me anymore, and that she paid attention to me, so I went along with it, I learned to like it…and here I am."

Chloe grabs Daniel and gives him a big hug, saying,

"I'm glad you're here, Daniel…"

"You're the only friend I've ever really had." Says Daniel as he hugs her back.

Chloe takes a step forward to give Daniel a hug again, and he immediately grabs her and hugs her back, holding her tightly.

"Daniel…"Says Chloe.

But before she could finish the sentence, Daniel turns around and runs out. Chloe watches as he runs down the hallway, then she hears him running down the staircase, the kitchen door opens, then shuts. Chloe runs over to her window and sees him running to the apartment.

"What did they do to you, Daniel?" Chloe whispers.

Chapter 7: It's Showtime!

Two weeks later, Saturday night, it's fight night! And the Bloodbath arena is filled with spectators. Food vendors walk up and down the aisles offering hot dogs, popcorn, and other snacks to the people. The announcer gives the play-by-play over the PA system as two wrestlers battle it out on the center ring. The production team from the TV show captures everything with multiple cameras, close to the ring, some capture the crowd, and one camera on a jib. Chloe, Anthony, Jose, and his wife, Yolanda, are clapping and screaming as they watch the fight just a few rows back from the ring. One of the wrestlers pins the other, and the whole stadium begins to shout and count alongside the referee.

"ONE…TWO…THREE!" screams the crowd, and everyone goes wild, and the wrestlers slowly get up.

Yolanda taps Anthony on the shoulder and asks him,

"Hey, when is your girl coming out?"

Anthony looks over at Yolanda, surprised at what she just said.

"Don't look at me like that, Anthony. Anyone with any kind of sense can see that you two are together."

Jose looks at the pamphlet in his hand, then taps Yolanda on her thigh and says,

"She's coming out next! She's coming out next!"

The announcer gets on the P.A. Speaker and yells,

"Ladieeeees and gentlemeeeeeeen!"

The lights in the arena dim, and a spotlight shines on one of the doors heading to the dressing room. The announcer continues to say,

> "For our next match, we have a storm heading your way!! Help me welcome her to the ring! From the depths of the Atlantic, all the way from New York City…. The great terror of the deep… OOOOOORRCAAAAAAAA!"

The door opens and out comes a female wrestler dressed in black and white spandex. Her face is painted as a killer whale, and her long black hair, tied in a ponytail. Deep blue and green lights flood the place. As she makes her way to the ring, screaming and waving her hands, sounds of killer whales and ocean waves fill the auditorium. The crowd cheers her on as she smiles and waves. She climbs the ring and begins to jump around in anticipation.

The mood changes quickly when all the lights go dark, and the whale sounds subside. Jose begins to jump up and down as the spotlight travels to the opposite side of the ring and shines on a different door in the back of the stadium. Everyone begins to cheer in expectation. Blood red lights begin to shine; they fill the whole stadium, turning everything red. The former Soviet Union anthem begins to play through the overhead speakers, and the crowd gets more excited. People begin to scream. The announcer gets on the P.A. System and says,

> "Aaaaaaaand NOW! Left over from the former Soviet Union, a killer, left over from the Cold War, with a colder heart to match…Aaaaaall the way from Moscow! The Russian Death, or as we know her in these parts…
>
> LA MUERTEEEEEEEE RUUUUUUUSAAAAA!!"

Tatyana comes out of the back door dressed in a very tight red spandex body suit, with a yellow sickle and hammer on her chest. Wearing knee-high black wrestling boots and her blonde hair tied in a bun, she slowly marches her way up to the ring.

As she walks up the aisle, she gives high fives to the spectators. An old man takes advantage and grabs her boob as she passes, she backslaps him so hard, she knocks him out cold. People love it and cheer her on even more. The old man is placed back on his chair by an old lady beside him, who slaps him repeatedly to wake him up.

Tatyana makes her way to the ring and begins to taunt her opponent inside the ring by running around it and screaming repeatedly,

> "It's time to die!! It's time to die!"

She climbs into the ring and stands in a corner watching her opponent as she grimaces.

Jose looks at Anthony, Yolanda, and Chloe and begins to chant Tatyana's stage name.

"Muerte Rusa! Muerte Rusa!"

They join in, and the chant catches on; soon, the whole stadium is chanting it. The bell rings, and everyone quiets down as the wrestlers rush to the center of the ring and begin to taunt each other. The Orca rushes Tatyana head-on, screaming like a banshee, but she is suddenly and violently stopped by Tatyana's boot in her face. The Announcer giving all the details says,

> "The Orca coming in for a bite of her soviet foe…Ouch! Gets a nasty foot in the face instead! A little bit of blood on the mat already, I think the Orca lost a tooth, she shakes her head, and the two wrestlers begin to circle the ring again!"

The two wrestlers interlock at the center of the ring. Tatyana quickly reaches down and grabs the Orca by her feet and knocks her onto her back. She begins to twirl her in circles like a helicopter, lets her go, the Orca hits one of the corner cushion guards, dizzy and out of balance, she stumbles and falls as she tries to get up. The announcer rallies up the crowd, saying,

> "The Orca and Muerte Rusa lock in the middle here. Oh! The Russian titan grabs the Orca's fins and starts up a helicopter move! Look at Orca's arms as she swings them wildly with every spin. The Orca throws up a little, Muerte lets her go! Unbelievable! The Orca slammed against the corner, looking more like a sardine at this point!"

Tatyana runs towards her opponent, grabs her by her left arm, and picks her up. Orca throws up on Tatyana's boot.

> "The Russian Mountain avalanches towards the little whale, grabs her fin…oops, the Orca spits out some more seawater." Says the announcer.

The two wrestlers look down at the throw up, then at each other. Suddenly, the Orca bites into Tatyana's forearm.

> "Unbelievable! The Orca literally takes a bite out of the Russian mama's arm!" Says the announcer.

Tatyana becomes enraged, punches the Orca right in the nose, and blood splashes everywhere, then she flips her onto the mat.

> "Strong punch to the nose by La Muerte! La Rusa flips the whale! We've got a bleeder!" says the announcer.

Tatyana reaches down and picks her opponent up. She elbows the Orca in the face repeatedly as blood splashes onto the mat as if from an open faucet. The announcer screaming on the mic,

> "She goes to work on the Orca, ladies and gentlemen! Looks like she wants to see what the inside of her skull looks like, La Rusa diggin into the head with her elbow!"

The Orca grabs Tatyana by her head and head-buts her in the forehead. They look at each other for a second, Orca expecting Tatyana to be hurt, but Tatyana is not moved and head-buts her right back, then again, then again, and again, deforming the Orca's face.

"It's a head-bashing dream!! Git sooooome!"
Screams the announcer.

Tatyana reaches down and picks up Orca by her feet. With
one fast movement, she swings her over her head and slams
her down on the other side of the ring, face-first.

"La Muerte reaches down again and grabs the orca
by her tail fins! And like a rag doll, she picks her up
feet first….over the top of her head she swings her
and slams her down face first onto the mat!! That
looked like it hurt!!" Says the announcer, and the
arena goes nuts!

Tatyana looks over to the Orca, and she's out cold, face-
first down on the mat, with splattered blood underneath her
face. The referee runs and lifts Tatyana's arm in victory.

"It's over, folks! La Muerte Rusa, dominating this
fight tonight! The Orca got a complimentary factory
reset to the head. She left it all on the mat, including
blood, teeth, vomit, and from the bulge on her ass, it
looks like she relieved herself into her leotard there
at the end! What a fight! What a fight!" Screams the
announcer as everyone is on their feet, screaming
and applauding.

Jose, Anthony, Yolanda, and Chloe run to ringside as
Tatyana climbs down from the ring. She sees them coming,
smiles, and waves at them. The four of them surround her
as she stands ringside.

"That was amazing! I've never seen you like that
before!" Says Jose.

"You were awesome!!" Says Anthony.

Tatyana smiles widely, reaches out, grabs Anthony, and hugs him hard.

"I've ever seen anyone just, completely beat the shit out of another girl!" Says Yolanda as she reaches out and hugs Tatyana herself.

"Thank you for inviting us!" Says Chloe.

Tatyana kisses Chloe on the forehead and says,

"Of course, honey!"

She puts her arm around Anthony and says,

"Come on, guys, let's go to the dressing room!"

As they all walk away from the ring and towards one of the back doors, Chloe looks back at the other wrestler. The Orca is unrecognizable as her face has almost doubled in size, she's covered in blood, her eyes are almost completely shut from the swelling. As medics lift her onto a stretcher, she tries to say something and opens her mouth, but spits out teeth instead, her eyes roll back into her head, and she faints.

Chloe turns to look at Tatyana walking ahead of her with her father beside her. She's a giant, almost two feet taller than her dad, her back twice the size with bulging trapezoids. Tatyana is a mountain of muscle and rage, and it is then that Chloe realizes the danger that her dad may truly be in.

Tatyana gives people in the crowd high fives as she passes them, they pat her on the back, and reach out just to touch her. They all go through the door facing the arena, walk down a short hallway, and enter a large set of double doors. The dressing room is badly lit, old rusty lockers surround the room, large open bins with towels in the corners, the old white tile floor is wet and dirty. Naked and half-dressed women walk around them as if they didn't even exist.

"Should we be in here?" Asks Jose

"Yeah, yeah, it's ok, just don't go into the shower area over there, that's where the naughty stuff happens." Says Tatyana as she points to the shower area.

"Oh yeah?" Says Jose as he turns to look.

Yolanda smacks Jose's shoulder, and he turns back around smiling.

Tatyana sits on a bench, begins to take a boot off, and says,

"I'm so happy that you guys could make it! It means so much to me!"

A camera crew comes into the locker room and begins to record Tatyana with her friends.

Daniel storms in right behind the camera crew. He runs up to his mother and hugs her as she takes her second boot off. Tatyana smiles, leans back, and hugs Daniel as she kisses his head

"Hi, Baby!" Says Tatyana,

"Hi, Mom!" Says Daniel as he pulls away from her.

Tatyana looks at Daniel up and down. He's wearing a white dress shirt, black dress pants, and a black tie. Before she could ask, Jessica, the director, walks in, kisses Tatyana on the cheek, and says,

"Honey, you were amazing! Great fucking show! I can't believe it!"

"Thank you, Jess!" Says Tatyana.

Jessica reaches into her front pocket, pulls out a business card, and hands it to Tatyana, who takes it and checks it out.

"This guy's big time, he's a manager, and part owner of… Well, I'll let him explain it to ya. I've worked with some of his clients before, and they all went mainstream, so…"

"Alright now! Says Anthony

"That's awesome!" Says Jose.

Jessica smiles widely and pats Tatyana on her shoulder, saying,

"Yeah, he watched the whole show, and I didn't even know he was here! This is big for you! Big Tatyana!"

Anthony, Jose, Daniel, Yolanda, and Chloe clap and cheer for Tatyana as they hear the news. They are happy for her. Jessica walks towards the door and says,

"Okay, I've got to get out of here. We got one more match for the guys tonight, but I'll catch you later!"

Everyone watches as she exits the dressing room, then they look at Tatyana, who is now staring at Daniel.

"So, how come you were not with everyone else?" Asks Tatyana.

Daniel gets a little bit nervous, swallows hard, and adjusts his tie.

"Well, ugh, I got here right before your match started, actually. I looked around and could not find the seats, so I watched from the balcony. I… I ran when I saw you guys coming back here!" Says Daniel

Tatyana looks him up and down, and with a serious face asks,

"You dress up just for me?"

Everyone looks at Daniel now, and he becomes a bit fidgety because of the attention.

"I ugh…came from church actually." Answers Daniel.

Tatyana's countenance changes at once to one of anger and disappointment, and everyone can see it and definitely feel it.

Before Daniel could answer, Chloe jumped in front of him and said to him,

"Daniel, I'm so glad you made it! We're going to get pizza after this! And there's this new ice cream parlor downtown we want to take you guys to, that I know you will love! It's going to be great!"

Daniel, with fear in his eyes, looks over at his mom, saying,

"Sounds like a lot of fun, I…I can't wait."

Tatyana throws her boot on the floor and says to everyone,

"Guys, can you give me a few minutes alone with Daniel, please?"

"Sure, we'll wait for you guys out here." Says Anthony.

"Come on, Yo-yo, let's wait outside." Says Jose to his wife, and they all exit the dressing room.

The cameraman recording Tatyana moves around to get a better shot of her, and Tatyana looks over at him with disdain and says,

"Can you guys give me five minutes, please? I need to talk to my son…please."

The cameraman stands up, disappointed, and slowly turns the camera off as he looks at her. The audio guy with the mic lowers the boom and quickly walks out of the dressing room, and the cameraman follows him.

Tatyana waits for them to leave, then she continues to undress. She takes the top part of her spandex suit off and lets it hang. She adjusts her sports bra, pats a bench right next to her, and says,

"Sit down, Daniel."

Daniel sits, Tatyana gets really close to him, Daniel cringes in fear as she turns to him and says,

"I never told you why I don't want you hanging around bible people."

Tatyana pats Daniel's head and adjusts his tie, setting him at ease; his countenance changes from fear to curiosity.

"Why?" Asks Daniel

Tatyana leans forward and looks out into the locker room, speaking as if she were re-living the past…she says,

"When I was a little girl, my parents were very religious. My dad was a construction worker, mama stayed at home. We went to church every Sunday. My mom, your grandma, she took me to church even on Wednesday night and Friday nights."

"WOW, really?" Says Daniel.

"Yup, but that's not all, because my mom also worked in the church. She cleaned it through the week with a few other ladies and even helped cook for church functions, I mean, she was dedicated." Says Tatyana.

"Doesn't seem bad." Says Daniel.

"Then, daddy passed away in a car accident, and mama couldn't make the mortgage payments anymore. We were in a lot of debt really quickly." Says Tatyana.

"What happened?" Asked Daniel.

"The preacher, he got a member in the church who was a real estate agent help my mom sell her house. She used most of the money to pay off old debts, and Reverend Thomas allowed us to come live with him and his family; he had a wife and six kids. Mom and I slept in a large shed in his backyard. We had to come into the house to use the bathroom and didn't have any running water, but at least we had a place to lay our heads." Says Tatyana as Daniel looks on. She continues,

"One night, not long after we moved in, mom left with the pastor and his wife to do some ministering, church stuff… he preached in the streets. Jimmy, his oldest son, was babysitting his brothers and sisters and me; he must have been about fifteen, maybe sixteen years old.

So we were all watching a movie on the TV, and I got up to go to the bathroom. I must have been about six years old at the time. And…while I was sitting on the toilet, I saw the door slightly open and I could see Jimmy looking in. I asked him to close the door, but he opened it more, and I could see that he was masturbating. I didn't understand it fully then, but I know now… Anyway, I felt uncomfortable and wanted to leave, so I stood up, but before I could pull my underwear up, her rushes in, locks the door behind him, and pins me down. Before I could say anything, his dick was up my ass."

"Oh my God!" Says Daniel.

"I cried, and cried, and bled a lot. When he was done with me, he undressed me and put me in the shower. He said he wanted to clean me up. I ran out of the shower naked and ran all the way out to the shed and locked the door. All the other kids laughed at me because I was naked.

 When mom came home, I told her what had happened, and she was very upset. She spanked me and told me to be more careful, as if I had done something wrong. She wanted me to keep it quiet because she was afraid we would get kicked out of the house and end up in the street." Says Tatyana as she gets up and pulls her spandex suit completely off.

"Mom, I…I'm so sorry," Says Daniel as he gets teary-eyed. Tatyana continues,

"Jimmy continued to rape me and got two of his brothers and a friend from down the street to join in from time to time. They would screw each other, but they all took their turn with me."

"Mom…" Says Daniel.

"I tried to tell my mom, but she didn't want to hear it, told me to shut up and stop lying. One time, one time the second-oldest son, Nelson was his name, he was on top of me, and as I looked away, I saw the bedroom door open, and his dad was looking in. He had come home early, and I thought… Finally! I was rescued; someone would finally save me from this hell. But he looked straight at me and then quickly closed the door." Says Tatyana.

"He knew, and didn't do anything?" Asks Daniel.

Tatyana takes he sports bra off, throws it with the dirty clothes, and smells her armpit. She looks at Daniel and says,

"He knew, and didn't do a damn thing. From time to time, I would catch him peeking from behind a door, or looking at the boys and me from another room, but he never stopped them; he never helped me. After six years of getting raped in every room of that house, the shed, and in the field behind the house, Mom was finally able to put money together to get her own apartment."

"So that was good, and what happened after that?" Asks Daniel.

"Well, mama continued to go to church, but I stopped going altogether. She could not understand why, and she would get so mad at me…But I was done with those people, DONE! But deep inside, I was always looking for love and kindness, something I never really got at home. Well, there was a girl at school, her name was Linda, and she was always nice to me. We became friends, and I developed a crush on that girl, and she was definitely crushing on me too!

On the way home from school one day, she mustered up the courage to reach out and kiss me on the lips; she left me stunned. I reached right back and kissed her as passionately as I could; it was like someone had opened the dam gates, and floods of emotions were pouring out of me. I'll never forget it. After that day, we became lovers.

I loved that girl; it was the first time I felt like someone understood me, you know, I felt intimate with her.

One day, Mama came home from church early and found me having sex with Linda on the couch. Mama had a fit, we had a big fight, Linda ran out the door, and that night I ran away from home." Says Tatyana as she smells her other armpit and rubs her underboob.

"Wow, and what happened to those boys?" says Daniel.

"Those boys, Jimmy and them, they were going to church the whole time they were raping me and having homo orgies on each other. Their daddy knew, and that's what still hurts me the most, that he did nothing." Says Tatyana.

"What did you do after you left grandma?" Asks Daniel.

"I lived with a few girlfriends, Linda went to college, and I eventually lost touch with her. I worked some odd jobs here and there. One of the girls I was with was into fitness, so I started lifting weights with her and got into wrestling soon after that, and never looked back…" Says Tatyana.

"How come you never told me?" Asks Daniel.

"I never really had a reason to tell you until now, I want you to live your own life, carve your own story, you know?" Says Tatyana as she reaches out and messes with his hair.

"And Linda?" Asks Daniel.

"Years later, I saw Linda at one of my matches. I was so happy to see her; she had finished college, gotten engaged, she had moved on… We still keep in touch from time to time, and I see her postings on social media. I still love her…" Says Tatyana.

Daniel reaches out and puts his hand on his mom's massive shoulder and says,

"I'm so sorry, Mom.."

Tatyana smiles and puts her hand on top of his and says,

"Don't be. If I had stayed with her, I probably never would have made you, and you are my life now! You are everything to me, baby! I'll kill a hundred men to protect you…believe me!"

They both look at each other for a few seconds. Tatyana can see that there's something bothering Daniel, she asks,

"What is it?"

"Can I ask you something?" Daniel asks, feeling a bit encouraged.

"Sure." Says Tatyana.

"Why didn't you tell me you were in prison?" Daniel asks.

Tatyana looks at Daniel, surprised that he knew the truth, and asks,

"What? How did you find out?"

"Mom, it's on the internet: your mug shot, the articles about you beating up those men, your extended sentence for bad behavior. Why did you keep all that from me? You told me you had been away working all that time! Grandma too!" Daniel asks.

Tatyana leans forward, resting her elbows on her knees, and looks at the floor for a few seconds. Then she leans back on the lockers, looks at Daniel, and says,

"Because I'm a bad person, I lie, and I cheat, and I hurt the ones I love…I was trying to save face with the son I gave birth to in a prison hospital. I made my mom lie to you all those years under the threat that she would never see you again unless she went along with it. I should have told you the truth, but there never seemed to be a right moment to do it. The longer I waited to say something, the harder it got, until I just gave up trying. I'm sorry, baby, I wish that I would have had the courage to tell you."

Daniel and Tatyana look at each other eye to eye for a minute without saying a word, then she says,

"Can you forgive me? I'm trying to do better. With this gig, I can make a lot more money for us than in that restaurant. I want you to be able to go to college, make something of yourself, get a sex change, the operations like we talked…"

"I don't know about that anymore, Mom." Says Daniel.

"Well, I want to provide for you, whatever you want, just… please give me that chance?" Asks Tatyana.

Daniel looks at his mom, she seems sincere about what she's saying, so he nods in agreement and says,

"I get it…I get it."

"I'm the one that's gonna take care of you, not those church people, believe me…?" Says Tatyana.

Daniel nods again and puts his head down. Tatyana leans over to him and kisses the top of his head. She slaps her knees and stands up.

"I love you, and will always love you, so believe me when I say, stay away from those church people, they will betray you." Says Tatyana.

"Mrs. June is nice, Mom…" Says Daniel.

"Stay away from them, Daniel." Says Tatyana.

Tatyana takes her panties off, rubs her crotch, and smells her hand.

"Damn, I need a shower. I stink." Says Tatyana.

She begins to walk towards the showers, turns around, and points at Daniel, who is still looking at her, and says,

"I'm going to take a quick shower, then we can go and celebrate, ok?"

Daniel smiles.

"Hey, I got you that red minidress you liked. I can't wait to see you in it!" Tatyana says with a smile.

Daniel slightly smiles and nods his head; Tatyana disappears in the steam coming out of the showers.

Later That Night

Mrs. June sits alone in the dark on her rocking chair in her backyard. Everything is quiet except for the sound of crickets in the air. She rocks back and forth as she looks up in wonder at the sky filled with stars. She sips her hot tea and turns to look as she hears a car come up Anthony's driveway, then suddenly stop. Truck doors open and slam shut. She hears voices getting closer, then Daniel and Chloe come around the corner, laughing and carrying on as they walk to their back door and go into the house.

Tatyana and Anthony slowly walk up the driveway, but head over to Tatyana's place instead. Mrs. June watches, underneath the shadows of her trees, the only visible light on her side of the property is her kitchen light.

Anthony and Tatyana slowly walk and talk until Tatyana turns and puts her hands around Anthony's neck, interlocking her fingers behind his neck, and walks him back to her door. She reaches down into his pants, unlocks the door with the other, and walks him into her place. Anthony closes the door behind them.

Mrs. June takes a sip of her tea and whispers to herself,

"You didn't have to ride this mare, Anthony…God had better for you."

Chapter 8: The Lioness, the Student, and the Ring

Six Days, Six Hours, and Six Minutes Later

It's a bright sunny day in Tonopah, the sun is high in the sky, and not a cloud to be seen. The back of Manuel's Taqueria is littered with spilled garbage, empty plastic crates, stacks of wooden pallets, and cardboard boxes. The back door to the taqueria slams open, and Tatyana comes out holding six exceptionally large, overfilled garbage bags. A dog sitting by the door, chewing on a bone, gets startled and runs away together with the multitude of pigeons that take flight from the rooftop. Tatyana looks up at them as they fly away, looks at the dog as he walks away, then spits on the concrete as she makes her way to the dumpster. Tatyana is sweaty, her hair is disheveled, and she looks very tired. She opens the dumpster lids and throws all the bags in at once. She wipes the sweat off her brow with her apron and frowns as she closes the lid; the smell of rotten meat coming from inside is disgusting. Then she hears a male voice that says,

"You never called me."

Tatyana hears the voice, but she does not see anyone. She takes a few steps towards the lot in front of her, then a few steps towards the taqueria, and looks around.

"Why? Says the male voice.

"Where are you?" Asks Tatyana as she walks around the wall encasing the dumpster.

Tatyana is surprised by what she sees on the other side of that wall. Leaning against the side of a Rolls-Royce is a middle-aged man with slick black hair and a very fancy black suit. He smiles when he sees Tatyana coming around the side wall.

"Who are you?" Tatyana asks

The man stands up straight, straightens up his suit jacket, and walks up to Tatyana, extending his left hand. Tatyana shakes it.

"My name is Lucious White. I believe Jessica gave you my card?" Says Lucious.

Tatyana looks at Lucious and takes it all in: the car, the suit, the mobster's slick back hair do, and she wonders as to what this is all about.

"Yeah, it was about two days ago…or something like that?"

Lucious smiles and says,

"Actually, six days, six hours and…" he lifts his hand and looks at his diamond-studded watch, "wait, wait…and six minutes ago, but who's counting right?"

"You're that mana…" Says Tatyana as she reaches out and shakes his hand.

Lucious takes her hand, softly kisses it, then gently lets it go.

"Yes, that's me. I did not get a call from you, so I figured I'd reach out to you in person, something I usually do not do…But for you, I had to make an exception. So I got into my car, drove out of Scottsdale, down the 17, got to Route 10, and drove and drove. Until I finally got to this, this filthy, god-forsaken shit hole of a restaurant truck stop thing." Says Lucious.

"Just for little 'ol me." Says Tatyana.

Lucious caresses his greasy black hair with one hand, smiles, and says,

"I wouldn't say little, but yes, just to see you."

Tatyana puts her hands on her hips, stands with her legs apart, at attention, looks him up and down, and says,

"And there you are…"

"Here I am…" Says Lucious.

He leans back on his car, looks Tatyana dead in the eyes, and says,

"Here I am, about to make you the offer of a lifetime. The type of offer that only comes once. The kind of offer that will make you glad, or sad for the rest of your life."

"Oh yeah?" Says Tatyana.

"Oh yeah!" Says Lucious.

Lucious pulls away from his car and begins to walk in circles around Tatyana as he looks her up and down. He says,

> "I'm part-owner of the World Action Network, and we broadcast sports on channels all over the world. Professional Wrestling is my baby, and I'm always looking for new talent, fresh faces, special people that I know would do well…
>
> But sometimes, I came across that one person who has that something extra. That someone who has something so special that it will make them stand out above everyone else.
>
> They have that special something that makes me want to get personally involved and make sure they get everything this fucking life has to offer."

With his index finger, Lucious reaches out and catches a drop of sweat that's about to fall off Tatyana's chin. He takes the drop, puts it in his mouth, smiles wide, and says,

> "And that is why I'm here."

"Oh yeah?" says Tatyana.

"Oh yeah…" Says Lucious as he stops right in front of her, he continues to say,

> "I know you're doing this little thing with Jessica right now. But…and here comes the offer, would

you be interested in wrestling in the big leagues for me? I would manage you personally. You'll be making at least four million in the first two years. I know it's not much, but the bag will only get bigger from there. I'm talking television commercials, toy collectibles, comic books, trading cards, cereal boxes, you name it, you'll be on it. Then, we'll transition to movies, Hollywood is looking for someone…just…like…you, and that's when the big money starts coming in. Action movies, comedies, you name it…it can all be yours." Says Lucious.

Tatyana looks up at the sun, wipes the sweat from her forehead again, and says,

"What do you get out of it, my soul?" Asks Tatyana jokingly.

Lucious bursts out in a wicked laugh. He quickly gathers himself, looks at Tatyana side-eyed, and says,

"Well…"

"WELL?" Asks Tatyana.

Lucious takes a deep breath, reaches into his inner jacket pocket, and pulls out a cigar. He bites the end off and lights it with a gold lighter. He takes a deep puff, exhales, and says,

"Inside of you is a fucking lioness waiting to get out. I saw it the other night. This is the right time, the only time for you to become what you were meant to be!"

Tatyana looks down at herself. She takes a good look at her sweaty shirt stuck to her body, the dirty apron, and she looks further down at her sweaty legs, her dirty socks, and filthy sneakers covered in food spills. Then she looks up at Lucious, who is looking straight back at her in his shiny suit, spotless leather shoes, leaning on a Rolls Royce while he smokes his fat cigar.

"Let me transform you! Let me make you the mega star that you were meant to be!" Lucious says.

"For my soul?" Asks Tatyana.

Lucious takes a drag off the cigar, blows circles of smoke into the air as he looks at Tatyana's eyes, and she looks back at him intensely. His eyes flash bright red for a second, and then he says,

"Just say yes…"

Lucious puts his index finger up slowly, then says,

"This offer comes once…and only once."

Tatyana takes a deep breath, then takes her apron off and throws it on the ground.

"Well?" Tatyana asks.

"Well, what?" Asks Lucious.

"Are you gonna open your car door so I can get in? Or do I have to do it myself?" Says Tatyana.

Lucious gives her a big smile, he quickly walks to the passenger side door and opens it. Tatyana nods and gets in, Lucious closes the door behind her, and slowly walks to the driver's side. He enters the car, takes a look at Tatyana, and smiles as he starts the car. Tatyana is wide-eyed as she looks around the inside of the car, touching the leather seats, the dashboard, and the ceiling. Lucious says,

"Open the glove compartment."

Tatyana opens the glove compartment, looks in, and quickly glances over at Lucious, who smiles. Inside, there's a single piece of cream-colored paper sitting on top of several bundles of money. She looks at the money, then over at Mr. White.

"Sign at the dotted line, and we can be on our way, we can begin our journey together." Says Lucious as he holds out a gold pen.

Tatyana takes the pen, picks up the paper, and quickly reads through it.

"Are you serious? This is very basic, I mean my previous manager had a lot more stipulations than this!" Says Tatyana.

"Think of it as a prelude to the actual contract. This is just a preliminary document; there's more to come, but this is enough to get us started." Says Lucious.

"And this money?" Asks Tatyana as she signs the document on her lap, and hands it to Mr. White, who quickly takes it and puts it in his inside jacket pocket.

"That's to get you started, baby, a little sign-on bonus for you. I can't have you walking around looking like a homeless person, driving that thing you call a truck…" Says Lucious with a greasy smile.

Tatyana grabs the cash and begins to put it in her pockets. Lucious smiles and drives away.

At the very exact moment, all the way across town…

Chloe sits in a large corporate office waiting room filled with young adults, some standing around, others sitting as they all wait their turn. Large windows on one of the walls allow the sunlight to flood the waiting room. ASU posters splatter the walls.

A receptionist by the door on a large desk talks on the phone, and a teenage girl wearing sweatpants stands in front of her desk, waiting to talk to her. The desk is covered with ASU paraphernalia and fully decorated with university posters. The receptionist takes an ASU pen from one of the many university mugs on her desk and gives it to the girl in front of her. She motions to the girl to take a seat as she still talks on the phone. The girl reluctantly takes the pen, walks away with an attitude, and sits next to Chloe.

Chloe looks at the girl who just sat down next to her, nervously looks at the time on her phone, then over to a closed office door in the corner. The sign on the door says *Linda Shultz*. The door opens, and Chloe perks up as a young man exits the office door. A beautiful, tall black woman wearing a gray suit comes to the door. The woman looks over the waiting room area and says out loud,

"Chloe! Chloe Borgia! You're next!"

Chloe raises her hand with excitement and says,

"Coming!"

Linda places her eyes on Chloe and smiles as she plays with a few curls from her Afro. Chloe grabs her bags, the architectural presentation tube, and walks towards Linda. Linda is tall, so tall that Chloe has to look up when she finally stands in front of her, smiling, Linda says,

"Hi Chloe! Come on in, girl! 'I've heard some really good things about you!"

Chloe smiles and walks into her office filled with excitement. The office is small, but bright and fully decked out in ASU posters and pictures of sports events. Linda walks over to her desk and motions for Chloe to take a seat on the other side of the desk.

"Have a seat, Chloe. Give me just a second, I'm finishing up an email." Says Linda.

"Of course. Thank you." Say Chloe.

As Linda types on her laptop, Chloe looks around. Linda's desk is stacked with piles of papers and binders. The wall behind her has pictures of Linda's family, her kids, her husband, and even several pit bulls. There are framed awards hanging as well, right next to her diplomas. Chloe nervously looks at Linda as she types. Linda takes a sip from her ASU cup and continues to type with one hand, without looking at Chloe. She asks,

"Why are you so nervous, hun?"

Chloe fidgets a bit in her seat. She drops her tube and quickly picks it up.

"Sorry." She says.

Linda stops typing and looks over at Chloe with a big smile and says,

"Relax…I'm gonna take care of you."

Chloe fixes her collar, swallows, then says,

"I'm just grateful you're seeing me. Th…this scholarship means everything to me, without it I, I…"

Linda puts her mug down and says,

"I'm glad that Tatyana reached out to me and told me to look you up! You are perfect for this scholarship!"

Chloe smiles really wide and straightens up in her seat. Linda turns around and continues to work on her computer. She looks over her screen and says,

"So, I'm enrolling you for the next semester, that's two months from this coming Monday…"

Linda turns to look at Chloe for her approval, and she smiles and nods her head.

"The scholarship is pre-approved for the first three people who apply with your type of financial situation. And because it is based on household income, residence, and the fact that it's for women only…I can squeeze you right in!"

Chloe smiles really wide, stands up suddenly, and tries to give Linda a hug over the desk, but does not quite reach her. Linda laughs, stands up, and walks around her desk saying,

"Hold on, hold on, let's do this right."

Chloe hugs her tight, and Linda is pleasantly surprised by that and hugs her back.

"Thank you, thank you, thank you!" Says Chloe.

"You're welcome, honey." Says Linda as she pats Chloe's back.

Chloe pulls away from Linda and wipes tears from her eyes.

"How do you know Tatyana?" Asks Linda as she walks back to her chair.

"She lives with us." Says Chloe

"She lives with you?" Asks Linda as she hands Chloe a paper tissue box dispenser.

"Well, not with us exactly, she's renting the RV garage behind my dad's house." Says Chloe.

Linda is taken aback and shakes her head, saying,

"I know baby girl is not living out of a garage!"

"My dad converted the space into an apartment a little while back. It's actually quite nice.

"There's a kitchen, bedroom, small living room…" Says Chloe.

Linda looks at her family pictures on her desk, contemplates for a moment, then says,

"Tati…still living in people's back yards…wow, not much has changed, has it?"

Chloe looks in the same direction as Linda and sees a small, framed picture of two young teen girls, one black and one white; it's Linda and Tatyana from years ago.

"How do you know her?" Asks Chloe.

Linda does not respond but is lost in thought as she looks at the small, framed picture. Chloe looks at Linda as her face fills with emotions, obviously of times past. Linda turns around, faces Chloe, and smiles.

"So?" Asks Chloe.

Linda is still daydreaming and did not hear Chloe's question.

"What?" She softly asks.

"How do you know Tatyana?" Asks Chloe.

Linda chuckles and says,

"Ha! Well, Tati and I go waaaaay back. We've known each other since we were in our teens."

"WOW! You guys have been hanging out that long?" Asks Chloe.

"We still see each other from time to time, but we don't really hang out much, at least not like we used to…"

Linda unbuttons her blouse and caresses her neck, she says,

"We were really close when we were younger, she was my everything back then…my Mon Cheri, my…first love really."

Chloe, incredibly interested, asks,

"What happened?"

"What happened?" Asks Linda.

"Yeah, with the two of you. If you don't mind me asking." Says Chloe.

Linda straightens up in her chair a bit and says,

"No, not at all. Tatyana is a real sweetheart; she's just been through a lot…And some of the things that happened to her in her life have, well…let's just say it messed her up real bad. She has a… really bad temper because of it."

Linda wanders off in thought for a few seconds, then says,

"I still love her, though, and always will. We lost touch after she had a big fight with her mom. Came over to my house punching the walls and shit…it was bad. My dad threw her out, she took off in a rage, and I didn't see her for a long time. I caught back up with her in Texas, many years later, when I was visiting my husband."

Linda looks back at the small framed picture of her and Tatyana and continues to say,

"He took me to a wrestling match at this popular, nasty old bar…and there she was. She had put on so much muscle by then that I could hardly recognize her. She was beating the crap out of this biker-looking guy in the ring. She was dressed up in some Russian soldier get-up."

"La Muerte Rusa" says Chloe.

"You know about it, ugh? It was bittersweet to see her. We had a few drinks after her match, but we could both tell, we had both moved on with our lives. But we promised each other that night that we would always keep in touch going forward." Says Linda.

The two look at each other for a few moments. Linda takes a deep breath and says,

"We have kept in touch ever since."

"So, that night when she was angry, she just left you?" Asks Chloe.

Linda nods and says,

"She said she was trying to protect me from herself, whatever that means. But…that Tatyana when she gets angry, she gets reeeeeally angry, you know what I mean?"

"Not really, she's always been nice to us." Says Chloe.

"Well, let's just say that she can get to the point of complete scorched earth nuclear destruction….and you don't want to be there when it happens." Says Linda.

Chloe's mouth drops as she looks at Linda, who continues to say,

"I remember one time we were at a diner close to my house, and this middle-aged guy slapped my ass as we were going in. He was a pretty big guy compared to her back then, but that didn't matter. Tatyana immediately put herself between me and him and told the guy to step off. He pushed her, and she pushed right back, and then some. They got into a fight; Tatyana beat him so bloody we thought she had killed him. It took two other big guys and me to peel her off that man. When we finally did get her to stop, Tati and I ran all the way back to my house laughing. We ended up having frozen waffles for dinner, ha, ha, ha. So, yeah…scorched earth."

Chloe, a bit shocked, watches Linda intensely and asks,

"So what happened to the guy?"

"What guy? Oh, the one that got beaten up?" Asks Linda

Chloe nods her head.

"They put him in the hospital. The local paper did a story of a brawl at the diner and how a junkie broke his jaw, some ribs, and cracked his skull. She, she almost killed the guy." Says Linda.

"Oh my goodness," Says Chloe.

Linda smiles, stands up, and lightly slaps her hands together, saying,

"But anyways….listen, welcome to ASU, we are glad to have you, honey! That's what this is about in the first place, right?"

Chloe stands up and picks up her bags and tube. Linda grabs a large folder on her desk and puts a whole lot of papers in it, saying,

"You should begin to get emails regarding enrollment, class selection, all that good stuff. And you'll get a few emails from me as well in the next coming days, so be looking out for those."

"Okay…thank you," Says Chloe.

Linda hands the folder to Chloe, who takes it and puts it in one of her bags. Linda steps out from her desk and holds her arms out to Chloe, saying,

"One last hug before you go?"

Chloe smiles and hugs Linda for a few moments. They walk to the door together, Linda pats her on the back and says,

"It was so nice to meet you. Tatyana was right, you're a sweetheart."

Chloe smiles as Linda winks at her and pats the back of her head.

"Reach out to me if you need anything, ok?" Says Linda as Chloe walks out of her office.

Chapter 9: Daniel Brakes

Anthony gets home and parks his truck in the driveway. Tatyana gets out of the passenger side, celebrating.

"Yeeeeeaaaah!" Tatyana screams as she raises her arms in victory.

Anthony gets out of the truck, smiling as he looks over at Tatyana.

"I can't believe it, this is such great news!" Says Anthony.

Tatyana takes her sneakers off, runs around the truck, and hugs Anthony, saying,

"I'm so happy, baby!"

She picks him up off the ground and carries him like a baby, a she kisses him for a few steps. Then they hear some loud music, people talking, and the sound of hammers banging. Anthony looks towards the back of the house; Tatyana slowly puts him down, and Anthony quickly walks towards the backyard.

"Yeah…I meant to tell you earlier. Hold on!" Says Tatyana as she quickly walks to catch up to Anthony.

Anthony gets to his backyard and stands there in shock. There is a full construction crew putting up a wrestling ring at the end of his property. Loud music coming from a stereo system in a pickup truck driven up to the RV garage cannot drown out the sound of saws, hammers, drills, and screaming people.

"What the hell is this!" says Anthony.

Tatyana quickly runs up, stands beside him, smiles, and says,

"Pretty cool, right?"

Anthony is not amused; he is shocked, upset, and tries very hard to maintain himself. He turns to her and asks,

"But…why?"

Tatyana takes his face into her hands and kisses him passionately on the lips. They kiss and kiss, so much so that some of the workers begin to take note. Then, Tatyana sucks his lips completely into her mouth and finally lets him go.

Anthony is flabbergasted, dazed really, she pets his head and says,

> "This is where we'll do the online multimedia stuff, baby! We'll do backyard matches, competitions, we can do tag team wrestling, and everything! The production company shooting the documentary is paying for it, they're setting it all up, and it's just for a few days, I promise! But I didn't expect it this soon! This is AWESOME!!"

Anthony tries to gather himself as he wipes her lipstick off his face and says,

"The movie company from the arena?"

"Yeah! It's all part of the shoot! Of course, they'll pay you for hosting, so don't worry about that! Be right back!"

Tatyana runs to the wrestling ring being constructed and starts talking to one of the workers as Anthony watches in dismay. Chloe happens to be watching the whole thing from the back window of their house. She runs out the back door and hugs her father from behind. Anthony turns around and hugs her back.

"I got it! I got it! I got it, Dad!!" Says Chloe.

Anthony smiles and asks,

"What? What are you talking about?"

Chloe jumps up and down, holding the ASU folder Linda gave her.

"You got in?" Asks Anthony.

Chloe nods and smiles while reaching into the folder. She pulls out the scholarship papers and hands them to her dad.

"What is this?" Asks Anthony as he takes them and begins to read.

"No way!" He says as he looks at Chloe.

Anthony puts his hands on her shoulder, and Chloe begins to jump up and down as she can't contain herself. Anthony continues to read and says,

"Yes! Yes! This is amazing, Honey!! I'm so proud of you!!"

Anthony hugs Chloe, picks her up, and spins with her. Tatyana walks up to them, laughing as she drinks a beer and asks,

"Good news?"

"She got into college…and has a scholarship!" Says Anthony, the pride for his daughter so evident on his face.

Tatyana opens her arms up to Chloe, and she runs into them, hugging Tatyana with all her might.

"We need to celebrate! You got into college, and I got a manager today!" Says Tatyana.

Chloe pulls away from Tatyana for a second and smiles at the news.

"She sure did!" Says Anthony.

Chloe embraces Tatyana again and says,

"I'm so happy for you, T! Such great news!

Tatyana pulls away softly from Chloe, looks at Anthony, and says,

"Hey, let me treat you guys to dinner tonight! C'mon, please?"

"That sounds good, but hey, I understand the workers being here, but what are these wrestlers doing here just hanging out?" Says Anthony as he points to two wrestlers drinking beer on his lawn as they watch the crew work.

Tatyana turns around, points to the wrestlers, and says,

"You guys need to get the fuck out! NOW! Let's go!"

The wrestlers slowly get up and fold their chairs. Tatyana watches them as they make their way down the driveway. When she turns around, she sees that the construction crew has stopped working, and they are all looking at her.

"Not you guys! You need to keep going, get this finished! A trabajar! Andale!" Says Tatyana, and the guys get back to work immediately.

"Well, let me take a shower real quick!" Says Anthony as he quickly makes his way to the house.

"Me too, I won't be long." Says Tatyana.

Chloe bends down to tie her shoelace, and Tatyana watches her carefully and lightly taps her on the butt. Chloe jumps up, startled, and smiles at her.

"I'm happy for you." Says Tatyana.

"And I for you…you know, Linda is a beautiful person, and she really loves you." Says Chloe.

"She is, I'm glad you met her…okay, I'll see you in a few!" Says Tatyana as she walks away.

Tatyana reaches the door of her apartment and looks back. She sees Chloe staring at her and says,

"Hey, your butt is almost as hard as mine…almost!"

"You wish!" Says Chloe.

Tatyana smiles and enters her apartment. The door closes, and Chloe continues to stare at the closed door. She puts her hand on her butt and squeezes it, then walks back towards her house.

Tatyana enters her apartment, grabbing her butt with one hand and the doorknob with the other.

"Hard as a rock…" she whispers to herself as she looks around and realizes it's dark in the apartment.

She looks around, wondering why all of the lights are turned off as she makes her way to the fridge. She walks cautiously, turning the kitchen light on, then the living room light as she goes, looking around carefully. Tatyana hears soft music coming from upstairs, but does not pay it any mind as she looks around. She gets to the fridge, pulls out a bottle of water, takes a sip, and places the cold bottle to her forehead. She hears the music a bit louder now, it's a soft instrumental piece, and she whispers to herself,

"What is Daniel listening to? Let me see this boy…"

Tatyana slowly makes her way upstairs, and when she walks to the bedroom, her countenance completely changes from pleasant to complete fury, her eyes become bloodshot, and she clenches her fists, crushing the water bottle she holds.

Daniel is sitting on her bed reading a bible, as he takes notes down in a notebook..

"DANIEL!!" Tatyana screams.

Daniel jumps up in terror

"MOM!!" Daniel screams.

"WHAT DID I TELL YOU!!" Screams Tatyana, then continues, "DIDN'T I WARN YOU TO STAY AWAY FROM THOSE PEOPLE!   "

Daniel quickly closes the Bible, jumps off the bed, and runs to a corner of the room in fear. Daniel immediately begins to plead,

"I'm sorry, Mom! I'm sorry, I'm sorry! I can explain, please!" Daniel pleads.

Tatyana runs to him in a rage, she grabs him by his hair and slaps him repeatedly in the face,

SLAP! SLAP! SLAP! SLAP!

"ARE YOU A BIBLE MAN NOW!!" Tatyana screams.

"Aaaaaaahhhh!!" Daniel screams

SLAP! SLAP! SLAP! SLAP!

"You're a faggot, Daniel! You're a fucking girl, DANIEL!!" Tatyana screams

"Moooooom!" Daniel screams as she splits his lower lip, and blood begins to fly.

Daniel tries to get away by running on top of the bed, but Tatyana slaps him so hard, he falls off the bed and onto the floor. Tatyana jumps on top of him and holds him down.

"Where did you get that bible?" She screams as she grabs him by his shirt.

Daniel tries to get away, but Tatyana is too strong for him.

"That bitch next door gave you that bible? ANSWER ME!!" Scream Tatyana.

"No!" Yells Daniel.

SLAP, SLAP, SLAP

Daniels' face is completely red from the slapping now.

"Who gave you that garbage! WHO!!" Tatyana yells.

"The pastor at the church…" Daniel whimpers.

"Fuck that! You're gay, Daniel! You'll always be gay, and I love you for it!"

Tatyana looks around the room and spots a paper shopping bag on the floor on the other side of the bedroom. She gets up, walks over to the bag, picks it up, and takes a beautiful yellow sundress out. She looks over at Daniel and throws the dress at him, saying.

"Put this on NOW!!"

Daniel looks at the dress that fell in front of him and says,

"Wh… what?"

Tatyana walks over and picks the dress up, still enraged, fury emanating from every expression. She holds up the dress in front of him and says,

> "You told me you liked this dress, and I went and bought it for you. You are not a bible man, you are a fucking girl! You're my little girl! So put this dress on NOW! I WANT TO SEE YOU IN IT!!"

> "But…but mom, please…" Daniel says as he touches his swollen, bloody lip.

Tatyana grabs Daniel, takes his shirt off, and then rips his gym shorts off of him. He tries to resist, but she completely overpowers him and violently undresses him against his will.

> "STOOOOOOP!!" Daniel screams as he tries to keep his underwear on, but she rips them right off of him.

SLAP! SLAP!

Tatyana slaps him again, saying,

> "Stop resisting, you little bitch!"

She throws Daniel on the bed, and throws the dress at him

> "Get dressed! Put it on NOW!" Tatyana says sternly.

> "mmm….mom, p….please." Daniel whimpers.

Tatyana points to the dress and says,

"NOW, Daniel! You put it on now! I'm not playing with you! You are not gonna become a bible person! You're my little girl!"

"I…I just need to expla…" Daniel tries to respond as he stands, but Tatyana slaps him.

SLAP!

Daniel falls to the floor.

"Explain what! You're gonna tell me you love church now! You gonna tell you you've been changed?" Tatyana screams.

Daniel weeps on the floor, blood gushing from his mouth.

"Answer me!!" Yells Tatyana.

"I….I don't know…" Daniel says slowly

Tatyana grabs her hair and pulls it; she's out of her mind now, her skin on her face and chest is so red it looks like she's boiling alive. She begins to pace back and forth as Daniel stares at her in horror.

"I told you how those boys raped me! That was hard for me to tell my own son! I told you how those church people are deceitful! I told you!" Tatyana begins to punch her chest muscles as she continues to say, "I never corrected you while you were growing up, Daniel! I felt bad because I wasn't there enough, I…I thought. I…. I never spanked you like I should have! You're spoiled! You're a spoiled little shit!" Tatyana rants.

Daniel holds his face as he cries in a fetal position on the floor, blood gushing out of his split lip. Tatyana stands over him and says,

"I let you get away with too much! You're disgusting, Daniel! Stand up!"

Daniel slowly begins to stand up as he tries to cover his nakedness. Before he can fully get to his feet, Tatyana violently grabs him by the back of his neck and brings him over to the bed. She sits down and places him face down on her lap. She holds him down with one hand and begins to spank his naked butt with the other, as hard as she can.

SPANK! SPANK! SPANK!

"You need discipline!" Says Tatyana.

"Mooom! Stoooop!" yells Daniel.

SPANK! SPANK! SPANK!

"You're a girl, not a bible man!"

"STOOOOOP," yells Daniel.

SPANK! SPANK! SPANK!

"Aaaaaaaaaah!" Daniel screams in horror.

Suddenly, Tatyana stops and pulls her hands away.

"I'm sorry, I'm sorry, I'm sorry!" Daniel says repeatedly.

Tatyana pushes Daniel off of her lap, he lands on the floor and looks back at her, horrified by what just happened.

Tatyana looks down at her lap, she's covered in urine, Daniel's bladder gave way out of fear.

"What… the…fuck…IS WRONG WITH YOU!!!!" Screams Tatyana.

"Aaaaaaaahh," Daniel screams in complete humiliation.

Daniel reaches for the shorts and the shirt lying on the floor.

"You're sick, Daniel!! It's…. It's everywhere!!" Says Tatyana as she looks down at herself.

Daniel runs out the door, down the stairs.

'Aaaaaaaahhh, Aaaaaaaahhh!" Daniel screams.

Tatyana stands up, takes her shirt off, and begins to wipe herself as she walks downstairs.

SLAM!

The door slams open. Chloe, who is sitting on one of the patio chairs in the backyard, jumps up, startled. The workers putting the ring together suddenly stop and begin to laugh as they see the naked teen. Chloe sees Daniel run out of the apartment naked with clothes in his hand, screaming and crying. She knows it's serious.

"Oh my God! Daniel! What happened!" Chloe says, but he does not answer.

Daniel runs away from her and makes his way down the driveway. He tries to put on his shorts, but falls face-first in the dirt.

"Daniel! Daniel, you ok?" Says Chloe as she begins to quickly make her way to Daniel.

Daniel gets up, puts on the t-shirt, and keeps running with his shorts in hand.

Tatyana steps out of the apartment wearing a bra and shorts, still holding onto the sticky shirt in one hand and the yellow dress in the other. She looks over to the workers and says,

"What are you looking at? You never saw a naked boy before?"

Tatyana looks over at Chloe and can tell she's very concerned about Daniel.

"He'll get over it." Says Tatyana as she approaches Chloe, holding out the yellow dress.

"What happened?" Says Chloe

"We had a fight." Says Tatyana.

"OH wow, you ok?" Says Chloe.

"Yeah, just, disappointed that's all." Says Tatyana.

"Is he going to be ok?" Asks Chloe.

"He'll be okay, he's just embarrassed, that's all. And this should not stop us from getting a good dinner." Says Tatyana as she resets in her mind, and takes a deep breath in and out.

"So, boys will be boys, and we are still going out to dinner and enjoying some good food, so that's that."

Says Tatyana, she looks down at herself and continues to say, "I definitely need a shower now, I'll be back in ten minutes, m'kay?" Says Tatyana.

"Okay." Says Chloe as she takes the yellow dress.

Chloe looks down the driveway again. Daniel is gone; just the settling dust of where he fell remains. Chloe looks back at Tatyana, who's already entered the apartment and is closing the door behind her.

On a small, narrow, desolate dirt road, Daniel frantically runs. Leaving a large dust trail behind him, as if his life depended on it, underneath purple, red, and yellow clouds of a glorious Sonoran sunset, he runs and runs. Wearing only shorts, and several bleeding scratches on his knees and face, he cries, tears fly off the sides of his bloodshot eyes and red and purple face.

Daniel trips on a rock and falls on the ground face-first. He slowly picks himself up and rests on his knees as he looks up at the sky, holds out his arms, and screams.

"AAAAAAAAAAAAAAHHHH!!!" Screams Daniel as he clenches his fists up to the sky.

"WHYYYYYYYYYYY!!!" Screams Daniel as he vehemently bangs on his head with his fists.

"I hate myself, I need to die! Why am I this way!!" Daniel tells himself as he cries.

An old white Mercedes station wagon slowly approaches Daniel from the front, and it stops just a few feet away from him; he does not even notice it. Mrs. June gets out of the car and quickly walks towards Daniel, saying,

"Daniel? DANIEL!!"

Daniel opens his eyes, drops his hands to the ground in complete defeat, and looks up at her as he weeps, his face covered in dust and tears.

"Oh my God!! Daniel, what happened?" Cries Mrs. June as she runs to him and kneels beside him.

Mrs. June begins to dust him off; he is covered in dust and dirt from the road. She takes her buttoned sweater off and covers Daniel with it. Daniel looks at her and continues to weep, and Mrs. June softly puts her arms around him and gets teary-eyed as well. It breaks her heart to see him like this.

Mrs. June takes a handkerchief from her skirt pocket and begins to dry his tears. She carefully wipes his eyes, making sure that none of the dust gets in there. Daniel continues to cry, his heart is completely torn, he tries to say something, but cries come out instead, he just can't form any words. Mrs. June pets Daniel's back gently as she continues to dry his falling tears. She gives him a big hug, and they slowly rock back and forth together. Mrs. June, feeling his pain, also begins to weep with him. Minutes pass, and Daniel slowly stops crying, and then there is complete silence, the only thing that is heard is the sound of the breeze picking up dirt, birds in the distance…there is calm.

"C'mon, honey, let me help you get up." Says Mrs. June.

Daniel looks at her and nods his head. Mrs. June gets up first, then reaches down and helps the young man to his feet.

"Tha…" Daniel tries to say thank you, but struggles. Mrs. June says,

"Let's go sit in the car, honey, it's better than this dirt here."

Mrs. June and Daniel walk towards her car together, her arm still around the broken boy. Mrs. June quickly makes her way to the back of her station wagon, and Daniel slowly follows along. She opens up the hatchback and asks,

"Wanna sit with me for a few, Daniel?"

Mrs. June opens up a little blanket she has back there, sits on the back of the wagon, and holds her hand out to Daniel. Daniel nods, takes her hand, and sits down beside her, carefully making sure that he keeps her sweater from dropping onto the ground. They sit there without saying a word for a while, Daniel looking down at the ground as Mrs. June looks up at the sky.

"Look at that beautiful sky!" Says Mrs. June as she points to the sunset.

Daniel looks up and sees the rays of the sun flaring up into the sky from behind a purple mountain range in the distance. The rays traveling through a sky filled with purple, yellow, and pink clouds, and his countenance softens a little bit. Mrs. June turns to her side, reaches into a grocery bag, and pulls out a six-pack of lemon soda.

"I'm getting a pop for myself, would you like one?" Asks Mrs. June.

Daniel nods, and she hands him a soda can. Mrs. June opens hers and quickly takes a sip.

"Mmmm. They're warm, I hope you don't mind. I'm just coming back from the store." Says Mrs. June.

Daniel opens his soda and quickly drinks from it as it spills onto the ground.

"I'm sorry about that; all the bouncing around in the car made it fizzy." Says Mrs. June.

"No, it's perfect." Says Daniel as he quickly drinks all of it.

He suddenly and unintentionally burps loudly and quickly looks over at Mrs. June.

"Excuse me." He says, a bit embarrassed. Mrs. June smiles and responds, "It's ok, baby."

Daniel's head slowly begins to sink as he thinks about the beating his mom gave him, she saw him completely naked, and how could he not control himself… how could he face his mom again… he thought.

"Daniel, stop thinking and look up." Says Mrs. June. Daniel quickly looks up again.

"Look at that sky, Daniel, look at the wonderful colors. The purples, the pinks, the pretty yellow clouds. It looks like someone took a brush and painted it…don't it? Look at it! Look!" Says Mrs. June as she points out the clouds and colors in the sky.

Daniel really begins to take in what she's saying; he sees the details in every cloud wrinkle and the colors as they shift right in front of him.

"Look over there, the way the sun travels through the clouds. The rays going through and all." Says Mrs. June.

Daniel looks in the direction she's pointing and says,

"It's…it's beautiful."

"You know what's more beautiful?" Asks Mrs. June.

"What?" Asks Daniel.

"Your precious soul, Daniel." Says Mrs. June.

Daniel turns and looks at Mrs. June, surprised at what she just said. Mrs. June turns to him and says,

"Well, don't look at me like that…you are. Just like God painted the sky for all of us to admire, He made you."

Mrs. June looks back up at the sky and says,

"That sunset right there will only be there for a few minutes, as beautiful as it is. God made it with his paintbrush, and it has a time limit."

Mrs. June looks back at Daniel, who is transfixed on her every word, and says,

"What are you trying to say?" Asks Daniel.

"God made you, Daniel, and when he makes something, He does not make mistakes, like this painted sky… You're precious son, you may not know it, you may not see it, you may not feel it right now, but you're a treasure." Says Mrs. June.

Daniel looks at her, flabbergasted at the words that are coming out of her mouth. No one has ever called him a treasure or made him feel as if he were of any value.

"…You don't really know me. If you did, you would not be saying that." Says Daniel.

Mrs. June takes a sip of her soda and says,

"God sometimes will let His people know things… From the moment I saw you, I could see the pain in your eyes. I know you've been through a lot of pain. People have disappointed you, taken advantage of you, and repeatedly hurt you. Your mama keeps you on a tight leash because she feels like she failed you somehow, and though you love her, you also resent her because she inflicts pain.

Her telling you she loves you after a beating does not make anything better. I also know that there's been someone in your life who has shown you love, and you received it gladly. You know what love is supposed to feel like, and you long for it every day."

There's a moment of silence as they both look up at the sky. Daniels' eyes water up, and a single tear falls from his eye.

"Not bad…" Says Daniel.

"I also sense self-hate in your heart; you don't think too highly of yourself, do you?" Asks Mrs. June.

"I'm garbage…I'm so messed up." Says Daniel.

Mrs. June places her hand over Daniel's hand as it lies on the bed of the station wagon and says,

"You're not garbage, Daniel. You are a precious soul, don't let anyone tell you otherwise. Don't you ever feel like you're not worthy of happiness, of love, of redemption? We're all messed up in one way or another, and we all need God to fix us. He's the only one that can!"

Daniel takes a sip of his drink and looks up at the sky, as he does a shooting star falls from the sky and disappears. The silence of the desert is calming, and the soft breeze and sounds of birds in the distance are a welcome sound to Daniel's ears. After a few moments of silence, he says,

"It seems like you know me pretty well, Mrs. June."

Mrs. June pats Daniel on the shoulder to comfort him.

"I'm tired, Mrs. June…so tired I don't understand it…" says Daniel.

Mrs. June looks at Daniel for a few seconds and takes pity on the boy; he looks so defeated in his spirit, and she knows that he feels hopeless. She says,

"All those years of pain will do that to you, son, trust me, I've been there."

"I wish I could just be normal; I wish I had a normal mom. Someone who would bake me cookies or help me with homework…Someone who was not self-centered, so commanding!" Says Daniel.

"Someone who would love you, love you unconditionally." Says Mrs. June

"…yeah," says Daniel.

Mrs. June takes a sip of her soda and becomes curious about a thought she just had, and asks,

"Why did you want to come to church with me that Sunday?"

Daniel looks over at Mrs. June, somewhat surprised at her question.

"Well, something about you told me that you were sincere about the things you were telling Chloe and me. And I… guess I wanted to know more." Answered Daniel.

"What was it?" Asks Mrs. June.

"I mean…It felt…good when you hugged me." Says Daniel.

"What did you feel?" Asks Mrs. June.

Daniel pauses for a moment, takes a sip of his soda, and adjusts Mrs. June's sweater so it does not fall off.

"It was warm, kinda nurturing…It… it was like medicine." Says Daniel.

"You felt love, son." Says Mrs. June.

"Love…" says Daniel as he looks back up into the sunset.

"When my mother and father forsake me, then the Lord will take me up." Says Mrs. June.

Daniel looks over at Mrs. June and asks,

"Who said that?"

Mrs. June looks over at Daniel and smiles.

"It's in the Bible. It means, when you don't have a mom or a dad to love you and take care of you, God will step in and be more than what you need. The love you felt…Jesus has an unlimited supply of it. All you have to do is believe." Says Mrs. June.

Daniel looks up at the sky again. He closes his eyes and takes a deep breath. He looks a lot more relaxed and pleasant now. He stands up, takes a sip of his soda, then looks over at Mrs. June and says,

"I like that…"

"Not my words, it's in the New Testament." Says Mrs. June.

"What else is in there?" Asks Daniel.

"Love your neighbor as yourself." Says Mrs. June, smiling.

Daniel smiles back at Mrs. June jumps out of the car, takes a few steps, turns around, and with his arms wide open says,

"You sat down and talked to me, shared a drink with me, you showed me love…Are you trying to be my friend, Mrs. June?"

Mrs. June holds her drink up to Daniel and says,

"To new friendships!"

Daniel holds his drink up to Mrs. June and says,

"To good friends!"

The two take a sip of their drinks.

But at that exact moment, just a block away, Anthony drives his truck onto that same dirt road, but heads in the opposite direction from Mrs. June and Daniel. Tatyana sits beside him, and Chloe is in the back seat of the truck; everyone is dressed for a night out, laughing and smiling.

"So what is this place you're talking about?" Asks Tatyana.

"You are going to love it! We're gonna have some red wine…" Says Anthony.

"Ok, ok." Says Tatyana.

"We'll start with bruschetta, garlic bread toasted to perfection, and they roast the garlic in olive oil, then mozzarella, sun-dried tomatoes, onions, basil…. Yes!" Says Anthony.

"That sounds soooo gooood," Says Chloe from the back seat."

"Then we'll have some chicken cacciatore, with delicious risotto Milanese, and finish up with their loaded tiramisu!" Says Anthony.

Tatyana grabs Anthony's shoulder and says,

"Say no more, I'm in, ha, ha, ha."

Tatyana then looks out the window and suddenly catches a glimpse of Daniel and Mrs. June in her side-view mirror. She leans in and sees them in the distance holding up a drink, and Mrs. June walks up to him holding up a drink as well. Daniel then gives her a big hug. Tatyana becomes infuriated, sits back into her seat, and looks straight ahead. Her lips and hands are tightly clenched, and her face begins to get supper pale.

Anthony looks over at her and asks,

"Hey, you ok? What's the matter? Looks like you've seen a ghost."

Tatyana quickly changes her demeanor, smiles widely, looks over at him, and says,

"For some reason, I started thinking about a dead woman I used to know, ha! No, I am fine, are you kidding me! I'm ready for this Italian dinner, how bout you, Chloe?"

"I'm ready, ha, ha, ha!" Chloe says

Anthony laughs, and Tatyana laughs right along with him. Slowly, Tatyana turns to look in the side view mirror and sees Daniel with his arm around Mrs. June as they head back to the car. Tatyana's eyes turn red, and her heart fills with rage and vengeance.

Four Hours Later

It's dark, the clouds in the sky hide the stars, there is a warm breeze that passes through the trees, and an owl can be heard in the distance. Tatyana, Anthony, and Chloe walk up the driveway of the Borgia house and into the backyard after having a big Italian dinner. They are all in a good mood, laughing and carrying on.

"I cannot believe I had so much spaghetti!" Says Chloe as she grabs her belly.

"That bruschetta… and the chicken scampi, it was sooo goooood!" Says Tatyana.

"Well, I'm glad you guys enjoyed it! Next time we'll try the chicken carbonara!" Says Anthony as he smiles, and the girls smile back.

They get to the middle of the back yard, and as they approach the patio set, Anthony gives Chloe a kiss on the cheek, then Tatyana a kiss on the mouth, and says,

"Good night, ladies. I am going to sleep. I got an early start tomorrow."

He looks over at the wrestling ring fully set up in the back of his property, and then looks at Tatyana, smiles, and says,

"I must really love you, to let you put that monstrosity back here, he, he."

Tatyana reaches out and hugs him, saying,

> "Thank you soooo much, it will only be a few weeks, I promise, just a few people taking pictures and video."

Anthony nods and smiles.

> "Well, goodnight."

> "Good night!" Tatyana and Chloe say at the same time as they watch Anthony go up the stairs and enter the house

Chloe looks over at Tatyana and sees that she is looking over at Mrs. June's yard. Chloe looks over in that direction and sees Mrs. June sitting on her patio chair by her house, looking up at the stars as she listens to music.

> "She's a nice person, a good woman, I'm glad she's our neighbor." Says Chloe.

Tatyana continues to look over at Mrs. June, hatred and resentment stir in her heart as she associates her with all of the pain and suffering that she experienced in the past from people who were supposed to be "good" church going folks. As Tatyana stoically looks over at Mrs. June, Chloe touches her on the shoulder to get her attention. Tatyana turns to her,

> "Hugh?" Says Tatyana.

> "You okay?" Asks Chloe.

Tatyana quickly smiles and lightly nudges Chloe on the shoulder, saying,

"Yeah… I was just deep in thought, that's all."

"Well, I'm going to bed. So, have a good night." Says Chloe.

"Me too. Have a good night, honey." Says Tatyana as she watches Chloe climb the stairs, open the back door, and enter her home.

The door closes, and when she hears the lock turn, Tatyana looks back over to Mrs. June in disgust. She quickly makes her way to her home, enters, and a few moments later comes out with the Bible that Daniel was reading. With anger in every step, she makes her way to the fence, leans over it, and calls Mrs. June, saying,

"Excuse me! Hello?"

Mrs. June turns her radio down and looks over at Tatyana and says,

"Hi there!"

Tatyana holds the Bible out to Mrs. June and says,

"Hi, can you please take this?"

Mrs. June gets up from her chair, walks over to Tatyana, and takes the Bible from her hand. She looks at it, then looks up at Tatyana, wondering what's going on.

"My son was reading this in my house." Says Tatyana.

"That's good." Says Mrs. June.

"No, it's not." Says Tatyana, then continues to say, "Did you give it to him?"

Mrs. June looks at Tatyana, and she sees the anger in her eyes, the rage in the folds of her expression, and says,

"No, I believe I saw my pastor give it to him when he visited my church."

"You're not taking my kid to your church anymore." Says Tatyana.

"I never brought the boy; he showed up one Sunday, came all by himself. He had a good time too." Says Mrs. June.

Tatyana shakes her head and says,

"You people are something else…Look, I saw you talking to him today, drinking in the back of your car! What did you say to him? Where is he?"

Mrs. June looks down at the Bible and softly caresses the leather cover with her hand, saying,

"The boy was upset about something; he was crying…

"That's none of your business!" Interrupts Tatyana.

"A young half-naked boy, crying and running in the street, is everyone's business. I stopped to help him." Replies Mrs. June.

"What did he say?" Asks Tatyana.

Mrs. June looks back at Tatyana and says,

"Not much, that he just wanted to be normal, whatever that means. The boy is looking for love; he just wants to feel cared for."

"Where did he go? Did you take him somewhere?" Asked Tatyana.

"He wouldn't let me; he got dressed in the back of my car and said he needed to walk and think. He's a mature boy for his age

Tatyana becomes emotional as her anger turns to pain. She says,

"I love my son."

"Then show it, because I know that the boy loves you...He needs all the love he can get," Says Mrs. June.

"I know that! Don't you think I know that! Who the hell do you think you are!" Says Tatyana, insulted by the comment, Mrs. June just looks at her for a moment, then responds with,

"I'm someone who's been round for a while and know that you can't push your will on people; it never ends well. You give the boy love, understanding, and guidance, and they will respect you. When you talk, they will listen." Says Mrs. June.

"I'm not gonna stand here and be lectured by you! I came over to tell you to stay away from my boy! You hear me!" Says Tatyana.

Mrs. June looks at Tatyana up and down and says.

"First of all, I live here and will talk to whoever I please, and you can't stop me. Second, no one will tell me not to help someone in need, not you, nor any devil in hell will stand in my way. You understand me!"

"My son is not gonna be one of you filthy bible people!" Tatyana says with disgust in her voice.

Mrs. June does not respond to that; she just stares at Tatyana, unmoved by her size or threatening demeanor. Mrs. June's countenance changes to that of sympathy, pity really, for Tatyana. She puts the Bible under her armpit and says,

"You have been obviously hurt by people who called themselves Christians. Seems to me that you were hurt at a young age, and people you trusted… broke that trust, over and over again. You felt unprotected, vulnerable, as these people who went to church had their way with you. You had no control of the situation, no control of the pain they caused you, no control of the fear they made you feel. Somewhere along the line, you made a decision to not be a victim anymore, you fought against the fear, you fought against the pain, and the sufferings you went through, but you never got rid of it, and it's all bottled up inside you right now.

Only God can get that out of you, so there's a bomb
in there, it's ready to explode at any moment. And
because you swore to yourself that you would not
be a victim, you became the perpetrator. Hurting
others before they could hurt you, destroying
everyone and everything that even resembles the
pain you harbor inside. That's one of the reasons
why you built your body the way you did: you want
to be so big, so intimidating that no one will ever
even think of hurting you again."

Tatyana's mouth drops open, completely disarmed now. As
Mrs. June speaks, she feels exactly what she is talking
about, the fear, the pain; she feels the pain of that little girl
again, back in that shed, getting raped by those boys. She
knows that everything Mrs. June is saying is the truth, and
she is reading her like a book. Mrs. June continues,

"God did not do that to you, mankind did, because
man without the true living God is evil, period. God
is not your enemy; He loves you and wants to
forgive you, and can help you to forgive and heal.
Only He can make you whole."

Tatyana puts her hands up to her ears and loudly says,

"Enough! Enough…. You got your bible back,
just…leave me alone!"

And with that, Tatyana walks away. Through the chain-
linked fence, then the yard, and in deep thought, she slowly
makes her way back to her house. She opens the door to her
apartment, but lingers at the door. She turns around, looks
back at Mrs. June dead in the eyes for a moment, Mrs. June

looks back and smiles, but Tatyana does not respond. Tatyana takes a step backwards, enters, and slams the door shut.

Chapter 10: Pain Incoming

The night of the celebration dinner

A small night-light illuminates Chloe's room with soft pink tones from an electric socket on the wall. Her book bag sits right beside it on the floor, with the ASU binder and fliers falling out of it. Chloe sleeps peacefully on her bed, wearing a large t-shirt, the bed sheet crumpled together on the floor beside her. Suddenly, faint screaming is heard outside. Chloe turns on her bed, her head hanging down from the side.

Fire truck sirens in the distance get closer and closer, louder and louder. A woman screams outside again. The fire engine blasts its horn, and Chloe stirs, then sits up on her bed, startled. She sees lights on the trees in her backyard through the window. Chloe runs to her window facing the back yard and opens it. She hears a woman screaming something, and her whole backyard is filled with emergency vehicle lights moving and swirling.

"It's coming from the front!" Says Chloe and runs out of her room.

Chloe runs to the hallway, down the stairs, and jumps the last four steps to the main floor. The sounds of the sirens are much louder now. She runs to the front door and opens it wide, and takes a few steps down the front steps of her house to the front yard.

Mrs. June's car is engulfed in flames next door on her pebble driveway. One of the tires suddenly explodes, making Chloe take a step back as she watches the firefighters scramble to get their hoses out, and the fire chief yells out orders. Police cars begin to arrive, the flames get even more intense, and the car horn begins to yell loudly.

> "Oh no! Wha...." Says Chloe as she watches the car being consumed right in front of her.

Some of the officers get out and begin to block the street on both sides. Others try to keep neighbors who are coming out of their houses from getting too close to the scene; the whole area is lit up by the light of the blaze.

Chloe wants to see if she can see Mrs. June and takes a few steps into her yard, but an officer quickly comes up to her with his hands out.

> "Stand back, young lady, it's not safe." The police officer says as the firefighters begin to spray the car.

BOOOOM!!

Suddenly, a very large explosion goes off, and the fire doubles in size. Everyone takes cover. Chloe looks over to Mrs. June's yard and is finally able to spot her a ways away, talking to an officer as they look at the car. Mrs June spots Chloe looking at her and sees her anxiousness to approach her, but Mrs. June motions for her to stay put with her hand. Chloe nods and takes a step back. Anthony comes out of the house and is taken aback by the whole scene unfolding before him. He slowly walks up to Chloe, stands beside her, and says,

"What happened?"

"Mrs. June's car…" Says Chloe.

"How?" Asks Antony.

"I don't know," Chloe answers as the car horn begins to get louder.

The firefighters eventually do put out the fire, there is foam everywhere, and even more smoke ascending up into the sky, rising from what's left of the car, now a black, churned frame. It's been more than an hour now, and the firemen are rolling up their hoses as police take down their perimeter, and some of the police cars begin to drive away. Mrs. June stands with Chloe and Anthony in her front yard; they were finally able to get over there and talk to her.

"Mrs. June, I'm so sorry. How could this happen?" Asks Chloe.

"I don't know, baby, I just don't know." Says Mrs. June.

"Did the car have a gas leak or anything like that?" Asks Anthony.

Mrs. June shakes her head and takes a deep breath, and says,

"No, the car was an '85, but I kept it up, nothing wrong with that car at all!"

The fire chief walks up to them and addresses Mrs. June.

"I'd like to show you something, ma'am." He says.

Mrs. June, Anthony, and Chloe follow him as he takes them to the car remains. He points to where the back seat used to be and says,

"This is where the fire started, we can tell by the intensity of the burn, then it spread inside the cabin, expanding to the extremities of the car. The explosion happened when the fire got to the gas tank, over here."

"How did it start?" Asks Mrs. June.

"Well, it was definitely arson, some type of accelerant was used to ignite the fire inside the cabin, in the backseat over here." Says the fire chief

"Like what?" Asks Anthony.

"It could have been a number of things, right now I'm not one hundred percent sure, but it looks like it could have been lighter fluid, or gasoline, maybe a type of alcohol. As we run more tests, we'll find out more, but I can tell you for certain that someone did this intentionally." Says the fire chief.

"I can't believe it!" Say, Mrs. June, flabbergasted by the news.

"Do you have any enemies?" Asks the fire chief.

"Enemies?" Asks Mrs. June.

Just as she was forming those words, Tatyana walks into Anthony's front yard wearing a nightgown and quickly made her way to them. They all watch her approach until she stands close to them and asks,

"Oh my god! What happened?"

Her question sounds hollow and uncaring, almost staged. Everyone looks at her without responding.

"Why didn't anyone come up and get me?" Tatyana asks.

"Sorry, what?" Asks Chloe.

Mrs. June shakes her head; she can't believe the ridiculousness coming out of Tatyana's mouth.

"Well, I wish someone had come and gotten me out of bed!" Tatyana says.

"Why?" Asks Mrs. June.

"Ugh?" Says Tatyana.

"Did you want to help them with the hose?" Asks Mrs. June.

"What?" Asks Tatyana.

"Or do you know more than the firefighters. What more could you have possibly done?" Asks Mrs. June.

Tatyana looks at Mrs. June, surprised by her words. Mrs. June is visibly upset. She looks over at what is left of her car, then looks back at Tatyana and says,

"I'm sorry, I should not have snapped at you…it's been a long night."

"Fine." Says Tatyana with a nasty tone.

There's an awkward moment of silence as they all look over at the car remains.

"Well, Mrs. June, I'm sorry about what happened to you. You have my card with all my information. Please reach out to me if you have any further questions." Says the fire chief as he pats her on the shoulder.

"Thank you." Says Mrs. June.

The chief walks away and heads towards his truck as everyone watches him. Suddenly and loudly, Tatyana declares,

"Well, I'm sorry for what happened!"

Before anyone could respond, an officer comes up to Anthony from behind, she puts her hand on his shoulder, and Anthony quickly turns around.

"We're wrapping up here, sir. Please reach out to me if you get any of that footage, ok?" She says.

"Footage?" Asks Tatyana.

"Yes! Of course. I don't know what happened. I could not get any of the video from the doorbell camera; my phone is not connecting to their network for some reason or something. I'm going to have to reach out to their customer support…I'm so sorry." Says Anthony.

"I understand, you have my card, please reach out to me if you find anything, okay?" Says the officer. She smiles and walks away to her car on the street.

"Dad, the app is not working?" Asks Chloe.

"Yeah, I'm completely locked out, can't get into it…" Says Anthony as he looks at his phone.

"You, you have a camera out here?" Asks Tatyana.

Chloe points to the doorbell and says,

"Yeah, it's on the doorbell right there."

Tatyana leans over to look past Chloe and sees the doorbell camera. She laughs nervously and says,

"He, he…isn't that something. I need to get me one of those."

Mrs. June looks at Tatyana with disgust; she can tell something is up, but does not address it at the moment. Instead, she turns to Anthony and Chloe and says,

"Y'all have a good night now. I'm going to bed."

Chloe reaches out and hugs Mrs. June, saying,

"I'm so sorry, Mrs. June!"

Mrs. June smiles, turns around, and heads home.

"Try and get some sleep, Mrs. June!" Says Anthony

"G'night," Says Tatyana as she immediately turns around and heads back.

Anthony and Chloe watch as Tatyana walks away from them without saying another word, turns the corner, and disappears. The two look at each other and take a deep breath. They can sense something is off with Tatyana's behavior, but they don't say anything.

"We should be getting to bed ourselves." Says Anthony.

"Yeah, Tatyana said she had invited people for a get-together later today?" Asked Chloe.

The two begin to walk back into the house, and Anthony says,

"Yeah, she told me it would just be a few wrestlers and a small camera crew to get some footage for a commercial or something."

Later that Day...

Anthony's back door opens, Chloe comes out to her backyard, stands for a few seconds, eyes wide open, and she takes in the whole scene. There's over one hundred people partying, dancing, drinking, and screaming, literally going wild right in front of her. There's a DJ dressed in a metallic jumpsuit set up close to the RV garage with multiple large speakers blasting dance music, wrestlers inside the ring fighting with people packed like sardines around the ring watching and screaming. There's a large camera crew capturing the action on the ring and off the ring as people carry on; there's alcohol everywhere.

"This…is…crazy…" Says Chloe.

A muscular woman dressed in blue wrestling spandex runs out of the crowd, approaches Chloe, and asks,

"Hey, are you Chloe?"

"Yeah?" Chloe responds.

"Great, I found you! I'm Sapphire. Tatyana sent me to come and get you. Can you meet her in her apartment? She said she needs your help with something." Asks Sapphire.

"Yeah, sure." Says Chloe as she notices that Sapphire is looking at her with desire.

Sapphire looks at Chloe up and down, smiles, and says,

"She's right, you sure are a pretty little thing!" Says Sapphire as she touches Chloe's curls.

Chloe slowly walks away from Sapphire; she can't help feeling like prey as she sees Sapphire watching her move through the crowd, like a lion would watch a gazelle through tall grasses. As Chloe navigates through the thick crowd, the DJ gets on the mic and screams,

"YEEEAAAAAAHHH!! Give it up for our two wrestlers up here, Graveyard and Tornadoooooooo!!"

Everyone in the backyard screams as the DJ blasts an air horn through the microphone, then says,

"We're gonna take a little break for a few minutes, folks, enjoy the music while we wait for the next match!"

The DJ puts on some heavy club music, takes the headgear off, and steps away from his console. He sees Chloe approach and, as she's about to open the door to Tatyana's apartment in the RV garage, he leans into her and asks,

"You, Chloe?"

"Yeah!" Screams Chloe as she tries to be heard over the loud music.

"Thanks for letting us party at your place, girl!" Says the DJ.

"My dad is going to have a heart attack when he comes home!" Says Chloe.

"Why, baby? It's all good here, we're just having a little bit of fun, that's all!" Replies the DJ.

Chloe raises her eyebrows at him and opens the front door. Before she could go in, the DJ put his hand on her shoulder, leaned into her ear, and said,

"You need a little somhm, somhm?"

Chloe pulls away from him and asks,

"What?"

The DJ partially pulls out a large bag of pills from his pocket, shows Chloe, and winks at her. Chloe becomes disgusted.

"NO!" Says Chloe, she enters the apartment and slams the door behind her. She takes a few steps inside, turns around, looks back at the door, and shakes her head. She can't believe that guy is selling drugs in her backyard.

"Chloe, is that you?" Yells Tatyana from upstairs.

Chloe looks at the ceiling and yells back,

"Yeah, it's me!"

"Can you come upstairs, please?" Yells Tatyana.

"Coming!" Yells Chloe.

Chloe quickly goes to the staircase and runs upstairs. When she gets to the bedroom, she finds herself greeted by tons of new shopping bags spread out all over the floor, clothing everywhere, and the song "Eye of the Tiger" playing from a large Bluetooth speaker on the bed, and a strong smell of cherry perfume. Chloe looks over to the dresser and there stands Tatyana, completely naked, putting on lipstick, her hair teased up like an '80s rock star.

"Hi, did you need something?" Asks Chloe.

Tatyana turns around, filled with excitement and a wide grin.

"Yes, thank you for coming! I'm gonna need help zipping up the back of my new costume!"

"Oh, ok...and Sapphire?" Says Chloe.

"Her hands kept trembling, so I told her to get you instead."

Tatyana hustles over to one of the bags on the floor, looks around, then runs over to the nightstand, grabs something, makes her way to Chloe, and puts the little bag in her hand. Chloe looks at the bag and says,

"Nipple pads?"

Tatyana runs back to the mirror and teases her hair a bit more, saying,

"I don't have the nails to peel those. Can you peel them for me?"

"Sure," says Chloe, and starts to peel the plastic off.

"Have you heard from Daniel?" Asks Chloe.

Tatyana looks at Chloe through the mirror and says,

"No, he didn't come home last night."

Chloe stops peeling the pad; she's concerned about Daniel and says,

"Shouldn't we call someone? Maybe let the police know that he's missing?"

Tatyana grabs some deodorant and applies it to her underarm, then grabs the hair dryer.

"That kid! It's not the first time he's stayed away from home." Says Tatyana as she turns the dryer on and touches up her hair with a brush.

"Really? I'm really worried…" Says Chloe as she continues to peel the other pad.

"Don't be! He's probably hooking up with a friend or something; he'll come home when he's ready. He always does." Says Tatyana as she carefully watches what she's doing.

"Ok, I got them ready for you." Says Chloe.

Tatyana looks at Chloe through the mirror and says,

"Can you put them on for me, please? I can't let go of my hair right now."

Chloe hesitantly walks over towards Tatyana, intimidated by her gigantic stature and the size of her muscles. Tatyana sees her in the mirror, smiles and turns around, both hands up in the air as she works on her hair, blow drying with one and teasing with the other.

"Oh, before you do, wipe the lotion off my nipples with those alcohol wipes over there?" Says Tatyana as she looks at the container of wipes on the nightstand.

Chloe walks over, gets the wipes, and comes back to Tatyana, who is looking at herself again in the mirror. Chloe takes a wipe out of the container and gently wipes one nipple clean, then the other. Then, carefully pressing one of the pads on, Tatyana smiles, turns her upper body to give Chloe better reach to the other breast. Chloe takes a deep breath and swallows as she presses the other pad on.

"Thank you, honey! Hey, aren't they cute?" Asks Tatyana as Chloe quickly walks back to the bed, sits down.

"Well?" Asks Tatyana.

"What?" Asks Chloe as she looks back at Tatyana.

Tatyana turns the hairdryer off and puts it down on the dresser along with the brush. She walks over to Chloe and deliberately stands just a few inches in front of her, her crotch at Chloe's eye level. Chloe gets stuck looking at Tatyana's large, shaved womanhood. Tatyana knows exactly what she's doing and moves her hips forward to give Chloe a stronger scent of her cherry perfume. Being the enticing devil that she is, she opens her legs slightly to give Chloe a better look. Chloe finally pulls away and looks up at Tatyana, who is lustfully looking down at her, smiling.

> "I'm talking about my titties, my girls, my boobs, how do they look? Are they cute?" Asks Tatyana as she cups her small breasts and moves her hips towards Chloe's face a bit more.

> "They're nice…" Says Chloe.

Tatyana reaches down and pats one of Chloe's breasts. Chloe becomes rigid and uncomfortable, completely taken by surprise.

> "I mean…they're not as big as yours, but they are round and shapely, they're not bad, right?" Asks Tatyana.

Chloe nervously looks up at Tatyana, who is smiling back at her. From her point of view, sitting on the bed, Tatyana is a mountain of broad and bulging muscles standing over her. Chloe swallows again and nervously says,

"You have nothing to worry about; they are beautiful, just like you."

Tatyana smiles wider, bends down, and kisses Chloe on the cheek.

"Thank you, Baby!" Says Tatyana, then quickly runs to the closet and pulls out her new costume and holds it out for Chloe to see, she says,

"Look, I got this new costume, my manager wants to rebrand me."

"Really?" Asks Chloe.

Tatyana begins to put on the spandex pants as she says,

"The Soviet Union is long gone, the Russian thing was getting old. He wanted me to be something fresh; he suggested I come up with something new."

"Well, new could be good…hey, aren't those a bit tight?" Asks Chloe as she points to Tatyana's crotch.

"Is it that bad?" Asks Tatyana.

"You tell me." Says Chloe.

Tatyana turns to the mirror, looks at herself, and sees the large cameltoe. She takes a pair of tight white sports underwear and puts them over the spandex pants; they blend in so well that it looks like part of the costume.

"Well?" Asks Tatyana as she turns to show Chloe.

"Well done," Chloe says.

"So, my manager said he had something in mind for me, but he wanted to see what I would come up with, so…" Says Tatyana.

Tatyana reaches for a white sleeveless top with a lot of white fur around the wide collar. She puts it on and points to a small zipper in the back and says,

"Ok, this is the little crappy zipper I was talking about. Can you help me?

Chloe stands, walks over to Tatyana, and quickly zips her up while Tatyana looks at herself in the mirror. Chloe walks back to the bed, turns around, and looks at Tatyana, checking herself out in the mirror. Tatyana turns around, holds up her hands like a cat, and snarls, waiting for Chloe to respond.

"Eighty's rocker chick?" Says Chloe.

"No, no! The White Lioness!" Says Tatyana.

Chloe plops down on the bed with her mouth open, all of her energy suddenly escapes her, and she feels faint. She cannot believe what just came out of Tatyana's mouth.

"You're kidding…" says Chloe.

"Grrrrrrrr." Says Tatyana.

A few moments later, the RV garage door opens wide, Tatyana stands at the threshold of her apartment with her hands on her hips, and everyone close to the door that sees her starts to cheer, clap, and scream. Chloe stands inside the apartment behind her and watches the spectacle unfolding. The DJ at his station sees Tatyana, smiles, turns the music slightly down, and gets on the microphone saying,

> "Aaaaalright, everybody! If I could have all eyes over here, please!! Everyone look this way!"

The whole crowd now looks over at the DJ, he begins to play "Eye of the Tiger" and begins to announce,

> "It is with great pleasure that I introduce to you, for the very first time!

> THE WHITE LIONESS!!"

Tatyana raises her arms and flexes her biceps, taking in the adoration of the crowd. She then begins to walk to the ring, bouncing to the music as people cheer her on, and touch and caress her muscles as she passes, all the cameras are on her now. Tatyana climbs into the ring, followed by a cameraman, she begins to run around, flex and growl at he crowd. The DJ announces,

> "And her opponent, the only one brave enough to get into the ring with the White Lioness….Please help me welcome…

Hip Hop music begins to play.

> "The Beautiful…Sapphire!!" Yells the DJ.

Sapphire raises her hands, she's on the other side of the backyard, and begins to make her way up to the ring.

Chloe, now standing in front of the steps leading up to her back door, with her arms folded, shakes her head, not amused. Anthony slowly opens the door to the backyard, sees Chloe, and goes down and stands next to her.

"What…the hell…is all of this?" Anthony asks.

"Tatyana is introducing her new persona," Chloe says.

Anthony looks over at the ring in the back of his yard and sees Tatyana dressed in white, inside the ring with Sapphire. Anthony looks back at Chloe, who is looking at him in disgust.

"No more Muerte Rusa, she's the White Lioness now." Says Chloe

"Lioness?" Asks Anthony.

"YES! A lioness dad, remember what Mrs. June warned you about?

"She warned me? About what?" Asks Anthony.

"DAD! The very first day, when Tatyana was walking up the driveway!" Says Chloe, observing her father's expression as he thinks. Then Chloe continues,

"She said she had a dream of you riding a beautiful horse, the horse became a lion, then it became a dragon! Remember?"

Suddenly, Anthony gets a vision in his mind of that very morning when Tatyana was walking up his driveway in a see-through dress. He hears Mrs. June's words echoing as she warns him about the beautiful white horse, how it becomes a devouring lion, then finally a destroying dragon.

"I…I remember. Why did I not realize it before?" Says Anthony to himself.

Anthony looks over at the ring and sees Tatyana body slamming Sapphire face-first, unmercifully, onto the mat, blood splatters everywhere.

"I don't know any of these people, I can't recognize one." Says Chloe.

"How? Where did they come from?" Asks Anthony.

Chloe points to the DJ and says,

"And the DJ tried to sell me drugs!"

"WHAT!?" Says Anthony, as he looks over at Chloe, who looks back at him with folded arms and says,

"You have to put a stop to this, Dad."

"This ends now!" Says Anthony as he storms off.

Anthony walks into the crowd of people and makes his way up to the ring. Inside the ring, Tatyana helps a shaking Sapphire to her feet. Tatyana and a bloody-faced Sapphire hug, then raise each other's hands in victory.

"And there you have it!! The White Lioness and Sapphire!!" Screams the DJ as the crowd cheers.

Anthony finally reaches ringside and yells up to Tatyana,

"Tatyana!"

The DJ begins to play more dance music, and everyone begins to dance.

"Tatyana!" Anthony screams again.

Tatyana sees Anthony and quickly goes up to him and squats down to talk.

"I'm so glad you're here, babe! Isn't this incredible!!" Says Tatyana as she caresses Anthony's hair.

"Everyone needs to go home, right now!" Says Anthony.

Tatyana can see that he's upset, but it does not faze her; she smiles and says,

"We're just getting started, baby! What are you talking about?"

"The DJ is selling drugs, I don't know any of these people, this is completely out of control! We need to stop this now!" Says Anthony.

Tatyana nods her head and says,

"Okay, I got this…"

Tatyana stands up, points over to the DJ to get his attention, and motions for a microphone. The DJ takes a cordless mic, hands it to a biker, and motions for him to give it to her. The biker takes the mic, walks it over to Tatyana, she blows him a kiss, and takes the mic from him. The music volume lowers a bit, and Tatyana's mic turns on. Everyone looks over at her as she begins to say,

"Hi everyone!"

The whole backyard cheers, and Tatyana smiles widely; she loves the attention.

"I just wanted to take the time here to… to thank you. Thank everyone of you for coming out here tonight." Says Tatyana.

"You better not be quitting now!" Says the biker who gave her the microphone.

Tatyana smiles at him and flexes her bicep. Everyone begins to cheer again, she flexes her right leg, and her muscles pop through the tight spandex. Everyone gets excited. Tatyana feeds off the energy of the crowd and says,

"I hope you like the White Lioness!"

"Let's fuck!!" A woman in the crowd yells, and everyone laughs.

Tatyana laughs as well. She looks over at Anthony, who is looking straight at her, then she looks over at the large crowd before her and begins to say,

"But at this time, I'm gonna have to ask you…"

People know where she's going with it and begin to boo. One man in the crowd close to the ring yells,

"C'mon, we want more lioness!"

"Yeah! bring out the lion again!" Yells a woman from the back, then the whole back yard begins to chant,

BRING OUT THE LION!

BRING OUT THE LION!

BRING OUT THE LION!

Tatyana closes her eyes and extends her hands outwards as far as she can, receiving the energy from the crowd, soaking it all up, and realizing, as tears flow from her eyes, that this is her destiny, that this is what she was meant to do, and nothing is going to stop her. After a few moments, and just like that, her mind and heart are changed. She opens her eyes and smiles, and everyone cheers, she says,

"Please help me welcome to the ring…." Tatyana points at Anthony, "The Plumber of Destruction!"

The whole backyard goes up in a roaring cheer.

"No! No way, NO WAY!" Says Anthony as he gestures in the negative with his hands.

"He looks a little timid. Can we give him some assistance, please? Let's get him up here!" Says Tatyana over the mic.

Three large men from the crowd grab Anthony, and though he tries to push back and break free, they overpower him, pick him up, and push him into the ring. Anthony stands up and looks over at the crowd. They begin to clap and cheer. Tatyana walks up to Anthony, holds the mic away, and whispers in his ear, saying,

"Let's give them a good show and then I'll send them home, okay?"

"I don't know anything about wrestling." Says Anthony.

"Just follow my lead, and you'll be fine," Says Tatyana.

Tatyana hands the mic to one of the women in the crowd, then turns around and looks at Anthony, who is still bewildered by the whole thing.

Tatyana begins to walk around Anthony in circles.

"Hit me." Says Tatyana.

"No." Says Anthony.

SLAP!

Tatyana slaps Anthony, and he shakes it off and says,

"No!" Says Anthony.

Tatyana slaps him again.

SLAP!

"Come at me!" Says Tatyana, then taps him in the groin.

Anthony pushes her, and she smiles, because she knows she got him now, and the two begin to circle the ring.

"That DJ's got to go!" Says Anthony as he slaps Tatyana.

"Oh yeah?" She says, and punches him in the mouth, splitting his lower lip. Anthony begins to bleed.

Anthony wipes the blood off his lip, looks at it, and swings at her. Tatyana dodges out of the way and laughs. Tatyana slaps him again, but this time Anthony grabs her arm, pulls her in, and grabs her from the waist. Tatyana stumbles backwards, with Anthony on top of her.

"Stop!" Anthony says as he tries to hold her to the mat, but she is too strong for him.

"Don't forget I love you, baby…" says Tatyana, then head-butts him right in the nose and violently pushes him off of her.

Chloe sees her father fall backwards with a stream of blood flowing up in the air from his nose, she panics and yells.

"Stop! Stoooooop!"

Anthony lands on his back, Tatyana goes to the other side of the ring, and just stares at him, waiting to see what he's going to do. Slowly, Anthony gets up, takes his work shirt off and wipes his nose, and looks into the crowd. He sees people screaming at him, all kinds of things.

"You gonna let her do that to you!" A woman says.

"Get in there and fight like a man!" An old biker yells.

"Don't be a pussy, fight!" Yells another woman from the back.

Anthony looks over at Tatyana, and she's egging him on with her hands. Anthony runs over to Tatyana, but she easily grabs him and picks him up over her head and begins to spin him like a helicopter. The crowd gets wild with excitement. People begin to throw food into the ring, water bottles, soda, pieces of hamburgers, they are going crazy as she begins to walk around the ring while spinning him up in the air.

"Put me down!" Yells Anthony.

"I will, honey." Says Tatyana as she body slams him on his back.

BAM!!

"Aaaaaah!" Anthony yells.

Tatyana picks him up again and lifts him over her head; the crowd goes wild! Someone in the crowd begins to chant the word BODYSLAM and it quickly grows louder until the whole backyard is chanting,

"BODYSLAM, BODYSLAM, BODYSLAM!"

She sees Chloe upset and screaming at her from ringside, but can't really hear what she's saying due to the screaming people. Tatyana walks up to the edge of the ring, stands in front of the ropes, and faces the crowd with Anthony still up in the air, and watches as everyone has their hands raised and chants,

"BODYSLAM, BODYSLAM, BODYSLAM!"

Tatyana turns around and faces the ring. She takes a step forward and suddenly slips on a wet, waxed paper cup lying on a small puddle on the mat. She drops Anthony, who falls backwards into the crowd. When people realize what's happening, they get out of the way, and he lands back-first onto the back of a metal folding chair. Tatyana falls on her butt and quickly turns around to see Anthony.

"Aaaaaaah! Oh my God, aaaaahhh!" Moans Anthony.

Chloe runs to him and pushes past the crowd and reaches Anthony's side, pulls out her cell phone, and dials 911. She begins to tell the operator while looking up at Tatyana, now standing, looking down stoically at them from the ring. Chloe cries as her hand trembles while holding the phone to her ear.

"Nine one one operator, please state the nature of your emergency." Says the operator.

"Hello? Yes, my dad is hurt, he's fallen and hurt his back…I don't know, maybe fifteen feet? He landed on the back of a metal chair…" Says Chloe with a trembling voice.

Hours later, in a room at a Phoenix Hospital, surrounded by medical equipment, Anthony sleeps on a bed. The room is large and aesthetically clean with a single large window; the lights in the room are dim, allowing the moonlight to enter the room and shine on the closed bathroom door. Chloe and Mrs. June sit and keep watch beside him. Chloe's eyes are red and swollen from crying. She looks at her dad with wires and tubes coming out of his arms and mouth; she can't believe he's here. Mrs. June looks at her without saying a word; she has her bible on her lap.

"Lord, have mercy." Mrs. June whispers.

There's a knock on the door. Mrs. June and Chloe turn to look. A doctor comes into the room, nods at them, walks over to Anthony, and checks him out. He looks over some of the monitors, then turns around, looks at Chloe, and says,

"You're the daughter?"

"Yes." Says Chloe.

"I'm Dr. Banders. I'm treating your father. Well, your dad is going to be ok, but he will need to use a wheelchair." Says the doctor, but before he could continue, Chloe interrupts.

"Oh no!" Says Chloe

"My God!" Says Mrs. June.

"Hold on, hold on. It's not permanent," says the doctor.

"Okay…" says Chloe

"Your father suffered a lot of internal trauma, especially on his spinal cord. Two of his bones on his lower back are slightly bruised, so we have to be very careful with treatment." Says the doctor.

"So will he walk again?" Asks Mrs. June.

"Mr. Borgia was very close to severing nerves and connective tissue in his spine, and if that had happened, he would not have been able to walk, but

that did not happen; he is very, very lucky." Says
the doctor.

"God was looking out for that boy." Says Mrs. June.

"Yeah…well, in time, he will be able to walk. Every
person is different, and how long it will take will
depend on a lot of things. But from the results
we've seen, I'm very hopeful." Says the doctor.

Chloe and Mrs. June look at each other with hope.
They reach out and hold hands, then look back at
Anthony, still asleep on the bed.

Chapter 11: Birth of the Dragon

Towels and clothes on the floor, overflowing garbage cans, and broken lockers, the Bloodbath Arena dressing room is disgustingly dilapidated and unclean. The door to the stadium swings open, a camera crew with a sound man enters, followed by Tatyana dressed in her lioness costume. The mic man pinches his nose due to the smell, and the door slams shut. The camera crew follows Tatyana as she angrily and rapidly walks towards her locker. She kicks one of the garbage cans, sending it flying along with all the garbage inside it, and punches a locker, breaking it in half. She pulls and rips the lower part of the broken locker door, throws it on the floor, and grabs a clean towel from within. She turns around, and her face and vest are splattered in blood. She tries to clean herself, but the blood is not coming off.

> "She got her blood all over my face, my new vest…" Says Tatyana as she sits on one of the benches.

The locker room slams open violently again, and another wrestler comes in dressed in a green spandex bodysuit. The girl is completely covered in blood, her front teeth are missing, and a nurse is trying to hold a towel to her face, but the wrestler is pushing her aside. The production crew quickly turns its attention to her,

"It's Viper! Get a shot of this! Quick!" says one of the crew members.

The camera operator begins to zoom in on Viper as she sees Tatyana on the other side of the room and screams,

"You fucking bitch!"

"Fuck you!" Screams Tatyana.

"You broke my nose, my front teeth! What the fuck is wrong with you!" Screams Viper.

"Good! Your face looks a lot better now!" Scream Tatyana.

Viper pushes the nurse and runs up to Tatyana. Tatyana quickly stands up and readies herself for a fight. The nurse quickly runs and gets in between the two wrestlers. She tries to hold Viper back, but is not strong enough. Viper plows forward until she gets right in front of Tatyana's face, the two wrestlers square off, Tatyana towering over Viper by two feet.

"You're an asshole!" Says Viper as she splatters more blood on Tatyana's face.

"I know! So you better get the fuck out of my face before I break your fucking spine!" Screams Tatyana as she looks down on Viper.

"STOP!! That's enough!" Screams the nurse, wedged between the two.

Viper presses her chest towards Tatyana, pinning the nurse in the middle.

"I'll take you on right here bitch!" Says Viper as more blood continues to flow from her mouth and nose.

"You're bleeder…I fucking love bleeders." Says Tatyana. ·

"MAKE A MOVE!!" Screams viper

Suddenly and out of nowhere, there's a single loud handclap that echoes through the whole locker room, and everyone turns to see where it's coming from. Standing on the other side of the locker room is a very tall and muscular black man dressed in a black suit and tie. Everyone is captivated by his presence as he comes out of the shadows and walks up to the women; all eyes are on him.

The man stands a few feet away from the two wrestlers. He is so tall that when he looks over at Tatyana, he has to look down.

"Ms. Johnson, if you would excuse us, I have some business with Ms. Ivanova. Please, take a shower and cool off." Says the tall, mysterious man.

"No one tells me what to do! Who the fuck do you think you are!

Viper raises her fist to hit the man and takes a step towards him, but he quickly grabs her by the throat with one hand and stops her in her tracks. The man lifts Viper off the floor; his hand is so big that his fingers meet in the back of her neck. Higher and higher he lifts Viper as he chokes her and brings her face right up to his. Viper tries to break his grip with her hands, but she can't; her face quickly turns red, and she is hardly able to breathe.

"You need to go take a shower and cool off." Says the man.

"Damn…" whispers Tatyana.

Viper's eyes begin to bulge, tears begin to flow, and her face turns blood red. The man looks in her eyes and says,

"Nod if you understand."

Viper slightly nods, and the man immediately releases her. She falls to the floor and lands on her side. She holds her throat and looks up at the giant in front of her.

"I did ask nicely at first. Now, hit the showers. Everyone else, OUT…NOW!" Says the man.

The camera crew and the nurse quickly make their way out the door. Viper gets up and walks to the showers, leaving a trail of blood and urine behind her. Tatyana stands alone, looking at the giant in front of her with anticipation. The locker room is quiet. Viper exits the room, and the man turns to Tatyana and says,

"Ms. Ivanova, I am the Associate. It's a pleasure to make your acquaintance."

The man reaches into the inner pocket of his suit, pulls out a small matte black envelope, and hands it to Tatyana.

"What's this?" Asks Tatyana as she takes the envelope from his hand.

"This is an invitation to a very special event at Mr. White's residence." Says the Associate.

"A Party?" asks Tatyana as she looks down at the envelope.

She opens the envelope and pulls out a small plastic matte black business card. The card has no writing on it, no symbols, nothing. Tatyana looks up at the man and says,

"There's nothing on this card. He could have just called me or emailed me the invitation; this is weird."

"Mr. White insists that invitations to this event be delivered in person." Says the Associate.

"WOW, ok." Says Tatyana.

"The event starts at ten at night." Says the Associate, then points to the card and says,

"Without this invitation, you will not have access, and Mr. White would be very disappointed if you miss it. Please, do not lose it, or forget to bring it."

Tatyana nods her head, taps on the card, and says,

"Can I bring some friends?"

The associate smiles and reveals that all of his teeth are covered in precious diamonds, he says,

"You can bring one guest. They will not have the access you have, but I'm sure they will enjoy themselves. Make sure, however, the person you bring is someone…someone you are very comfortable with."

Tatyana nods her head. The associate straightens out his suit, looks Tatyana dead in the eyes, and says,

"Very well then, thank you for your time."

The associate walks over to the locker room door, opens it, and Tatyana asks,

"Hey! What's your name?"

Without turning his head to look back at Tatyana, the man says,

"Have a good day, Ms. Ivanova." And exits the locker room.

The next morning, Chloe sits at Mrs. June's kitchen table. The kitchen is well lit, flooded with natural light from the windows, quaintly decorated in an old country farmhouse style with yellow flowered wallpaper and white see-through curtains. There are black and white pictures of family members on one wall, and a collection of small silver spoons hanging on another wall. Mrs. June stands at her stove watching over a kettle as Mahalia Jackson plays from an old CD player on the countertop.

"So did you hear from the insurance company about the car?" Asks Chloe as the kettle begins to whistle.

Mrs. June takes the kettle off the stove and begins to pour water into two cups holding tea bags.

“Yes, the man said that they would have to inspect the remains of the car. He said I would probably get a few thousand dollars, if anything at all.” Says Mrs. June.

“Well, I hope you get at least what the car is worth, Mrs. June!” Says Chloe.

Mrs. June brings the two cups to the table, puts one in front of Chloe, and says,

“Here’s your tea, baby, you like mint tea, right?

“Love it.” Says Chloe.

“I got some oatmeal cookies, want some?” Asks Mrs. June.

“No, thank you.” Says Chloe.

Mrs. June gets a jar of sugar and a spoon from the counter beside the stove and brings it to the table. She sits in front of Chloe.

“When is your father coming home?”

Chloe pauses as she spoons sugar into her tea and says,

“They said in a few days, they just want to make sure he’s stable enough, I guess.”

“I see.” Says Mrs. June.

Chloe holds the spoon up while asking Mrs. June if she wants some sugar.

“Yes, please.” Says Mr. June.”

Chloe slides the sugar over to Mrs. June, who takes a small teaspoon of sugar and carefully dumps it into the hot tea. As she stirs the tea, Chloe looks at Mrs. June,

"I know you warned my dad about Tatyana…"

Mrs. June gently holds he index finger up and says,

"The Lord warned your dad about Tatyana. I was just the messenger."

"Did you see her the night my dad got hurt?" Asks Chloe, then remembers and says,

"No…no, you weren't there."

"I was not home at that time." Says Mrs. June.

Chloe leaves the spoon in her cup, puts both hands down on the table, and says,

"She was dressed like a lion, Mrs. June! Like a lion, just like you told my dad!"

Mrs. June takes a sip and puts her cup down.

"I'm telling you, this phase is a short one; she will get worse." Says Mrs. June

"But you said the lioness later became like a dragon, right?" Asks Chloe.

"These new people she's around will feed her ego. They will feed it and feed it, swell her pride so much that her hubris will consume her. She will think she's invincible, invulnerable…untouchable.

She will be deadlier than she has ever been." Says Mrs. June.

"What about my dad? What do we do? And, am I safe?" Asks Chloe.

"We watch out for your dad. And we pray, honey, we pray and you trust God, He'll keep you safe." Says Mrs. June.

Looking out the window into Chloe's backyard, Mrs. June sees the RV garage and asks,

"Have you heard from Daniel? It's been a few days, and I have not seen that boy."

"No, I haven't heard a word…I'm so worried." Says Chloe.

Mrs. June puts her cup down and stares at the RV garage where Daniel and his mom stay, and wonders.

At That Exact Moment

On the other side of the valley, Mr. Lucious White, Tatyana's new manager, sits at the end of a large, black, shiny table in an upscale corporate office downtown. The city below is vividly seen through floor-to-ceiling windows. At the head of the table filled with people, Mr. White taps his fingers down with anticipation. To the right of the large corporate table, there's a small lounge area filled with assistants and other staff members, many of

241

them standing because there is no more room. At a wet bar behind Mr. White, a voluptuous red-headed woman in a tight suit and skirt mixes a drink. She finishes the drink with a garnish and quickly brings it to the table and sets it in front of Mr. White. He looks at it with disgust and says,

"No olive, Katherine?"

"The Russian Mule does not take an olive, Mr. White." Says Katherine.

Mr. White squints his eyes and pushes the drink towards her, and says,

"But I do! Put it in a larger glass and give me an olive, Katherine, fuck it, give me three!" Says Mr. White as he looks over at Katherine in disgust.

The young girl quickly takes the drink and goes back to the bar. Lucious looks at everyone on the table; every eye is on him, and the only sound that can be heard is Katherine working at the bar. Katherine quickly makes her way back to Lucious, puts a little napkin down, and his drink on top of it. Mr. White looks down at his drink and smiles. He looks up at Katherine and says,

"This is why I love you, Katherine."

"I love you too, sir. I'm sorry." Katherine quickly responds as she slightly bows in reverence.

Lucious holds up the drink with four olives in it, for everyone to see, and says,

"Katherine always gives me more than what I want, see! That's why I love this fucking girl!"

Katherine slightly smiles and takes a step backwards.

> "As you always say, it's the little things that matter, sir." Says Mr. Willard Johnson, one of the executives at the table.

Lucious puts the drink to his mouth and drinks it all in one shot, olives and all. He slams the glass down on the table and says,

> "Yes, Will, it's the little things, the details, that's what makes the difference!"

Mr. White looks over at another executive at the table and asks,

> "How much longer, Virginia?"

Mr. Johnson looks over at Katherine, raises his hand, and asks,

> "Katherine, could I have some water, please?"

Katherine looks at him, but she does not make a move.

> "They should not be much longer, sir." Says Mrs. Virginia Longington, head of marketing, answering Mr. White.

Lucious gets up, walks up to Willard, puts his hand on his shoulder, and as he leans into his ear, he says,

> "Get up and get the water yourself. Katherine is my assistant, not yours…m'kay?"

Lucious looks over at Katherine and smiles. She smiles back and nods her head. Mr. White walks and stands in front of a set of large black double doors at the very end of the conference room. The doors are shiny black, with demonic designs and images engraved on them. As he looks out the window, Lucious hears the door unlock. He takes a few steps away from the door and smiles as loud music begins to play behind the door.

The doors open wide, and the Hip-Hop music blasts into the room. And out comes Tatyana surrounded by makeup artists, hair stylists, wardrobe designers, and all sorts of assistants, Lucious and everyone in the room begin to clap.

Tatyana is dressed in a maroon and red bikini top and spandex pants that look like they are made of red and black reptile scales. Her black knee-high boots look like they are made of reptile skin; they are also covered in scales. Her hair is teased up with red and black highlights, and her face is painted to resemble red and black reptile scales as well. Tatyana is all oiled up, and the bulging muscles on her shoulders, back, and arms look extra big with the lighting of the room.

Lucious holds his hand out to her as if presenting an idol and says,

"Ladies and gentlemen, I present to you....The Red Dragon!"

Everyone stands up and claps vigorously. While everyone continues to clap, Lucious begins to slowly walk around Tatyana as he speaks, saying,

"She used to be Muerte Rusa, and for a few weeks they knew her as the lioness, but…This right here is our future! This is the future of professional wrestling! She's too mean, too powerful, too big to be anything else but a DRAGON!"

Tatyana puts her hands on her hips and raises her head. Everyone loves it and claps harder as Mr. White continues to say,

> "That's right! There's no one more powerful than you, my dragon! You will destroy the bones of every woman wrestler that gets into the ring with you! Not one of them will want to fight you!"

Lucious walks behind her and lifts her arms. Tatyana raises them and flexes her gigantic biceps as Lucious caresses them, then continues to walk around her, saying,

> "No woman will want to face you, after you destroy those that dare to try, we will put you in the ring with men! And they will also fear you!

Everyone in the room continues to clap and cheer. Tatyana is eating it all up, Mr. White continues,

> "Within a year, you will be wrestling champion of women's and men's categories!"

> "YES!!" Screams Tatyana as she raises her hands.

Lucious pumps his fists and says,

> "That's fucking right! No one, no one will stand in your way!! Movie studios will come begging for you to do action movies, and toy companies will make all sorts of toys and costumes with your image! You will be the queen of social media, and

everyone will know your name. A goddess of red and black! The world will worship at the feet of…THE RED DRAGON!!"

Mr. White opens his arms as he showcases Tatyana, and everyone in the room goes wild. Tatyana takes it all in, her chest swells with pride, and she believes all of it.

"Don't you love her? Look at this muscle goddess! Don't you want her even though she looks dangerous?" Lucious screams into the room as everyone cheers and screams.

Lucious points to one of the men at the table and asks,

"Isn't she delicious?"

The man opens his jacket and rips his shirt in madness. Lucious nods and continues to clap, then he points at another man and asks,

"Don't you want her to slap you around, Marty?"

"YES! She can do it anytime!" Screams Mr. Martin Wilthrow, head of Analytics.

Lucious walks up to an older woman at the table and asks,

"Mrs. Green, what do you think? Is she dangerous? Does she make you hot?"

Mrs. Rhonda Green, head of Human Resources, opens her blouse and fans herself, saying,

"Yes, yes she does!"

Lucious nods, smiles in approval, and continues to clap with everyone else.

> "We're gonna make so much fucking money, it' gonna be diabolical!" Says Lucious as he and Tatyana look at each other in the eyes and smile.

Everyone claps even harder, papers go flying in the air, and people begin to jump up and down. One of the assistants in the back throws her panties, and they land at Tatyana's feet.

Tatyana looks around the room and smiles. She sees people clapping, smiling, and cheering her on.

> "I'm a goddess…a god…invincible…untouchable," Tatyana whispers to herself as an evil countenance takes over her face and her eyes become void of life or light.

She looks again at Mr. White, now standing back at the head of the table. He is not clapping, but simply stares at her; he's taken note of her change, smiles widely, and nods at her.

The next morning at the Borgia residence, Anthony is finally coming home. Chloe pushes Anthony's wheelchair up the driveway, Mrs. June following close behind.

> "I'm so glad you're home, son!" Says Mrs. June.

> "Me too, Mrs. June, and thank you for all your help with Chloe!"

> "What!" Says Chloe.

"Chloe can take care of herself; she did just fine!"
Says Mrs. June.

"You tell 'em, Mrs. June, ha, ha!" Says Chloe.

As they get close to the backyard, Anthony sees the beauty
around his property and sighs,

> "Look at these blue skies and white puffy clouds,
> listen to those birds in the trees! And the mountains
> all around! I missed this place so much, except for
> that stupid ring over there."

> "Only been a few days, mister, but I understand
> where you're coming from, he, he." Says Mrs June.

A car alarm beeps twice from the street, car doors are heard
opening and shutting, and they can hear Tatyana screaming
something unintelligible from the street. Everyone turns to
look at the driveway as they hear footsteps approaching.
Tatyana, in her dragon get-up, comes walking up the
driveway; she's joined by two wrestlers, a camera crew,
and a few assistants. One cameraman records her from the
front, the other from the side as she walks with her
entourage.

As she talks with the wrestlers and is headed to her
apartment, she looks around and sees the whole gang by the
patio furniture. Tatyana smiles and casually makes her way
over to them. She places her hand on Anthony's shoulder
and says,

> "Anthony, you're back! It's so good to see you!"

> "No thanks to you!" Says Chloe.

“Chloe!” Anthony snaps back.

They all get surrounded by the production crew, cameras, mics, even the wrestlers come over and stand around them.

“I’m so sorry you got hurt,” Says Tatyana to Anthony.

“You didn’t visit once at the hospital, I thought you cared about him.” Says Chloe.

“Chloe, enough!” Says Anthony.

Tatyana gets closer to Anthony, puts her hand on his shoulder, and says,

“She’s right, I’ve been so busy, I never made time to come see you, I’m sorry.”

Tatyana turns to the camera crew and says,

“Okay, guys, you need to give me a break here for a bit, go wait in the car or something.”

She turns to the wrestlers and says,

“Can you guys wait for me by my door, please?”

The guys nod and walk away.

“Well, I’m gonna head on home. I’ll see you guys later. Anthony, I’m so glad you’re home.” Says Mrs. June.

“See you later, Mrs. June.” Says Chloe.

“Thank you for everything, Mrs. June!” Says Anthony.

They all watch as Mrs. June walks over to her house, waves goodbye, and enters.

"I'm glad I got you here, Anthony, you too, Chloe. I'm going to be going on the road and I won't be around as often, but I wanted to run a few things by you, is that ok?" Says Tatyana.

"Uhm…yeah sure. Let's go to the house and talk." Says Anthony.

"Okay, great. I know you're just getting home, so get settled in. And I'll join you in a bit? Says Tatyana.

"Sounds good." Says Anthony and motions to Chloe.

Chloe takes the wheelchair, brings him to the door, then helps Anthony slowly climb the stairs and enter the house. Tatyana gets halfway to the apartment, and her cellphone rings. She looks at it, and it's the Phoenix Police Department.

"Hello?" Says Tatyana.

"Hi, is this Mrs. Ivanova?" Officer Guerra says.

"Let me guess, you have information about my son?" Says Tatyana.

"Hi, this is Officer Guerra. As a matter of fact, I do have information on your son." Says the Officer.

"Where is he?" Asks Tatyana.

“He’s right here. We picked him up a few hours ago.” Says Officer Guerra.

“Oh my god! Is he ok? Is he in trouble?” Asks Tatyana.

“Your boy is fine, he was hanging out with some transient folk in one of the junk yards, looks like he had been living with them for a few days.” Says the officer.

“What the fuck!” Says Tatyana.

“Yeah, well, they were very defensive of your boy. It looks like he made a lot of friends down there. He didn’t want us to call you; it seems he’ a bit angry with you about some domestic issues, but he didn’t want to elaborate on that. Anything you want to tell me?” Says Officer Guerra.

“We had an argument, you know how teenagers get, so rebellious and such. But I never thought he would run away from home for this many days…” Says Tatyana.

“I understand, anyway, when can you come get your boy?” Asks the officer

“Right now, right now. Thank you for calling me! I’m going to pick him up right now! Can you text me the address, please?” Says Tatyana.

“Of course, as soon as I hang up, I’ll text it to you.” Says Officer Guerra.

“Thank you.” Says Tatyana and hangs up.

Tatyana looks at her phone and says,

"What am I gonna do with you, Daniel?"

She walks over to the crew waiting for her and says,

"I'll be heading back to the gym in a little bit. Can you guys take the production team and meet me there? I need to settle a few things here before I head back, and I also have to pick up my son at the police station, so I don't know how long I'm gonna be."

"Yeah, sure, that's fine, we'll grab some food on the way back, we can take some preliminary shots and get the place ready, not a problem." Says the assistant.

Tatyana nods, then walks over to the two massive, muscular men standing by her door, and watches as the crew and assistants make their way to the car. When they are pulling away from the driveway, Tatyana turns to the guys and says,

"I need you guys to do me a favor."

"Anything." Says the wrestler known as the Elephant Man.

"I need you to come with me and pick up my son from the police station, and watch him tonight for me. I have to get back to the stadium and do another shoot tonight." She says.

"Yeah, that's fine," Says the other wrestler.

"You sure he'll want us around?" Asks the Elephant Man.

Tatyana looks at them, leans in, and says,

"Daniel needs more than just his mama; he needs a man in his life."

"Look, I don't want to burst your bubble, but we're not the fatherly type, ok." Says the elephant man.

"Just show him a good time, that's all I'm asking. My kid is gay; he likes men. Take him to a gay club, let him get someone in his face, get him some lap dances from some boys. I don't care what you guys do with him, just bring him home in one piece." Says Tatyana as she pulls out a large roll of cash and puts it in the wrestler's hands.

The guys look at each other, then they look at Tatyana.

"How did you know we were gay?" Asked the Elephant man.

Tatyana condescendingly looks at them and says,

"Let me just say that, I see the way you guys look at each other's burritos, hunger is an understatement, or am I wrong?"

The guys look at each other, then look back at Tatyana.

"No, you're right, you're right, but are you sure about this? What if he doesn't want that kind of…attention? How old is he?" Asks the Elephant Man.

"He just turned eighteen." Says Tatyana, knowing the boy is underage, then continues to say, "Trust me, the boy has been needing some fun like this for a long time."

The guys look at her, a bit concerned about what she's saying. Tatyana points to the roll of money in the guy's hand and says,

"Do this for me, and I'll make it worth your while; there's more where that came from, I promise."

The guys nod.

"Good, good. Now wait here for me, I have to talk to Anthony real quick, then we'll be on our way." Says Tatyana, then walks towards Anthony's house.

As she gets some distance from the wrestlers, Tatyana thinks to herself...

I gotta get you back, Daniel. I need to make you love who you were, what we had. You will always be my little girl.

Tatyana turns around and walks up to the Borgia house. She reaches the back door, looks inside through the door's window, and sees Anthony sitting in his wheelchair at the kitchen table, and Chloe stands at the stove cooking something. Inside, the mood is light in the kitchen. Chloe is so happy that her father is finally home; she's cooking him some eggs.

"Dad, did you want some ketchup for the eggs?" Asks Chloe.

"I'll get it." Says Anthony.

Chloe runs to the fridge, saying,

"No, I'll get it, Dad. You stay put!"

Chloe opens the refrigerator door, gets the ketchup, and quickly brings it to the table so she can get back to cooking. There's a knock on the back door.

"It's gotta be Tatyana." Says Anthony.

Chloe leans towards the center of the room and sees her smiling and waving outside.

"Yeah, it's her." Says Chloe.

"You were pretty nasty to her out there, you know." Says Anthony.

"I know, I know, I'll apologize." Says Chloe as she quickly makes her way to the door.

Chloe opens the door and says to Tatyana,

"Look, T, I'm sorry about…"

Tatyana immediately hugs Chloe, taking her by surprise, and says,

"You have nothing to apologize for. I'm the asshole, remember? I'm so sorry."

Tatyana quickly runs over to Anthony and gives him a hug and says,

"I'm sorry, Anthony, can you please forgive me?"

"Of course, baby, you got nothing to apologize about. I know you're busy." Says Anthony.

Tatyana pulls away from Anthony slightly and says,

"I never meant to drop you like that; it was a complete accident."

"I know, I know it was." Says Anthony.

They both smile at each other. Chloe seems to be more at ease now that she heard an apology, and slowly makes her way back to the stove to finish up the eggs she was cooking. Tatyana turns around and closes the door as Anthony asks,

"So you're going to be going away?"

Tatyana looks at him and quickly turns around, walks over to the kitchen table, and takes a seat. She puts her hand over Antony's and says,

"Just for a little bit. They've scheduled a wrestling tour to promote the documentary, and I definitely have to go. The problem is that I can't take Daniel, he has school, and he will have to stay here."

Anthony takes his hand back from underneath Tatyana's hand, reaches for his glass, and takes a sip of his drink, then says,

"I see, when do you leave?"

"In two weeks." Says Tatyana.

Tatyana nods her head and smiles. Chloe brings the eggs to the table and sets them down in front of Anthony. She points to his plate and asks Tatyana,

> "Want some eggs?"

Tatyana shakes her head negatively, then says,

> "What I'm really saying is…I need someone to watch over Daniel. He can take care of himself; you don't have to worry about feeding him or anything like that. I'll leave him some money. But I just want to be able to tell him he can come to you guys if he needs anything?"

> "Of course, baby, we will be here for him, without a doubt!" Says Anthony.

> "Chloe, you're really good with him. Would you be willing to spend some time with him while I'm gone? Asks Tatyana.

Chloe looks a bit concerned and asks,

> "I love Daniel, of course, I'll help. But how long are you really going to be gone? I start at the University in a few weeks myself, and things will change then. My dad's not working, so I have to take care of him as well…"

> "Don't worry about me, honey…" Says Anthony as he reaches back and holds Chloe's arm.

> "He won't be a bother to anyone, I promise; he's a good kid," Tatyana says, beginning to get a bit anxious. Chloe quickly interjects and says,

"It won't be a problem! Daniel's like my little brother, he'll be fine with us!"

Tatyana takes a deep breath and smiles, saying,

"Are you guys sure?"

"He'll be fine with us." Says Anthony with a smile.

Tatyana puts both hands on the table and says,

"Okay! Well, thank you guys! And that brings me to the other thing I wanted to talk about."

Chloe and Anthony look at Tatyana with anticipation as she pauses and stares at them for a moment. The room is eerily quiet, then she says,

"So I've been invited to a party, and it's actually a very big deal for me. There's going to be all sorts of industry people there, media folks, promoters, you know, very influential people."

"That actually sounds really good, T. You need that exposure." Says Anthony as he chews.

Tatyana puts her hand on Anthony's hand and says,

"Well, I wanted to take you with me, baby."

Anthony puts his fork down and says.

"I can't go like this."

"Why not?" Asks Tatyana.

"He just got out of the hospital. When is this party?" Asks Chloe.

“It’s this Thursday coming up.” Says Tatyana.

“That’s a weird day to throw a party, isn’t it?” Asks Anthony, then he gets an Idea.

Anthony looks at Chloe, then he looks back at Tatyana, then he looks back at Chloe.

“What?” Asks Chloe.

Anthony looks over at Tatyana and says,

“Take Chloe.”

Tatyana smiles widely. She is very pleased with the idea. She looks over at Chloe and asks,

“That would be nice! What do you say, Chloe?”

Chloe is taken by surprise; she wants to be upset with Tatyana for what she did to her dad, but at the same time, she sees Tatyana wanting to make peace, so she knows she should be nice to her.

“I mean…I don’t know.” Says Chloe.

Anthony turns to her and says,

“You should go, honey! Get out of the house and do something fun!

“It’s gonna be great! High-class atmosphere, top-notch food, they’ll probably have a live band and everything! C’mon, it’ll be fun!” Says Tatyana.

“That does sound nice, I like it.” Says Chloe.

"They said they were going to send a car to pick us up and everything!" Says Tatyana excitedly.

"Wow…you are going to have a blast, honey!" Says Anthony to Chloe.

"You should come…" Says Tatyana playfully.

Chloe throws her arms up in the air and proclaims loudly,

"Okay! Okay! I'm in, I'll go with ya!"

Tatyana slaps her hands and says,

"Awesome! Thank you, thank you, I know we'll have a good time!"

Chloe feeds off her energy, she begins to jump up and down with excitement, Tatyana gets up and starts jumping with her as Anthony smiles and takes it all in.

"I have to go see what I'm gonna wear! Aaaaaaah!" Yells Chloe.

Chloe runs out of the kitchen, runs through the living room, and they hear her footsteps running upstairs to her bedroom. Anthony backs up on his wheelchair and moves himself closer to the living room door to hear her as she moves around in her bedroom. Tatyana notices his checkbook on the table and quickly takes it and hides it in her pocket. Anthony turns around and comes back to the table. He slides his lap underneath the table again and says,

"It's really good to see her so happy like this."

"Sure is!" Says Tatyana.

She gets up, leans over to Anthony, kisses him on the lips, and says,

"I gotta go, baby. Please call me if you need anything, ok?"

"Okay, I will, and thank you!" Says Anthony.

Tatyana smiles and walks out the door as Anthony watches her leave. The door closes, and Anthony is all alone. He looks around the room for a few seconds, wondering how he could be so blessed to have a wonderful daughter and such a great girlfriend. He looks down at his eggs and begins to eat.

Tatyana walks down the back stairs to the house. She looks over at the wrestlers by her house and motions for them to follow. They quickly walk towards the driveway and make their way to the car waiting for them at the front of the house.

A Few Hours Later

Tatyana stands in front of a bulletproof window at the front desk of the Phoenix Police Station. The air in the precinct is thick with the stench of stale coffee, sweat, and desperation. The fluorescent lights buzz overhead, casting a sterile glow on the whole place. Tatiana looks to the right and sees the booking room, which is a chaotic spectacle. A gaunt woman is shrieking obscenities at a bored-looking desk Sergeant while a tattooed man in ripped jeans, handcuffed to a chair, slumps against the wall with his eyes glazed over, saliva dripping from his lower lip gathering on his lap.

A young woman in a torn dress, her makeup smeared and mascara running down her cheeks, sobs uncontrollably into her hands as she fills her seat with urine, which overflows on the floor and marinates her bare feet. A hulking figure of a man with multiple cuts to his face stumbles into the room hands handcuffed to the back, being led by three police officers. He talks to himself and mutters threats under his breath. The room is a petri dish of society's underbelly, a place where despair, addiction, and desperation collide.

The booking desk area itself is a monument to forsaken order, as cups, discarded food wrappers, containers, and bottles litter the surfaces of the whole place. Officer Stanley, his face etched with weariness and his eyes glazed over from being overworked, looks at Tatiana and says from the other side of the glass,

> "So yeah, we're releasing the boy into your custody tonight. He will have to face the judge on this day, right here. And these are the fees that will need to be paid." Says Officer Stanley as he points to the paperwork he's handing to Tatyana

Tatyana barely looks at the paperwork and says,

> "Fine, Fine, where's my boy?"

Suddenly, a side door opens up, and Daniel comes out. He sees Tatyana and immediately tenses up he lifts his head and slightly turns his head in fear. The door closes behind him, and both stare at each other for a minute. Daniel looks like he's been through hell. His hair is greasy and stuck together, his shorts and shirt are dusty and stained, his skin is covered in what looks like car exhaust, he's almost unrecognizable.

Officer Stanley pushes the paperwork through the small opening at the bottom of the window and says,

>"And there he is, and here's your paperwork."

Tatyana takes the papers as she continues to look over at Daniel, who continues to look at her with distrust. She puts the papers under her armpit, walks over to Daniel, and says.

>"What the hell is wrong with you! Hugh! It's been days!"

>"I'm not going anywhere with you." Says Daniel.

Tatyana feels anger begin to build inside. She tries to contain herself and says,

>"That's fine, that's fine, Daniel. I figured as much, so I made some preparations. I have two friends in the car outside. You're going with them. They're gonna get you cleaned up, get you some new clothes, some food, and show you around town a little bit, then they're gonna take you home. Tomorrow, we'll sit down and talk. How does that sound?"

Daniel looks at his mother up and down and says,

>"I don't know your friends."

"Let's go." Says Tatyana.

Tatyana takes Daniel by the arm and leads him outside. A short distance away, the two wrestlers stand by Tatyana's truck waiting. Daniel sees them, stops walking, and says,

"Nope, no way."

Tatyana grabs his arm now and begins to force walk him down the sidewalk.

"No, Mom, I'm not going with them. Just take me home."

"Dam it, Daniel! I can't take you home because I have to work." Says Tatyana.

Daniel breaks away from Tatyana's hand, she immediately grabs him again, turns him around to face her, and sternly says.

"You're going with them because I don't trust you to take care of yourself, Daniel. You're not gonna be alone tonight, they are your fucking babysitters whether you like it or not. So, you can play along, get new clothes and food, and go out with them, or you can spend the whole night in the car, dirty, hungry, and stinky, with two guys looking at you until I get home later tonight. What's it gonna be!"

Daniel looks over at the guys. One of them raises his hand and waves. Daniel looks back at his mother and says,

"You're not going to say anything about what happened?" Asks Daniel.

Tatyana looks down at Daniel, as he looks up at her, wanting a response. She can tell that he's been wounded by her, and though she knows that the easiest thing to do would be to just apologize, she cannot bring herself to do it. She looks into her heart for pity, for some type of acceptance for finding her son reading a bible, but instead finds the engulfing canyon of hatred she has for religion, so great, and so vast, she has to compose herself before she answers.

> "I love you, Daniel, and though I should not have reacted that way, you should have known better than to bring that book into my house."

Daniel looks down at the sidewalk, in his heart, he was hoping for a simple *I'm sorry,* maybe a hug, but he got nothing of the sort. With a broken heart, he looks over at the guys by the car and says,

> "If I go with them, who's taking you?"

> "I called someone to pick me up here. Just go with them, please! C'mon, Daniel!" Says Tatyana.

Daniel looks back up at his mother, and she says,

> "They'll show you a good time, I promise! I gotta go to the stadium to do a shoot, otherwise I would go with you…please."

Daniel does not answer her; he slowly turns around and begins to walk towards the guys. Tatyana watches as her boy reaches the truck, is greeted by the two men, and jumps into the front seat. The truck drives away, and Tatyana turns around and sees a sports car on the sidewalk; it's a brand-new Camaro. The tinted window slides down, and from inside, someone says,

"You're getting in or what?"

Tatyana leans down to see who it is. She's surprised to see it's the DJ who was dealing drugs at the party; he's smiling at her from the driver's seat.

"This is your ride now?" Asks Tatyana as she opens the door.

"Yeah, yeah, get in here!" Says the DJ.

Tatyana gets in and throws a roll of money on his lap.

"You got my juice?" Asks Tatyana.

The DJ looks down at the paper, quickly puts it in his pocket, and says,

"This is the good stuff from Russia, it's a bit more…"

Tatyana takes Anthony's checkbook out and throws it on his lap, saying,

"I figured as much. Buy yourself a few things with this for the time being until I get more cash, now hand it over!"

The DJ puts the checkbook into his pocket, saying,

"Really? Checks? You know what I have to go through to use these nowadays?"

"I don't care, give me my stuff!" Says Tatyana.

The DJ opens the center console door and takes out a bag filled with vials of steroids. Tatyana snatches it from his hand and says,

"Good, now take me to the stadium!"

He nods, puts the car in drive, and they take off through a side street. They get on the highway traveling west, and the skyscrapers begin to get smaller in the distance as they put more distance between them and Phoenix. They exit the highway, get to the streets below, and when they are finally there, he pulls in front of the Bloodbath arena. Tatyana's phone rings. She looks at it, it's the Elephant Man, she answers, and says,

"You guys having a good time?"

"Well, we got him some clothes, took him to the hotel room to clean up, and went to get a drink. When we got back to pick him up, he was gone!"

"WHAT!! YOU LEFT HIM ALONE!" Tatyana screams and, in a rage of anger, she jumps up and down in the car's seat and continues to say, "You idiot! You were supposed to stay with him! Where is he now?"

"We don't know, we gave him the money…" Says the elephant man.

"You gave him the money? You're so stupid, you are, so brainless…You guys are useless…I cannot believe it, I cannot fucking believe it." Says Tatyana as she opens the door and gets out of the car.

"Should we call the police?" Asks the wrestler.

"No, just leave it alone for now. We won't find him unless he wants to be found…just forget it." Says Tatyana and hangs up the call.

She looks down at the DJ, he makes eye contact, and quickly drives off. Tatyana turns around, takes a deep breath, and walks towards the large glass doors of the arena.

CHAPTER 12: THE PARTY

Thursday morning, it's a cloudy day in Tonopah, Arizona. There's a haze over the mountains in the distance, and a light wind blows through the tree tops. The front door to the Borgia house opens, Chloe comes out and walks down the walkway of her home, and sees a large tow truck taking away Mrs. June's car remains. She sees Mrs. June watching from her yard as the truck rips the carcass of her car out of the ground, as it had been slightly buried.

Chloe approaches Mrs June and notices that she's holding something in her arms, wrapped in a soft blanket. Chloe waves at Mrs. June as she approaches and says,

"Good morning, Mrs. June!"

Mrs. June smiles, waves back, and says,

"Good Morning, dear!"

Chloe walks up to Mrs. June, pointing at the tow truck, saying,

"I see they finally took your car."

"Finally, ha, ha." Says Mrs. June.

Chloe tries to take a peek at what Mrs. June is holding.

"What you got there?" Asks Chloe.

Mrs. June opens the blanket that she's holding and reveals a little gray kitten.

"Oh, Mrs. June, it's adorable! When did you get it?" Asks Chloe.

Mrs. June smiles and says,

"So I got a call from the tow truck company saying they were coming. I started getting ready, got dressed, put the kettle on the stove, and when I went to get the tea bag, I heard meowing right outside my door. So I opened the door, and there he was, looking straight at me!"

Chloe begins to pet the Kitty, moved by her story, she says,

"Oh my goodness! Oh my goodness! He's so cute!"

Mrs. June hands the kitty over to Chloe, she takes it and begins to pet it.

"So what are you going to do when your other cat comes back?" Asks Chloe.

Mrs. June begins to pet the kitty on the head and says,

"He's not coming back, that's why God sent me this little treasure right here."

Chloe looks over at Mrs. June, surprised by the confidence in her voice in knowing that the other cat would not come back. She hands Mrs. June the kitty and asks,

"Have you heard from the insurance company yet?"

"Not yet," says Mrs. June, "But I'm fixing to call them today."

Mrs. June and Chloe turn to look as they hear loud footsteps coming down the Borgia driveway on the other side of the house. It's Tatyana, she's making her way to her new black truck. Tatyana points at the truck and disables the alarm as she hurries.

"I was wondering who owned that big ol' shiny new truck." Whispered Mrs. June.

Tatyana walks down the driveway, looks at them without saying a word, and hurriedly gets into her new truck. As soon as she closes the door, Tatyana peels off and drives right up the street and stops short right in front of Chloe and Mrs. June. The window rolls down, and Tatyana is leaning towards the window,

"Chloe, they're picking us up at nine tonight. It's a fancy party, so you got something nice?" Asks Tatyana.

"Yes, I do! I'll be ready!" Says Chloe, then quickly adds, "Have you heard from Daniel?"

"Nothing…" says Tatyana.

Chloe nods, then says,

"Don't worry, I'll look nice!"

Tatyana smiles, pumps her fist in the air, and says,

"Excellent! See you then!"

Tatyana takes off, leaving a small cloud of dust behind. Chloe looks back at Mrs. June, who is looking straight at her as she pets the cat. Mrs. June does not say anything, but Chloe feels convicted and says,

"Don't worry, Mrs. June, I'll be ok."

"You know you can call me anytime." Says Mrs. June.

Later that night, up in Scottsdale, Arizona, Tatyana's limousine pulls up a large circular driveway of a very fancy, well-lit mansion. The limousine stops at the top of the driveway, and a member of the valet staff quickly runs up and opens the door. Tatyana steps out wearing a blood red, low-cut, V-neck, strapless mini dress. The dress is so small it looks painted on; her muscular legs press so tightly against the fabric, the dress looks like it's about to rip. Her skin is covered in sparkles, making her enormous shoulders and arms glisten in the night lights. Her hair straightened out beautifully, falling to her right side. She has very classic but elegant-looking makeup on; she looks like a movie star.

Tatyana reaches back to the car and helps Chloe get out of the back seat. Chloe wears a long, elegant black dress, a little bit of blush, and lip gloss; her thick curls bounce as she turns her head to look around. The valet man gestures toward a very beautiful stone walkway nearby.

"This way, please." The man says.

Tatyana and Chloe make their way to the opening of the large walkway and are greeted there by a very tall, bald, and pale woman dressed in a long black robe. The woman stands behind a small black podium. The girls turn as they hear their limo drive off. They look back at the tall woman who is staring at them motionless. Tatyana and Chloe look at each other and slowly walk up to the intimidating person. As they get close to the podium, the pale woman says,

"Good evening, Mrs. Ivanova. My name is Vanessa. I hope you had a good ride up. Do you have your invitation?"

Tatyana takes the solid black invitation from her purse and hands it to Vanessa. Vanessa takes the solid black card, places it on a handheld tablet, and Tatyana's information immediately comes up.

"Thank you." Says Vanessa as she gives the invitation back.

Tatyana takes it, nods her head, and so does Chloe. Vanessa walks out from behind the podium and places a beautiful rose pin on Tatyana's dress. Tatyana smiles as she admires it. Vanessa then places a pin on Chloe's dress and walks back behind the podium. Chloe checks out the pin as she caresses it.

"It's beautiful." Says Chloe.

"Ladies, I welcome you to the White residence. The pins will grant you full access to all of our amenities tonight. Please follow Susan…Enjoy." Says Vanessa as she motions towards a young and tall redheaded girl standing on the walkway leading up to the house.

Susan wears a long black robe as well, but has a welcoming smile. As she extends her hands and helps Tatyana and Chloe get onto the walkway, she says,

"Thank you for joining us this evening, ladies. Please follow me."

Susan smiles and begins to lead the two to the front door.

"As Vanessa said, your pins grant you access; without them, you will not be able to move around the complex, so please do not lose them. Inside, you will find four wet bars, two fun bars, a spa with a massage room, three pools, and, of course, there will be buffet tables throughout the house. Later tonight, we will open the special rooms for you to enjoy."

"Excuse me." Says Tatyana.

Susan stops, turns around, and smiles.

"Yes?" Asks Susan.

"What exactly is a… Fun bar?" Asks Tatyana.

"Yeah, and what are these special rooms you're talking about?" Asks Chloe.

Susan looks at them both for a second, as if she knew something they didn't, and was hesitant to reveal the secret.

"First time, yeah?" Asks Susan.

"First time." Says Tatyana.

Susan smiled widely, showing super white, shiny teeth.

"I can assure you, there's nothing to worry about. I am more than confident you will enjoy yourselves tonight."

Susan turns around and continues to lead the girls down the walkway. As they walk up to the house, loud music can be heard coming from inside the mansion. The place is huge, and the stone on the outside makes it look like a fortress. It's four stories high, with towers extending higher up into the sky, adorned by little gargoyles.. There are beautiful trees and shrubbery everywhere you look, manicured landscaping, and flowers of all different types, bringing life to the place. The illumination of the house is top-notch; the lights move and change color as they hit different parts of the enormous castle-looking home.

Through the windows, they see multitudes of people inside dancing and having a good time. They approach a large set of black double doors, four large men in black suits stand in front of it, but when they see Susan, they stand aside, and one of them opens one of the doors for them. Susan turns to the girls, slightly bows, and says,

"I leave you here, ladies, enjoy your night."

"Mrs. Ivanova." Says the doorman.

"Yes," Tatyana says.

"I was told you would be bringing something for Mr. White." The doorman says.

Tatyana takes a small USB drive from her purse and hands it to the man. He quickly takes it and puts it in his vest pocket.

"Thank you. Please come in." Says the man.

Tatyana and Chloe enter the mansion, and they are in awe of its size. The vestibule of the mansion is breathtaking, its grandeur and opulence evident, and resounding in every detail. The walls are adorned with shimmering silk wallpaper, the colors subtly changing from a light cream to a deep gold that ascends towards the ceiling. The floor is made of the most intricate marble tile designs, each one a unique pattern, creating a dazzling artwork that flows beneath their feet.

 A grand double staircase, sweeping towards the upper floors, dominates the space. It's steps covered in plush carpeting, the same luxurious color fabric used for the window treatments that hang elegantly from the ceiling to the floor. The windows themselves are enormous, reaching from the floor to the ceiling and framed in sleek modern metal work designs. The curtains are drawn back to reveal stunning views of the manicured garden beyond.

In the center of the ceiling, there's a magnificent chandelier of crystal pendants, sparkling like diamonds under the soft glow of the lights. The chandelier is so large and elaborate that it seems to float, casting intricate shadows on the walls, ceiling, and floor below. The air is filled with the subtle scent of expensive perfume that overwhelms the senses. The overall effect is one of luxurious comfort and refined elegance. It's a space that's suited to wealth and sophistication, a fitting entrance to a home of such grandeur.

A server walks up to them wearing a white tuxedo, holding a tray loaded with glasses of champagne.

"Champagne?" The young man says, holding the tray down for them. The girls take a glass each.

As they sip on their drinks, Chloe points to a large room to their right and says,

"That's where the music is coming from!"

Tatyana looks and sees a large, elegant ballroom filled with people dancing, jumping, or swaying to the music blasting from speakers as a DJ on a platform points to the crowd. Laughter mingled with the beat of the music charges the room with excitement. Cristal chandeliers with lights beaming from them cast a soft, glowing sea of reflections below. Champagne flutes clinked as guests mingled, their conversations punctuated by sudden bursts of laughter. The whole room is a sea of movement, a tapestry of joy and celebration.

"I'm not going in there yet, let's take a look around?" Asks Tatyana.

"Ok, sounds good to me." Says Chloe.

The girls continue to walk deeper into the extravagantly decorated house. There are people everywhere, some dancing in the hallways, talking in groups, or moving from one section of the house to another. At the end of the large entranceway, they see a young lady wearing a tiny black dress, covered in tattoos, sitting behind a glass counter. It looks like a bar, but with no drinks. This intrigues Tatyana, who walks up to her and asks,

"So, what do you do?"

The young teen takes a binder from a shelf behind her and places it on the countertop, saying.

"Welcome to the Fun Bar, what would you like?"

Chloe opens the binder and begins to see pictures of drugs with summaries and explanations of what they do.

"Coke, heroine, weed, ecstasy, fetynol….damn what the hell?" says Chloe and closes the binder, shocked at what she saw.

"No, thank you! C'mon, T, we don't need any of that, let's go get some food."Says Chloe as she walks away.

Tatyana watches Chloe as she enters a large room across the hall, and then asks the young girl,

"What's your name, baby?"

The girl whips her eyelids, smiles, and says,

"Alexis, you delicious mountain of sin." Says Alexis, making Tatyana smile.

"Alexis, you have anything to help me relax a little…you know, something to get me in a horny kinda mood?"

Alexis smiles, turns around, and digs through some bags behind her. She comes back to Tatyana and places a small little baggie with two large capsules on the glass top.

"Here, this will take a little time to kick in, but when it does, you'll get a warm fuzzy feeling of well-being, happiness, and then contentment. Then

you'll feel hot and sexy all over." The teen says
with a devilish smile.

"Perfect." Says Tatyana.

"Maybe you can come see me later, I always
wondered what it would be like to be with a large
amazon like you…" Says the young girl.

 Tatyana looks her up and down with a devious smile and
says,

"I might take you up on that…maybe, baby."

Tatyana blows her a kiss, takes the pills, and follows Chloe
into the room.

Tatyana enters the large dining hall and is taken aback by
what she sees. The grand dining hall is a sight to behold, a
feast for the eyes as much as the stomach. Long, ornate
tables groan under the weight of tremendously large
culinary delights. Platters of caviar, oysters on ice, and
smoked salmon sparkle under the moving lights. The
carving stations display succulent roasts, while pastry chefs
meticulously assemble towering desserts. Guests mingle
with laughter echoing through the room. On every table,
there's either a naked woman or a man covered in fruit and
hors d'oeuvres or some other type of food that people eat
from.

Champagne and hard liquor flow freely, and the air is filled
with the intoxicating aroma of fine food and expensive
perfume. Crystal chandeliers, again hanging from the
ceiling, cast a soft glow on the whole scene. Plush velvet
drapes adorn the walls, and the floor is a mosaic of intricate

tiles. This is a world of luxury, extravagance, and indulgence without limits.

Chloe stands close to the entrance of he room, completely frozen by what she is looking at. Tatyana walks up to her, points to a bar on the side of the room, and says,

"Hey, let's go refresh our drinks over there. You want another?"

"Yes." Says Chloe.

The girls move through the large crowd, squeezing through the press of some groups of people talking and standing around, asking others for permission to pass. They finally get to the crowded bar. And find a small opening and squeeze right up against it.

"This place is packed!" Says Chloe, Tatyana nods.

The bartender at the other end of the bar places a drink in front of an old man. He sees the girls and quickly comes up to them.

"What can I get you?" He asks.

"I'll take a beer." Says Tatyana.

"Rum and cola." Says Chloe.

"Coming up!" says the bartender and heads to prepare their drinks.

Tatyana laughs and pats Chloe on the back, asking,

"Your daddy knows you drink hard liquor?"

Chloe smiles and says,

"One of my friends made one for me a while ago, and I liked it so…"

"Okay, okay, I won't say a word, I promise." Says Tatyana.

Tatyana turns to one of the large windows nearby and says,

"Chloe, look at that backyard!"

Chloe turns around and looks out the window. She sees a beautifully manicured Japanese garden, which looks like a park more than a backyard. The bartender puts down the drinks in front of the girls, saying,

"Here you go!"

Chloe continues to look out the window, Tatyana quickly takes Chloe's drink, opens one of the capsules she got from the fun bar, and puts it in. She notices the bartender looking straight at her as she does.

"It looks beautiful out there." Says Chloe.

"Mr. White has four Niwa Shi on staff to look after his gardens." Says the bartender as he looks into Tatyana's eyes.

Tatyana stirs Chloe's drink with her finger, wipes it on her dress as she continues to look at the bartender to see if he will say anything.

"Niwa what?" Says Chloe as she continues to look out the window.

The bartender continues to look at Tatyana as he says,

"Niwa Shi, it means Grand Master Gardner in Japanese. Mr. White wanted to create an atmosphere so authentic to Japan that people would actually lose themselves in the moment while they visited. He wanted people to feel like they were in Japan."

Chloe turns around, takes a large sip of her drink, and smiles at Tatyana.

"Can we go out and take a quick look?" Asks Chloe.

"Sometimes we all need a little push in order to get to where we should be. I can understand that." Says the bartender as he looks deep into Tatyana's eyes.

"Of course, we can go take a look outside, baby." Says Tatyana as she smiles at he bartender.

The bartender looks over at Chloe, takes a stirrer, puts it in her drink, and stirs it once.

"You make a beautiful couple." He says

"Oh, we're not a couple, ha, ha…but, thank you?" Says Chloe

"If we were a couple, I would definitely have found a treasure in her, right?" Says Tatyana.

The bartender smiles and says to Tatyana,

"I get it."

As the bartender walks away, Chloe asks,

"He gets what?"

Tatyana takes a large sip of her beer and says,

"I don't know, he was weird. Let's go see this Japanese garden!"

"Yes!" Says Chloe as she grabs her drink.

The girls make their way through the sea of people and finally get to the large glass doors leading to the gardens. Tatyana opens one of the doors, and they step outside.

They find themselves standing in front of a Japanese garden that is a true masterpiece of harmony and tranquility, a place where nature and human artistry intertwine to create a serene and inspiring space. The garden is meticulously landscaped with every element carefully placed to evoke a sense of peace and balance. The garden is surrounded by a tall wooden fence that conceals it from the outside world, creating a sense of privacy and seclusion.

Inside, the garden is divided into several distinct areas, each with its own unique character and atmosphere. The central feature of the garden is a large, tranquil pond, whose surface reflects the surrounding trees and starry sky. The pond is home to a variety of colorful Koi fish, which swim gracefully through the water, adding to the overall sense of tranquility. A small wooden bridge arched over the pond, leads to a small island in the center. The island is covered in lush greenery, and a small stone pagoda stands at its highest point.

The garden is home to a variety of trees, including pines, maples, and countless cherry blossoms. The trees are carefully pruned and shaped, creating a sense of order and harmony. Below the trees lie a variety of colorful flowers, whose blooms add splashes of color to the garden. The flowers are arranged in carefully designed beds, and each bed is home to a different variety of flowers.

The garden also has a variety of small decorative elements, small stone lanterns, water features, and small bamboo fences. These elements add to the overall beauty and tranquility of the garden. Tatiana and Chloe are completely blown away.

"This is so beautiful…" Says Chloe as she takes it all in.

"Look at the fish!" Says Tatyana as she quickly makes her way towards the pond.

Chloe quickly follows her.

"Hey, let's go up on the little bridge!" Says Chloe.

"Okay!" Says Tatyana.

The two slowly walk up the wooden bridge leading to the island in the middle of the pond. They stop at the top of the bridge and look down at the pond loaded with fish of all different colors.

As they hold on to the rail of the bridge and look around, Tatyana says,

"Funny how he called us a couple, ugh?"

"I know…that was odd." Says Chloe.

"I've dated women before, and got really serious with one of them." Says Tatyana.

"Yeah….that's cool." Says Chloe

After a few moments, Tatyana breaks the silence and asks,

"Have you ever been with a girl, I mean, dated a girl at least?"

Chloe looks over at Tatyana, who is already looking at her, and says,

"No, never."

"You must have been curious about it at one point or another, right? I mean, did you ever wonder what it was like to be with a girl?"

Chloe takes a good look at Tatyana; she can see desire in her eyes, a longing in her expression.

"I…well, sure I've wondered sometimes, but never did anything about it. I, I don't think it's my thing, really." Says Chloe.

Tatyana puts her hand on top of Chloe's, leans in a little bit, and says,

"I'd probably be dating you if I weren't with your father."

"What?" Says Chloe as Tatyana leans in a little more.

"I think you're beautiful, Chloe." Says Tatyana as she leans in a little more and licks her lower lip.

"Don't you want to know what kissing a girl feels like?" Asks Tatyana as she gets closer to Chloe's face.

"Well…ugh…" Says Chloe, not knowing what to do as Tatyana's lips get closer and closer.

When Tatyana gets right up against Chloe's lips, she barks out loudly,

"Well, I'm dating your father, so I'm not kissing you, bitch! You'd better get another hoe to do it if you want to find out!"

Chloe takes a deep breath of relief and smiles. She takes a step back, and they both have a laugh.

"Gotcha!" Says Tatyana.

"You're an ass!" Says Chloe as she laughs

"Just kidding, just kidding, come here!" Says Tatyana.

Tatyana gives Chloe a hug and pats her on the back.

"Maybe one day you can join your father and me in bed," Tatyana says.

Chloe pulls away with her mouth open and says,

"Gross! Stop it!" Says Chloe as she playfully hits her on the shoulder.

Tatyana continues to laugh. Out of nowhere, a tall, pale-looking bald man dressed in a black suit walks up to the girls. He stops at the end of the bridge and says,

"Mrs. Ivanova?"

Tatyana looks over and sees the emotionless man looking at them. She straightens herself out and says,

"Yes?"

"Mr. White sent me; he is requesting to speak to you in his study." Says the man.

Tatyana turns, looks at Chloe.

"His study…" Says Tatyana.

"He's got a study." Says Chloe.

Tatyana looks back at the man and says,

"Lead the way, your paleness."

Tatyana and Chloe take a step towards the man, but the servant holds his hand up and says,

"I'm sorry, he only requested you, Mrs. Ivanova. Your guest will have to remain here with the other guests."

"Wait a minute now." Says Tatyana as she is about to argue, but Chloe takes her hand and says,

"It's ok, go ahead."

"You sure?" Says Tatyana.

"Yeah, I'll be fine. As a matter of fact, I'm feeling awesome! Go! Go ahead!" Says Chloe.

Tatyana takes a good look at Chloe; she knows the chems are starting to kick in. She smiles, turns around, and says to the man,

"Okay, lead the way, Mr. Manservant."

Tatyana and the man walk back up to the house together as Chloe watches, smiling. She takes a deep breath and chugs down the drink in her hand, then looks at the mansion, filled with people dancing, talking, eating, and moving around. She walks down the bridge and follows a little path adorned with flowers deeper into the gardens. There are a few people around, but the gardens are pretty empty.

"PSSSST," someone says, making Chloe look around.

Then out of nowhere, Daniel steps out of some large shrubs wearing a black suit, slicked-back hair, and a large smile. His arm open wide and says,

"TA-DA!"

Chloe jumps up and down, runs over to Daniel, and gives him a big hug.

"Daniel! Where have you been?"

"I was hanging out with my friend Charlie, who's a homeless man who lived under a bridge." Says Daniel.

"What! We've been so worried for you!" Says Chloe as she hugs him again.

"My mom picked me up from the police station a few days ago, but I ran away again. She didn't tell you?" Asked Daniel.

"What! No, she did not tell us. How, how did you know we were here?" Says Chloe.

"Her wrestling buddies told me she was taking you to this uppity party in Scottsdale, told me where to go…you know."

Chloe hugs Daniel again and gives him a big kiss on the cheek.

"I'm just glad you're ok." Chloe looks around and continues to say, "How'd you get in?"

Daniel steps back, brushes his suit, and says,

"I got in through the service entrance in the back…the people bringing wine are always allowed in! You need to remember that!"

"You're crazy!" Says Chloe.

"You know, there are four Rolls-Royces in the garage back there?"

Chloe points to the rose pin on his jacket and says,

"And that?"

Daniel leans over to the right and looks over to an old man passed out on one of the benches with a bottle of brandy in his hand.

"No, you didn't!" Says Chloe.

"Trust me, he won't miss it." Says Daniel.

Chloe shakes her head.

"So my mom left you on your own?" Asks Daniel.

"Her manager wanted to see her in his study…" Says Chloe.

"Oh, excuse me!" Says Daniel as Chloe laughs.

"C'mon, let's go get some food!" Says Daniel as he puts his arm around Chloe's neck.

The two run back up the walkway and into the mansion. They make their way through the large crowd until they get to the ballroom with all the tables of food.

"This is unbelievable!" Says Daniel.

"I know, I can't believe they have so much food here." Says Chloe.

"WAIT! WAIT A MINUTE!" Daniel says loudly to Chloe.

"What?" Asks Chloe.

"I don't see any chicken nuggets or con dogs here!" Says Daniel playfully.

Chloe chuckles and puts her hands on her waist as she looks at Daniel in a bit of disbelief.

"Really?" She says?

"Ha ha, just kidding." Says Daniel as he takes a plate and starts loading it.

As the two make their way through he table, Chloe points to a large platter and asks,

"What are those?"

Daniel takes a pair, puts them on his plate, and says,

"Frog legs."

"Not for me, yuck." Says Chloe

Daniel takes a bite out of one and says,

"They're actually really good!"

Chloe looks at him with a bit of disgust and curiosity. She asks,

"Well, how is it?"

"It tastes like chicken," Daniel says with a smile.

Chloe reaches for a platter of meatballs and says,

"I'm still not trying it, these meatballs look good though."

The two make their way through the table before them, putting food in their mouths as they load their plates. Chloe really begins to feel the effects of the drug Tatyana gave her now. She finishes the food in her mouth, swallows, puts her plate down, and grabs her forehead.

"Hey, are you feeling ok?" Asks Daniel.

Chloe smiles, wipes the sweat off her brow, and says,

"I'm actually feeling really good! WOW!! Like…I can't even explain it. I…I feel happy for no reason, Ha, ha!"

Daniel smiles as he puts some caviar into his mouth. Chloe puts her hands on Daniel's shoulders with a big, playful smile and says,

"I suddenly feel like dancing, you wanna go dancing with me?"

Daniel puts his plate down, saying,

"Yeah! Yeah, let's go! C'mon, let's hit it!"

He grabs her by the hand, and they press their way towards the door. It seems like more and more people keep coming; the place is packed. They get into the large hallway and press their way back into the ballroom. It's a rave-like atmosphere in there now. Electronic Dance Music blasts the room, flashing lights flood the walls and ceiling, and the DJ, now with a falus lighted helmet, works his table as he jumps to the music.

Chloe and Daniel press through the crowd until they get to the dance floor. It's hot and sticky, and people are shedding clothes as they dance. Chloe and Daniel join them. The music is entrancing, and the crowd jumps up and down in unison like waves in the ocean.

"I've never felt this good in my life!" Says Chloe.

Chapter 13: The Afterparty

Meanwhile, in another part of the residence, Tatyana is led by the manservant through a very large hallway, through automatic smoked glass doors, and into a large office. The office is a marvel of modern architecture and design, a firm statement to innovation and progress. The open plan layout is flooded with moonlight from the floor-to-ceiling windows, creating a cool and airy atmosphere. Sleek and tall minimalist sculptures are arranged in clusters throughout the office, the walls adorned with vibrant murals and thought-provoking artwork reflecting Mr. White's dynamic and artistic culture. Soft ambient lighting casts of warm glow on the thousands of books on the numerous bookshelves throughout the space, creating a comfortable and inviting environment. At the very end, there's a very large, sleek, shiny white desk, and Mr. White, dressed in a beautiful tailored white suit, sits behind it. Ms. Katherine O'Driscol, his personal assistant, stands beside him, also wearing a white suit.

The manservant stands at the door as Tatyana enters the office and looks down. There's thick, lush white carpeting wall to wall, with bristles so thick it feels like she' walking on soft cushions as she steps. Tatyana looks at Mr. White on the other side of the room, and he motions for her to come in.

"Tatyana, please come in!" Says Mr. White.

Tatyana walks through the valley of thin, explicit sculptures and stands about ten feet away from Mr. White's desk.

"Come closer, sweetheart." Says Mr. White.

Tatyana walks right up to his desk and stands right up against it, and smiles as she looks at him.

"Look at that gorgeous smile, isn't she a knockout out Katherine?" Asks Mr. White.

"She's gorgeous, sir." Says Katherine, as Lucious nods in agreement.

"It's good to see you. I hope you're enjoying yourself?" Asks Mr. White.

"I am, what an amazing party! You have such a beautiful home…I could never imagine myself living in a place like this." Says Tatyana.

"With me, baby, it won't take you long! But this is not where I live, I own this one to throw parties and such…nothing else." Says Mr. White.

"Oh…" Says Tatyana.

Mr. White motions with his hand to his assistant, and she quickly reaches down into his desk, pulls out a shiny white box from one of the drawers, and places it in the middle of the desk.

"You may be wondering why it is that you are really here. Why is it that you find yourself, while this awesome party is happening, here in this room with us, right now?" Says Mr. White.

Tatyana nods as she looks at the shiny box on his desk. The box is one foot by one foot, by one foot, a perfect square.

"I want to know. I…need to know that I can trust you." Says Lucious.

Tatyana looks a bit concerned as she says,

"You can trust me."

"How will I know your fealty?" Says Lucious.

"I, I signed a contract with you." Says Tatyana.

"I know, I know. But all you need is a few good lawyers, and contracts can be broken, we all know that." Says Lucious.

Suddenly, he gets out of his chair and quickly walks around his desk until he stands just a breath away from Tatyana, and says,

"I promised you fame, fortunes, a great career in wrestling, and film. The question is, how far are you willing to go in order to get what you want?"

"Anything." Quickly replies Tatyana.

"Really?" Says Lucious.

"Name it." Says Tatyana.

Lucious countenance changes, and it turns wickedly dark as he devilishly smiles and says,

"There is no turning back from this…"

Tatyana feels the change in the room, a darkness and oppressive atmosphere has taken over the office. Suddenly, there is a heaviness in her chest and spine, and she feels like she is dealing with the devil himself, but she tries to hide her emotions and show strength.

"All of my life, people have been fucking around with me, promising me things and never following through. Whatever it is, whatever price, I'll do it…what do you want!" Tatyana says.

Mr. White takes a small remote out of his pocket and presses the only button on it. A hidden door opens on one of the walls of his office, revealing a small room lit up in red. The room is filled with instruments of torture, there is thick, heavy plastic lining on the floor, and in the middle, sits a bloodied and wounded man gagged, tied up to a large thick iron chair.

"What the hell!" Says Tatyana as she takes a step back.

The man sees her and tries to plead for his life as he cries, but the gag around his mouth is so thick, he's completely unintelligible. Mr. White continues to smile as he walks over to the tied-up man. He taps the man on the head with his index finger and says,

"This is Dave. Dave was a trusted employee, and I emphasize the word trusted, until last week. He was one of my best drivers. You see…last week he was taking a very important person, a very close and dear friend of mine, to the airport. In the midst of putting lotion on her hands, this very important person left one of her rings in the back of the car that Dave was driving. Dave later found that ring. But instead of turning the ring over to me or to Katherine, Dave thought it was a better idea to keep said ring.

What good ol' Dave did not know, is that said ring is a family heirloom that has been passed down from mother to daughter in my dear friend's family. Passed down from one generation to the other all the way back to 1598, to be exact. The Edict of Navarre ascended to the French throne that year as King Henry the Fourth. And His Majesty the King… gave this beautiful ring to a young lady as a gift of appreciation for her clandestine help in ironing out some issue for him that year. That young lady was my dear friend's ancestor."

Lucious pauses, looks at Dave in disgust, and continues,

> "THAT RING IS OLDER THAN THIS FUCKING COUNTRY!!" Screams Mr. White, then catches himself, he takes a deep breath and continues,

> "When I heard the news of the missing ring, I was furious, of course. But we investigated, researched, did our due diligence, and after some good old detective work from our associates. Well, we found the ring in a small, little safe, hidden in a closet wall in Dave's house!"

Mr. White grabs Dave's face with one hand, looks at him dead in the eye, and says,

"So here we are…In a place where I have to make amends. I have to, and will, without a question, make things right with my dear, long-time friend and client." Lucious lets go of Dave and lightly slaps him on the face.

"But such a breach in trust to my client… this type of client, could only be remedied with one thing…and guess what that is, Tatyana." Says Lucious.

Tatyana shrugs her shoulders and says,

"Some kind of compensation, I guess."

"Some kind of compensation, exactly! You're smart, and guess what that is?" Says Lucious.

"A couple of million dollars?" Says Tatyana.

Mr. White smiles and says,

"HA! That would be easy!"

Luscious opens his arms wide and proclaims loudly,

"They want Dave's head on a fucking silver platter!! Literally!!"

Katherine pulls out a beautiful sterling silver platter decorated with jewels from a cabinet and places it on Lucious' desk beside the box. Tatyana looks at it, completely shocked.

"You see, Tatyana, trust is everything! Without trust, there is no way to do business, to have relationships, to look at someone face to face and actually have an understanding." Says Mr. White.

Tatyana nods her head, buying into everything she's hearing.

"Okay, what do you need from me?" She asks as Dave begins to squirm.

"I need to know that we can trust each other… with the deepest darkest secrets," Lucious says.

At that point, Katherine takes a large bone saw and places it on the desk as she looks at Tatyana in the eyes and smiles. Tatyana is quite alarmed and asks,

"Wh…what are you asking me to do right now, exactly. You, you want me to cut his head off?"

Dave begins to squirm. He tries to move around and scream, but his muffled mouth does not allow for much sound to come out, and his steel restraints don't budge. Mr. White looks at Dave and smiles, then he goes to the desk and opens the white box, revealing a Glock .45 and a red sealed envelope.

"Katherine will do the cutting. What I am asking you to do is to put a single bullet through Dave's heart. His death is your birth, this is the seal to your contract."

Tatyana is frozen solid, every muscle still, she feels a coldness come over her, and a reality of what she is being asked to do…take a life. Her heart races as she looks at Dave, his eye pleading for mercy, then she looks over at

Lucious, and he is looking back at her with a stoic, cold stare. Mr. White pulls Tatyana's contract out of his inner pocket and points to a clause within it as he holds it up to her and says,

> "This clause… this clause right here gives me authority to break the contract for failure to adhere to company expectations before work begins. That's what this is. If you don't do this…"

Lucious holds up his hands, painting a picture of grandeur,

> "Lights… cameras… heavyweight champion… movie star…world-wide fame…millions…the world will sit on your lap. You will have a lifelong career in entertainment, travel the world, and work with people at the top of the industry. I will take care of you for the rest of your life…"

Then Lucious puts his hands down in disappointment and says,

> "But if you don't…" Lucious pulls his hair back with both hands then puts his hands down in defeat and pauses, looks right into Tatyana's eyes and continues to say, "Well… if you don't… your wrestling career will dry up, because no one will hire you, promoters will avoid you like the plague because you turned me down and you won't be able to get management. You won't be able to get a job as a personal trainer in any of the major gyms because of your record or any other type of formal job in a major company out there.

Every day you wake up, you will hate yourself because you will feel like nothing, because you will know… that you are nothing. You will become a footnote in the pages of the people who could have been. Before you even know it, you will find yourself back in that shit hole of a taco shop flashing your tits for tips. Your muscles will fade, your beauty will go, and you will shrivel up and die. Then they'll bury your skinny dried-up shit course in a desert grave, and no one will remember or care to remember who you were. That will be your life without me…It's your choice, honey."

Tatyana looks at Dave, then looks at Mr. White. She quickly walks over to the desk, picks up the gun, and points it at Dave,

BAM, BAM, BAM, BAM, BAM, BAM

 She swiftly puts six rounds into Dave's chest.

Then, there is complete silence. The smell of the gun smoke enters Tatyana's nostrils, and she drops the gun on the carpet, staring at the bloody mess she made of Dave. The silence is broken by a trickle of liquid falling on the carpet. Mr. White looks down and sees Tatyana urinating on herself, her hands trembling. She drops to her knees in disbelief at what she's done.

Mr. White picks up the red envelope inside the box and brings it over to Tatyana. He stands directly in front of her and looks down.

"Tatyana," Says Lucious, and Tatyana looks up at him, teary-eyed.

"From this day on, you are no longer your own. I own your mind, body, heart, and soul. But fear not, because in return, you get so much more… I will give you the whole world, I promise… and everything in it will be your playground. Everything you do will be a success, everywhere you go, people will love you, they will give you gifts, and honors and awards!"

Tatyana looks at Lucious as tears fall down her face, nodding her head.

"One last thing," Lucious says.

Tatyana reaches up with both hands and softly says,

"Anything…"

Mr.White's countenance completely changes, his skin takes on a grayish tone, and his eyes dim as he says,

"Bow down and worship me."

Tatyana immediately leans forward and completely bows before him, her head to the carpet and arms at his feet. Mr. White smiles. He looks over at Katherine, and she smiles back at him and nods. Mr. White leans down, places a kiss on Tatyana's head, and puts the envelope in front of her.

"Open it." Says Lucious.

Tatyana reaches out with trembling hands and takes the blood-red envelope. She slowly opens it, and there's a thick black card inside. She looks at Lucious, who slowly begins to smile again, then takes the solid black card out and opens it. Inside, in shiny red letters, it simply says,

WELCOME

Mr. White extends his hand, Tatyana takes it, and slowly stands up. Lucious plants a kiss on her cheek and whispers in her ear,

"Welcome to the family, baby."

Tatyana is stoic, looking at Dave as he hunches over, lifeless, bloodstained chest dripping onto his lap and the plastic below. Mr. White picks up the gun with a handkerchief, places it back in the box, and closes the lid. He takes the remote out of his pocket, clicks the button, and the wall closes back up, completely hiding Dave's little room, as if nothing had ever happened. Tatyana is still stunned, not making a sound or moving a single muscle. Mr. White walks to his desk and touches a digital display on top of it. Another wall, filled with books, on the other side of the room opens up. From this aperture, surprisingly, soft instrumental music, lavender, and pink moving lights come out and light up the study.

Katherine walks over to Tatyana and gently leads her to the opening in the wall.

"This is just for you." Says Katherine.

Tatyana sees a balcony and what looks like a very large room in front of it. She looks over at Katherine, who simply says,

"Go ahead."

Tatyana slowly walks through the opening in the wall and steps onto the balcony. There is a very large room below that looks like an old-fashioned library, or a study, something out of the 1800s. Wooden shelves filled with old books and beautifully detailed wooden walls. There are old-fashioned desks and chairs, and couches. Beautiful paintings of bygone eras decorate the walls, the whole place lit by ornate chandeliers. In the room, a small group of very well-dressed guests looks up at Tatyana, and each holds a glass of champagne. Lucious walks up to Tatyana and stands beside her. He hands her a glass of champagne, raises his glass as he toasts, and says,

"To Tatyana! Our newest sister!"

All of the guests raise their glasses and say in unison,

"Welcome, Tatyana!"

A few hours later, elsewhere in the enormous mansion, Chloe and Daniel enter a very wide and long secluded hallway. Both out of breath and sweaty, they stumble and fall to the floor laughing. They take a minute to look around. The hallway has soaring ceilings and elegant arches, creating an atmosphere of awe and wonder. The walls, adorned with carefully crafted tapestries and old paintings from long ago, the rich colors in the room, and the intricate details add a sense of opulence. The floor is a dark, solid marble; you could not see a seam anywhere. The hallway is also home to very strange and intriguing sculptures, each one a testament to the owner's eclectic taste. There are sculptures of mythical creatures, abstract forms, and some that seem to defy any type of description. Each sculpture is illuminated by a series of spotlights that cast a glow on the walls and ceilings, creating an impressive, dramatic effect, but also unsettling, adding to the mysterious and intriguing atmosphere. The hallway is so large you could lose yourself in a world of fantasy and imagination as you walk through it.

"Look at this place!" Says Chloe as she pulls herself off the floor and sits in the middle.

Daniel slowly does the same and says,

"Wow, this place is crazy…"

Chloe tries to fix her hair; some of it is stuck to her sweaty face and neck. She puts both hands on her face, runs them down her neck, breasts, and then lightly hits her stomach. Daniel looks over at her and asks,

"You feeling ok, you look drunk or something…"

Chloe fans herself with her hands and says,

"Honestly, I don't know what it is, but I've never felt this good."

"I didn't know you could be so much fun!" Says Daniel.

"What!" Says Chloe as she playfully pushes Daniel on the shoulder.

Daniel smiles and slowly leans, then falls sideways on the floor. They both chuckle. Daniel sits back up and looks over at Chloe, before he could say anything, a very tall and beautiful black woman dressed in white enters the hallway holding a long tablet in her hand.

"Excuse me, I'm very sorry to interrupt you." Says the woman.

"No, that's fine, I think we're lost, actually, he, he." Says Chloe.

The woman extends her hand, Chloe takes it and stands up, and Daniel quickly gets to his feet as well.

"Ms. Borgia, my name is Dahlia. I'm from hospitality. I'm here to escort you back downstairs to the party, please." Says Dahlia.

Daniel looks at Dahlia, points to Chloe, and asks,

"You know her?"

Dahlia looks over to Chloe, points to her pin, and says,

"Of course, you came with Ms. Ivanova. We keep close watch on our guests. If you would please follow me downstairs, you do not have access to this part of the house."

Daniel straightens himself out, Dahlia looks over at Daniel, and says,

"And you are definitely not Mr. Randall Glistenthorp."

Daniel looks at her with fear, not really knowing what to do.

"I…I can explain." Says Daniel.

"You don't have to. We know you took his pin and left him sleeping outside." She says.

"Well, uhm. You see…" says Daniel.

Dahlia put her hands on his shoulder and says,

"Mr. Glistenthorp has a new pin, and you have been grafted into the system. We know you're Ms. Ivanova's son. I won't tell anyone what happened if you won't."

"I won't." Says Daniel, Dahlia gives him a wink.

"Thank you." Says Chloe.

Dahlia smiles widely, exposing a full set of diamond-studded teeth, and says,

"Of course, now, if you please follow me."

The tall, beautiful model turns around and walks down the hallway. Chloe and Daniel quickly follow. When they get to the end of the hallway, they begin to descend a red carpeted staircase leading down to the lower level. Adorned with gold accents and beautifully decorated wooden rails, the steps end in a well-lit landing area. The landing itself leads to several more hallways, all of them highly decorated and extravagant in nature. Dahlia leads them down the middle one until they get to the end, where there is a set of large double doors guarded by men dressed in black suits, one on the left, the other on the right of the doors.

As they approach the doors, one of the men opens them to let them through. The doors open wide to one of the main

ballrooms. They walk in, the doors close behind them, and
Dahlia says,

"You too enjoy the party and stay down here,
please."

They both nod in agreement. Dahlia nods to a man standing
on this side of the door, obviously a guard, and walks away
into the crowd. Chloe and Daniel turn and look at the party.
The grand ballroom of the mansion is a whirlwind of
activity and energy. The air throbs with the beat of the
music, a pulsating rhythm that seemed to vibrate through
the very bones of the building. Chandeliers above, each a
masterpiece of crystal and wrought iron, cast a dazzling
glow over the scene, illuminating the people below as they
danced with abandon.

The room, a sea of designer gowns and tailored suits, is
definitely a testament to the wealth and influence of the
guests. Laughter and conversation mingled with the music,
creating a vibrant, almost electric atmosphere. The DJ
perched in a custom-built platform expertly manipulates the
music, seamlessly blending classic hits with the latest chart
toppers. Champagne flows freely as servants with trays
laden with exquisite hors d'oeuvres circulate through the
crowd, adding to the sense of lavish indulgence. The entire
scene is a spectacle of opulence and excess, a celebration of
wealth and privilege.

Chloe, now feeling the full effect of the drugs that Tatyana
snuck into her drink, feels loose and completely at ease;
there's an overwhelming feeling of well-being that has
taken her over, like nothing could go wrong.

"I love it here." Says Chloe, catching Daniel by surprise as he quickly turns to look at her.

"Hey, I have to use the bathroom." Says Daniel.

"I'll go with you." Says Chloe.

"No, you can't come with me." Says Daniel.

"Let me." Says Chloe.

"What?" Says Daniel, completely surprised by what she said.

"I won't bother you, promise." Says Chloe.

Daniel grabs Chloe's arms and looks into her eyes. He realizes she is under the influence of something and asks,

"Did you take anything, Chloe? What's going on with you?"

"If you let me hold yours, I'll let you hold mine." Says Chloe, her words slightly slurred.

"You're talking crazy right now. Someone must have given you something." Says Daniel as he quickly walks her over to a set of chairs by a table.

"I feel fine, I feel good actually." Says Chloe as she slaps her sweaty face to move her hair.

"Oh my god, my bladder is going to burst." Says Daniel, then takes Chloe's face, gently turns it to face him, and says, "I need you to stay right here. Do not get up from this table, don't go anywhere. I will be right back. I'm going to the restroom, and then I'm taking you home."

"But I was gonna hold…"Chloe begins to say.

"NO, you're staying right here, okay," says Daniel.

"Right here." Says Chloe.

"That's right, stay right here." Says Daniel as he takes a long look at Chloe, then takes the hair out of her face.

Daniel quickly walks into the crowded room, leaving Chloe alone at one of the tables. Chloe looks around and begins to nod her head to the music. She looks around and sees all of the people dancing, drinking, and having a good time, and she smiles as she begins to move to the music as she sits on her chair. Chloe looks up and sees Tatyana in one of the upper balconies of the ballroom. Tatyana is kissing and hugging a younger girl.

"Hey!" Screams Chloe, but her voice is completely masked by the loud music.

As she continues to watch, Tatyana begins to undress the other girl. She takes the girl's shirt off and walks with her out of the balcony and into an inner room, completely out of Chloe's point of view. Chloe looks back down at the crowd and shakes her head. The beat of the music is intoxicating, she begins to bounce in her chair.

"Forget this, I gotta dance!" Chloe says. She stands up and runs into the crowd of people dancing in the middle of the room, and begins to dance all by herself.

Lost in the sea of people, Chloe loses herself to the music as she opens her eyes wide, looks up, and begins to spin. She is suddenly in a kaleidoscope of twirling color and sound. The colors begin to meld together, the music becomes an unintelligible pouncing throb in her ears, she feels like she is flying, levitating into the ceiling as she loses herself in the moment.

Suddenly, she's brought to a complete stop. Slowly, she brings her head down and realizes that someone grabbed her and stopped her from spinning. She looks at the man in front of her, but does not recognize him.

"Who are you?" Asks Chloe, now in a complete daze.

"It's me, Nico!" Says the bartender.

"Oh, you da drink man." Says Chloe

"Yeah, yeah, the bartender from earlier. Where's your girlfriend?" Asks Nico.

"My girfwen?" Asks Chloe, then says, "Oh, shied not ma gurlfien."

"C'mon, let's get you out of this crowd." Says Nico.

Nico walks Chloe out of the ballroom, into the hallway, and continues to guide her down the hall.

"Whe we goin?" Says Chloe.

"Somewhere safe, where you can relax and rest for a minute." Says Nico.

They walk to the end of the hallway, through a doorway, and enter a storage area for tables and chairs. Chloe looks around and says,

"What is dis?"

"Storage area, c'mon this way, you need to rest." Says Nico as he leads her to the end of the room.

He opens a small door to a utility closet, turns on the overhead light, and sits Chloe down on a large stack of plastic containers. The utility closet smells like cleaning chemicals, the walls are lined with racks of cleaning supplies for the whole house, it seems. There's nothing special to this room; the walls are white, the concrete floor is completely bare, and water drips from a service faucet down to a drain on the floor, adding to the weird vibe in the room.

"It's a lot quieter here, no?" Asks Nico.

Chloe looks up at Nico. She does not answer, but smiles and tries to get her hair out of her face.

"We need to go back." Says Chloe.

Nico goes over to the door, closes it, and begins to take his shirt off as he looks at Chloe. Nico unzips his pants and sits beside Chloe, who at this point clearly understands what's about to happen. Nico begins to caress Chloe's hair, and even though she is not lucid, asks,

"What are you doing?"

Nico begins to reach under her dress.

"Please don't," Says Chloe as she tries to pull his hand away.

SMACK!

Nico suddenly smacks Chloe across the face, stunning her.

"We can do this the easy way, or the hard way!" Says Nico as he forcefully grabs her waist and brings her closer to him.

"NO!" screams Chloe.

Nico smacks her again, grabs the top of her dress, and begins to tear it. Chloe punches him in the jaw. Nico headbutts Chloe and takes her down, slamming her head on the hard floor. Chloe's out of it. Nico reaches under her dress and rips her underwear off. He quickly brings it to his face and smells it as he locks his eyes onto hers. He throws the undies to the side, holds Chloe down with one hand, grabs one of her legs, and pushes it towards her head, all the way up to her ear, raising her hips as he jumps on top of her.

SLAM!

The door bursts open, and Nico immediately turns around to look. It's a group of security guards, accompanied by Daniel.

"Chloe!" Scream Daniel.

"Help me!" Chloe says softly.

The guards immediately rush into the room, two of them pick Chloe up, and the other four grab Nico, slam him to the floor, and restrain him.

"Hey, Hey, what the hell are you doing! We were just having a good time, that's all!"

"He was… he was going to rape me." Says Chloe as she is escorted out of the closet.

"That's a fucking lie! Let me go! Let me go now!" Screams Nico, who tries to get free as the guards hold him down.

"Keep him here until the police arrive, then have them take this fool out through the kitchen exit." Says Mr. Brown, the head of security.

Mr. Brown takes his cell phone out, calls the police, requests a car, then hangs up. He walks over to Chloe and Daniel, now sitting on the other side of the large holding area for tables with two guards. Chloe holds onto Daniel as he tries to comfort her.

"Ms. Borgia, my name is Ernest Brown. I'm the head of security. Daniel here told us you were missing, and we were able to find you via the pin. First of all, are you ok? I will call an ambulance for you." Says Mr. Brown.

"I'm ogey, I dink he may have dlipped somethin indo ma drink earlier at de bar, but I'm not sure…I just wang go home." Says Chloe

"Can you let my mom know what happened? She should be here," Says Daniel.

"Of course." Says Mr. Brown.

Mr. Brown walks away for a few moments as he talks to someone on his walkie-talkie, then returns to them and says,

"Ms. Ivanova is not available at this time; she is in a meeting, but we will notify her as soon as she exits that part of the house." Says Mr. Brown, then looks over at Chloe and continues, "I know that the cops will want a statement from you…"

"No, no, just dake me home right now!" Says Chloe.

"Are you sure? Don't you want to wait for my mom at least?" Says Daniel.

"No, I need do get oud of here. Please, gan you guys just dake me home?" Chloe insists.

Mr. Brown looks over as one of the guards standing by and says,

"Bring one of the cars to the back."

Chloe looks over at Daniel and asks,

"You're goming home too, right, Daniel?"

Daniel looks at Chloe with sadness and replies,

"I can't, Chloe, my mom and I got into a heated argument last time I saw her, and I'm not ready to face her. Honestly, I don't know if I will ever be ready to face her. I'll make sure you get home, but I'm not staying tonight."

Chapter 14: Oh, the Treachery!

It's a beautifully warm, starry night, not a cloud in the sky. The full moon behind the mountains allows for their silhouette to be clearly seen in the distance. Chloe slowly drags her feet as she walks into the backyard from the driveway on the side of her house. She looks exhausted, her hair is a mess, her dress is torn, and her head is down.

"That was the longest ride ever…." Chloe whispers to herself.

Chloe rubs her tired eyes and yawns, but then she hears a man's voice. She looks around, and it sounds like it's coming from a radio, over at Mrs. June's backyard. Chloe slowly walks towards the voice and can hear what the man on the radio is saying,

"Admit it! Everyone in this room has sinned at one point or another. We've all done things that we knew were wrong, but deep down inside we loooved those things, right? But Jesus said Be ye perfect even as your Father in Heaven is perfect!"

Chloe walks closer to the fence that divides Mrs. June's property from hers and sees Mr. June sitting on her rocking chair with a Bluetooth speaker on her lap. Mrs. June smiles and waves at Chloe when she sees her. Chloe smiles and waves back as they continue to listen to the preacher saying,

"Jesus also said, 'Come to me all you that labor and are heavy laden, and I'll give you rest.' Rest from what? Well, I will tell you, rest from the pain you feel, rest from the troubles in your mind, rest from the wounds you suffered from your loved ones…rest from your life! Stop running, stop sinning, stop rejecting God. You want peace? Jesus says you can have it right now; come to Him. You want love, Jesus loves you right now, come to Him."

Mrs. June lowers the volume on the speaker and says,

"He's a right now God. Hi Honey, it's a little bit late for you to be out and about, no?"

Chloe swats her hair back, but it falls right back on her face.

"It most definitely is, Mrs. June." Says Chloe as she grabs the fence for support.

Mrs. June takes a good, long look at Chloe and says,

"It didn't go the way you thought it would go?"

Chloe looks at Mrs. June, and her eyes begin to tear up, her upper lip begins to quiver, and she says,

"No, no, it was… it was a complete disaster."

"I can see that. Well, go inside and get some rest, baby. I'll be praying for you." Says Mrs. June.

Chloe smiles, opens the gate, walks over to Mrs. June, and kisses her on the cheek.

"Thank you, I love you." Says Chloe.

Mrs. June smiles back and says,

"You know you're like a daughter to me, right?"

Chloe leans down, hugs Mrs. June, and says,

"And you're like a mother to me, Mrs. June! I love you!"

They two hold onto each other for a few seconds, then Chloe slowly pulls away, saying,

"I saw Daniel tonight, he snuck into the party."

"Really! How is that boy doing? I've been praying for him!" Says Mrs. June.

"He seems to be doing ok, he…he did not want to come home though." Says Chloe.

"Oh my Lord." Says Mrs. June, as she places her hands on her mouth.

"Yeah, I'm supposed to meet him tomorrow at the skatepark so we can talk about it." Says Chloe as she places her hand on her forehead, then continues, "I've got to get to bed, have a good night, Mrs. June."

"You too, honey." Says Mrs. June, smiling.

Chloe walks back to her yard as Mrs. June watches her, rocking back and forth on her rocking chair. Chloe slowly climbs the back stairs, opens the door, and looks back at

Mrs. June. Mrs. June blows her a kiss and smiles. Chloe smiles back and enters her house.

The night passes, and so does the morning; the afternoon sun now washes over Chloe's bed as she sleeps deeply with her head underneath a pillow. Noises come from downstairs as Anthony hits a piece of furniture with his wheelchair and knocks something down.

"Chloe! Hey Chloe!! Wake up, baby, daddy needs you!!"

Chloe turns in her bed and continues to sleep, snoring now as her head hangs over the side of her bed. Chloe's cell phone rings; it's on her dresser on the other side of the room. Chloe turns again as the phone continues to ring. Chloe sits up with a disgusted look on her face. She takes a deep breath and sighs as she slowly gets out of bed, walks over to the dresser, and picks up her phone. She shakes her head when she looks at the screen, and it's her father. She walks over to her door and yells downstairs,

"Dad, why are you calling me?"

The phone stops ringing, then Anthony yells back,

"Do you have my checkbook? Have you been writing checks?"

"What! No, of course not!" Chloe replies.

"Well, my checkbook is missing and my bank account got hit with some checks I never wrote!" Says Anthony.

"Hold on!" Says Chloe as she reaches for her sweat pants on the floor.

Chloe runs downstairs and sees her dad in his wheelchair at the kitchen table; there are bills and papers all over the place. He's got his laptop on the table and is holding a cup of coffee. Chloe walks in barefoot, her feet slapping against the cold tile floor. She wipes her eyes, opens the fridge door, takes a bottle of water out, and sits next to her dad at the table.

"What's going on?" Chloe asks.

Anthony points to his laptop and says,

"I was paying some bills, and saw these checks over here. Look, three thousand to a nightclub, one thousand for a catering company, and look at this one, five thousand to some type of security firm thing."

"What the heck! Did you call the bank?" Says Chloe.

"Yeah, I told them my checkbook got stolen, but still, everything is frozen while they investigate," Anthony says, shaking his head.

Chloe begins to look through her phone and says,

"So what did the bank say?"

"I just told you, they're freezing everything, they're doing some type of escalation investigation thing, and I may have to change my bank account… they said they would let me know."

"Where did you last have it?" Asks Chloe, as she continues to read something on her phone.

"Well, I know I had it here a few days ago, I thought I had brought it upstairs to my night table, but it's not there." Says Anthony.

"I can't believe it!" Says Chloe, then her mouth drops with astonishment.

"Don't worry, they'll figure it out." Says Anthony.

Chloe holds her phone up to her dad and shows him an email and says,

"No… this!"

Anthony squints his eyes and tries to read.

"What is it? The words are too small for me to read." Says Anthony.

"ASU is doing an evaluation on me, and they put my acceptance and scholarship on hold!"

"How can that be?" Asks Anthony.

"I don't know!" Replies Chloe.

"Can you call…ah…what's her name?" Asks Anthony.

"Susan, the admittance officer?" Says Chloe.

Anthony taps his forehead and says,

"Yeah! That's her!"

Chloe quickly gets up from the table, she's very troubled, and looks through the numerous business cards and papers held by magnets on the fridge door. She finally sees Susan's business card and quickly grabs it, saying,

"There you are! Great, I can call her right now, she works on Fridays, so she should be in her office!"

"Today is Saturday…" Says Anthony.

Chloe slowly turns around, her mouth open, in complete shock.

"…what?" Chloe asks.

"After you came back from the party Thursday night, well, Friday morning, you plopped on your bed and went to sleep. You slept and slept, I checked on you several times, you were completely knocked out, baby!"

"WHAT!" Chloe yells, then says, "You didn't try to wake me up, Dad?"

"I mean, you were sleeping so soundly, so deeply, that I just felt you needed it. I thought maybe you got a little tipsy or something, so I figured I'd just let you sleep it off."

"NO!" Says Chloe as she grabs her head with both hands.

"It's okay…" replies Anthony.

"No, Dad, it's not!" Says Chloe as she walks over to the kitchen door facing their backyard.

Anthony turns to look a her as she walks to the door and looks outside at the RV garage.

"I've been there, I know what it's like…" Says Anthony.

Chloe continues to look outside from the glass pane on the door and asks,

"Have you seen Daniel? Has he been around?"

Anthony does not answer, but just looks at Chloe, a bit bewildered. Chloe suddenly turns around and looks at her dad; she's scared and alarmed.

"DAD! Have you seen Daniel? Have you seen him in the past two days?"

Anthony shakes his head and says,

"Ah, no. No, I haven't seen Daniel or Tatyana since you guys went to that party on Thursday night."

"Daniel's in trouble!" Says Chloe, she runs out of the kitchen, and makes her way upstairs.

Anthony follows the sounds that Chloe makes as she moves around upstairs and looks up at the ceiling. He follows her footsteps in her room, back down the hallway, and then he looks at the doorway when he hears her coming back down the stairs. Chloe burst into the kitchen fully dressed, with a baseball cap on her head and phone to her ear, she's trying to reach someone.

"Dad, can I borrow the truck?" Chloe asks.

"Where are you going?" Asks Anthony.

"C'mon, pick up, pick up." Says Chloe, she looks at her dad and says, "I need to find Daniel."

Anthony points to the key holder on the wall, Chloe sees the keys, and grabs them.

"Thanks!" Says Chloe.

"Where are you going to look for him?" Asks Anthony.

"I don't know, I'm going to the skate park first." Says Chloe as she checks her pockets.

"Chloe, we're in the middle of the desert, he could be anywhere!" Says Anthony.

Chloe grabs her water bottle from the table and takes a long drink. She slams the bottle back on the table and says,

"Dad, I have to try!"

"Chloe, think! What is your plan here?" Anthony asks.

Chloe paces back and forth anxiously.

"Don't let your emotions rule you; think, make a plan of action as to what you're going to do." Says Anthony.

Chloe continues to pace back and forth in the kitchen as she thinks about what she's going to do next.

"Okay, okay. I got it, I'll go back to the mansion where I last saw him. Then make my way back to our house, there are a few stops along the way where he could be hanging out with friends, the high school, a skate park, and a few eateries. I'll stop and ask to see if they know his whereabouts." Says Chloe.

Anthony nods his head and says,

"Well, that's a good start. I'll call the police and the hospitals in the area to see if they have him." Says Anthony.

Chloe smiles and heads for the door.

"How long do you think you'll be gone? You haven't eaten anything!" Says Anthony.

Chloe opens the back door, looks back at her dad, and says,

"I'll grab something while I'm out. Want me to bring something back?"

"Large pepperoni with extra sauce." Says Anthony.

Chloe smiles and says,

"I got it!"

The door slams shut. Anthony looks at the door for a few seconds, takes a deep breath, and closes his laptop.

Later that night, out in the backyard, Mrs. June and Anthony sit on his patio set and talk. They hold large glasses with lemonade that Mrs. June serves from a ladle in a large metal pot sitting on the table.

"I can't believe how good this lemonade is, Mrs. June! I taste strawberries, mint…" Says Anthony.

"Family recipe, everything from scratch." Says Mrs. June as she smiles and takes a sip.

The two turn their heads as they hear Anthony's truck pulling up the driveway, then stop.

"That's Chloe," Anthony says.

The two watch in anticipation as they hear the truck door open and shut, then footsteps, getting louder and louder from the side of the house. Then Chloe enters the backyard from the driveway, holding a pizza box in her hand. She looks sad and defeated as she approaches them.

"There she is! Did you find him?" Asks Anthony.

Chloe does not answer. She walks up to them, puts the pizza box on the table, and flops down on one of the patio chairs.

"That bad?" Asks Mrs. June.

Chloe shakes her head and says,

> "I looked everywhere, I even drove up to Scottsdale, drove all around the neighborhood up there. I stopped at every high school, every middle school, every park, skatepark on the way back down here…I don't know where he could be."

Mrs. June puts her hand on Chloe's shoulder and says,

> "Don't give up hope, baby."

> "That's true. We have to believe he's ok." Says Anthony.

Chloe takes a deep breath, opens the pizza box, and asks,

"You guys want some pizza?"

Anthony immediately grabs two slices and puts them on a napkin as he says,

"I've been waiting for this all day!"

"Sure, I'll take a slice. You want some lemonade?" Asks Mrs. June as she points to the pot.

"I would love some." Says Chloe.

Mrs. June smiles, gets up, and begins to walk towards her yard, saying,

"Ok, I'll be right back, let me get you a glass."

Chloe and Anthony begin to eat when, suddenly and out of nowhere, Tatyana shows up, walking up the driveway slowly. She's barefoot, dressed in tight black leather pants and a black leather bikini top, her hair is a complete mess, her makeup is smeared, and she has drool coming down from her lower lip.

"Tatyana, are you ok?" Asks Anthony.

Tatyana slowly turns around to look at him, and she says,

"Heeey baby…yeah…yeah I'm just very tired."

Tatyana looks over at Chloe, who is staring back at her while she chews without saying a word. Anthony, concerned, rolls his wheelchair over to her to get a closer look. Her eyes are completely bloodshot, and she looks like she hasn't slept in days. Tatyana slightly smiles, bends down, and kisses Anthony on the lips.

"T, I've been calling you and texting you for the past two days now. You don't look so good, you sure you're ok?" Asks Anthony.

Tatyana rubs her crotch, wipes the drool from her mouth, and says,

"I'm sorry, baby, I've…I've had a lot of work, been distracted. I just need some sleep, let me go in here and get some sleep, ok?"

"Sure, yeah, of course, I'll check on you in a while and see if you need anything." Says Anthony.

"No…no baby just…just let me sleep." Says Tatyana.

"I'm feeling a little bit stronger, I can move my feet and everything!" Says Anthony.

Tatyana looks back at her apartment, then looks back at Anthony, puts her hand on his head, and says,

"Yeah, that's great…that's really good."

Tatyana begins to waver back and forth as she stands there, completely spaced out for a moment.

"Have you heard from Daniel?" Asks Chloe, immediately bringing Tatyana back.

"He hasn't been around? I thought he was with you guys." Says Tatyana.

"No, it's been days, where is he?" Asks Chloe.

Tatyana grabs her forehead and closes her eyes slightly as she thinks.

"That boy…he's done this before. I hate it when he gets into these moods and disappears when he gets upset." Says Tatyana.

Chloe looks at Tatyana intensely and says,

"He was at the party two nights ago, but did not want to come home afterwards."

"How? what?" Asks Tatyana.

"He snuck in, but I haven't heard from him in 2 days now," Chloe says.

Tatyana looks straight into Chloe's eyes. Tatyana becomes stoic and responds by saying,

"I will call him."

"I hope he answers you." Says Chloe.

"I hope so, too." Says Tatyana.

Anthony reaches up to give Tatyana a hug, saying,

"Get in there and get some rest, baby."

Tatyana reaches down, gives Anthony a sloppy kiss in the mouth, then hugs him as she looks straight at Chloe with a very stern, serious face.

"Good night," Says Anthony.

"Good night," Says Tatyana and begins to walk to her door.

"Bye!" Says Chloe, but Tatyana does not respond.

Anthony and Chloe watch as Tatyana staggers to her door, the butt cheeks of her pants have been cut off, and they can clearly see her skin out in the open. She fixes her pants around her crotch, then reaches down to get a good scratch. She wipes her forehead, turns around, and sees Anthony and Chloe looking at her. They hold up slices of pizza as a salute to her. Tatyana nods, slightly smiles, but struggles to get her door open.

"Need help?" Asks Anthony.

"I got it!" Says Tatyana, and finally unlocks her door.

Tatyana opens her door, almost falls, farts, then quickly enters her apartment and closes the door. Chloe puts her slice down and says,

"Dad, she's having sex with other people!"

Anthony puts his slice down on his napkin and says,

"No, Chloe, don't start now, you know how you get when…"

"Dad, I can tell, she's having sex with other people!" Says Chloe.

Anthony takes a deep breath, obviously upset because he has strong feelings for Tatyana, and gives Chloe the side eye. He is about to say something when Mrs. June comes back to the backyard holding a large glass mug in her hand.

"Sorry I took so long, I had to wash this one." Says Mrs. June as she approaches.

Mrs. June gets to the table, grabs the ladle, and begins to pour lemonade into it. She looks at Anthony and Chloe and says,

"Here's your lemonade, baby. What I miss ya'll?"

Anthony picks up his slice, and so does Chloe.

"Nothing." They both say at the same time.

 Mrs. June senses something is off, but she does not say anything, just sits down and hands Chloe her drink.

"Thank you." Says Chloe, Mrs. June smiles and nods.

Mrs. June sits down, looks at the two of them, and says,

"You have to stay together, fight for each other, listen to each other…it's the only way you're gonna make it."

"Did you hear our conversation?" Asks Anthony.

Mrs. June smiles and says,

"No, baby, that's just love talking to you."

The tension lifts, Chloe and Anthony smile at each other, and continue to eat.

Tatyana, dressed in a sweatsuit, sits in a large tour bus by a window, as she waits to depart on her wrestling tour. The bus is pretty full with other wrestlers, assistants, press, and staff also getting themselves situated as they talk and laugh. As people walk up and down the aisle of the bus, finding their seats, Tatyana fixes her hair using her phone camera as a mirror. She takes lipstick out of her pocket and begins to apply it, adjusts herself on the seat, and then begins to record a video of herself saying,

"Hi, Guys! I hope you're doing ok! I'm sorry I didn't have time to say goodbye; they moved up the departure date for the tour. They picked me up this morning when you guys were sleeping." She looks out the window and looks at the bus at the crew waiting to get in, and continues to say, "I'm heading to Texas right now, our first stop is Houston, then San Antonio, then Dallas. After Texas, we're heading to Louisiana, and we'll do a few stops there, some recreation halls. On the way back, we'll hit Oklahoma City, Albuquerque, New Mexico, and a few other spots. I'm sending you the list so you can come out and see me if you can I know you're busy. But just let me know when you're coming, give me a heads up. Anyways, I love you guys. Thank you for looking after Daniel!"

Tatyana smiles, hits the stop button, and puts her phone down on her lap. A young black man dressed in a blue suit approaches her from behind, leans into her seat, and says,

"Hey, I'm going to get some water. You want one?"

Tatyana looks at him and sees that he is blushing. She takes a good look at him, recognizes him, and says,

"I know you, don't I?" Asks Tatyana.

The young man smiles, opens his suit jacket, and sits down next to her. He extends his hand out to her and says,

"I was hoping you'd remember me." Says Bobby.

"The ballroom, yes, I remember. I got everything from you except your name that night." Tatyana says, smiling as she shakes his hand.

"Name's Bobby, I'm one of the promoters." Says Bobby.

"Hi Bobby, with the light brown eyes." Says Tatyana.

"You know, I had never been with a muscle girl before. I've been thinking about you ever since." Says Bobby as he puts his hand on her inner thigh and slowly begins to rub it.

Tatyana smiles at Bobby and says,

"I can already tell this is gonna be a good tour."

Later that day, inside a run-down grocery store, Anthony and Chloe are shopping for food. The overhead lighting is bad, there are numerous lamps that are out, and the place is unswept as pieces of cardboard boxes and swept garbage pile up at the end of some of the aisles. One of the workers, wearing a winter jacket and a hat, takes meat packages from a small grocery cart and stocks one of the open fridges.

Chloe looks through the ground beef and checks the dates, as Anthony sits on a motorized shopping cart as he watches Tatyana's video on his phone.

"…Thank you for watching after Daniel!" Says Tatyana on her video.

Anthony closes the video in disgust and puts his phone in his pocket.

"Have you seen that crap?" Asks Anthony.

"Tatyana's social video post from this morning?" Asks Chloe.

Anthony drives closer to the open fridge and starts moving the meat packages around in anger.

"Yeah! That video. I can't believe it, I'm her boyfriend and she just leaves me like that, she could have called me or texted me at least!"

Chloe looks at her dad and puts one of the packages of ground beef in his cart, saying,

"Dad, she's not your girlfriend, she's like, the neighborhood taxi, everybody gets a ride."

Anthony looks up at Chloe in disbelief and says,

"Stop."

"I saw her kissing another girl at that party!" Says Chloe as she goes to another fridge.

"Well, you know how those parties are, and if it happened, it was another girl; it's not the same." Says Anthony.

Chloe comes back to the cart with a package of frozen potatoes and says,

"Dad, I told you, there's a lot that she's hiding about her personal life, and it's dark! I can feel it! She said Thank you for taking care of Daniel? No one has seen Daniel in days, and she just leaves anyway? Not knowing where her son is?"

Anthony takes the potatoes from Chloe's hands and nods his head as Chloe looks at him with raised eyebrows, then turns away and walks down the aisle.

"Well, we have her itinerary here, so when Daniel comes back, maybe we can go see her in another state! That would make a nice road trip, right?"

Chloe turns around again and says,

"I'm not going anywhere to see her, and I'm sure Daniel does not want to see her either."

Four Weeks Later

Jose pushes Anthony in his wheelchair, down a very large, well-illuminated hallway inside Tingley Coliseum in New Mexico. Anthony looks through his phone at a montage of videos on Tatyana's social media account. He sees in one video Tatyana getting off the tour bus late at night in a city, she smiles into the camera as the other wrestlers walk by and give her a kiss on the cheek. Another video shows Tatyana in the ring, throwing another wrestler into the ropes and screaming in a rage. Another video shows Tatyana drinking and partying at a bar, followed by a video of her climbing the ropes of a ring and then jumping on top of a wrestler.

"You've looked at those a thousand times, man…" Says Jose.

Anthony looks up and stares at posters of wrestlers and past events on the walls of the hallway. The place seems deserted at the moment; there's no one around. He carefully counts the numbers on the doors on both sides, then slowly looks back at Jose and says,

"I know, all I've gotten from her is a few text messages saying she misses me, she doesn't answer my calls, so… here we are, ha, ha."

The guys slow down as they get to one of the doors. Jose pats Anthony on the shoulder and says,

"You sure this is a good idea? You should have told her you were coming."

Anthony puts both of his hands on the handlebars of the wheelchair and says,

"Yes! Yes, it is a good idea. I haven't seen my girl for weeks now. And thank you for helping your friend out, because I couldn't do this by myself. So, thank you for letting me ride with you, Jose."

Jose shakes his head and replies,

"Well, good thing I had to deliver that shipment to Albuquerque, otherwise I would have said no. Man, I'm still saying no, you can't just drop in on someone like this. Give her a call at least, let her know you're coming to see her."

Anthony ignores Jose as he continues to count the numbers on the doors and says,

"It was a good match tonight, ugh?"

"She kicked some serious ass, I'll tell you. Those guys got their asses handed to them, ha!" Says Jose.

Anthony points to a door a few feet away and says,

"This is it, this is it!"

There is a computer printout with Tatyana's picture taped onto the door, and a badly handwritten title on top of the printout reads,

Dragon Lady's Dressing Room

Jose looks at the door and says,

"Yup, that's definitely her. You know, I liked the name *Muerte Rusa* much better for her…I mean, Dragon Lady? What is that!"

Anthony gets excited and gets fidgety in the wheelchair, saying,

"Ok, ok, ok. Never mind that, let me get the flowers."

Jose takes a bouquet of flowers out of a bag hanging from the back of the wheelchair and hands it to Anthony. Anthony quickly grabs the flowers and wheels himself forward towards the door, and gives it a knock. Nothing…he knocks again. Nothing.

"Maybe she's not here, man." Says Jose.

Anthony knocks again and says,

"No, she's here, all the security guards at the entrance said they saw her come in about an hour ago after the match, and she never left."

Anthony knocks again, and after a minute, he reaches for the handle and turns it. The door is unlocked, and it opens wide. Anthony looks up at Jose, smiling, but Jose shakes his head and simply says,

"No."

"Yes, yes, this is going to be great, she's gonna be so happy!" Says Anthony, smiling.

Jose lets go of the wheelchair and holds up his hands as if surrendering to Anthony's will. Anthony slowly wheels himself into the threshold of the dressing room, saying,

"Just wait here for me, ok?"

"Oh, I will. Trust me." Says Jose.

Anthony enters the dressing room and looks around the dimly lit room. Trance music plays loudly out of a speaker on a small corner table in one of the corners of the filthy room. The dressing room is large, filled with suitcases and bags resting on chairs, and loveseats loaded with clothing. The place is littered with water bottles, food remains, and garbage that is scattered everywhere.

"Tatyana!" Anthony says loudly, but there is no reply.

With the flowers on his lap, Anthony slowly maneuvers his wheelchair through the room. He's looking at the many bottles of booze scattered throughout the room, ashtrays overflowing with cigarette buds, and a large coffee table with prepared lines of coke, a large bag of weed that spilled over onto a small bag of meth rocks, and several used pipes.

"What the fu…" Anthony begins to say, but is interrupted by a loud noise.

He hears the loud bang again coming from behind a closed door at the end of the room.

"Tatyana, is that you?" Asks Anthony, but again, there is no reply.

Anthony moves his wheelchair to the closed door and hears more music inside, along with moaning and grunting. He slowly reaches for the doorknob, his hand trembling. He then slowly opens it and pushes it open. To his surprise, he finds Tatyana having sex, sandwiched between two large muscular wrestlers.

Anthony's mouth drops as he looks at the animalistic scene. Tatyana looks up and sees Anthony, but does not recognize him. The woman is drugged out of her mind, her eyes are completely bloodshot, with deep dark rings around them, and so puffy she can hardly open them; her countenance is changed, she does not look like herself at all.

"Who the fuck is this cripple! How'd you get in here!" she says.

The two guys look up and laugh.

"Get out of here!" yells Tatyana.

She passionately kisses the guy below her, then turns around and kisses the guy above her, completely forgetting that Anthony is there watching as his heart breaks.

"I gotta get out of here," Anthony whispers to himself.

As Anthony slowly backs his wheelchair up, he rolls over a plastic cup on the floor. Tatyana slowly opens her eyes again and screams,

"You're still here, loser? Get the hell out of here, cripple! Go on, get out!"

The two guys laugh at Anthony as he drops the flowers onto the floor and rolls backwards into the previous room. He watches one of the guys put coke on his index finger, kisses Tatyana, and brings it up for her to inhale.

Anthony can't take much more of it; he quickly makes his way past the dressing room and back out to the hallway with his head down. Jose helps him maneuver through the threshold, then closes the dressing room door.

"I'm not gonna say I told you so." Says Jose.

"Then don't." Says Anthony.

"Let's get some food." Says Jose as he pats his friend on the shoulder.

Chapter 15: The Dragon's Fire

The Borgia residence, it's late in the evening, and Chloe sits at the kitchen table staring at her dirty dinner plate. She takes a deep breath, stands up, grabs the plate, and her dad's on the other side of the table, and brings them to the kitchen sink. Deep in thought, and under the fluorescent light of the kitchen, Chloe turns the handle on the faucet, breaking the complete silence of the room. She looks out the kitchen window towards Tatyana's apartment, and the lights are on.

"Daniel?" Whispers Chloe as she turns the water off.

Chloe runs to the back kitchen door, quickly opens it to take a closer look. The lights turn off in the apartment, and Tatyana comes out, closes the door, and begins to walk towards the driveway. She has not spotted Chloe. Chloe watches as Tatyana continues to walk towards the driveway, and as she's about to leave the backyard, Chloe says loudly,

"Hey! You were not gonna tell us you were back?"

Tatyana suddenly stops and looks over at Chloe, with a surprised look. Tatyana smiles and laughs nervously.

"Oh, Hey Chloe! Yeah, I was going to put something in my car real quick, and then I was coming up to see you guys!"

Tatyana smiles and begins to walk towards the house. Chloe, with disgust, watches her approach and enter the house. Tatyana comes into the kitchen and closes the door behind her. Chloe takes a good look at Tatyana, now in the light, and sees she is dressed in a beautiful designer red shirt, with silk black pants, and very expensive pumps.

"You're looking good, looks like you're making pretty good money now." Says Chloe.

Tatyana smiles and says,

"Yeah, got rid of that black truck too, I got a brand new Benz up front."

Chloe looks at her without showing any reaction. She moves her long curls from her face and says,

"It's been six weeks…"

"I know." Says Tatyana as she takes a few steps closer to Chloe, looking her up and down.

"You know… You get used to someone being around, you love them, care for them, and they say they love you, but then they're gone." Says Chloe.

Tatyana walks a little bit closer to Chloe and says,

"Well, I've missed you guys, especially you, Chloe."

Chloe looks down at the floor, so deep in her thoughts that she does not realize that Tatyana reached out and is now caressing her shoulder with her hand.

"Daniel is gone, and you've been gone for so long. We've hardly heard from you, just a few texts here and there. I mean, you and my dad are you guys still…" Says Chloe.

"I don't think so, I haven't talked to him yet, but I think he's moved on, at least it feels that way." Says Tatyana.

Tatyana traces her index finger from Chloe's belly to the bottom of her chin, saying,

"We never talked about that night at the party. I know you saw me with that other girl on the balcony."

Chloe looks up at Tatyana, a bit perplexed, and says,

"Wait, I think you're misunderstanding what I'm trying to say…"

Before she can get another word out, Tatyana grabs her by the back of the head, leans in, and forcibly kisses Chloe in the mouth and pushes her other hand down the back of her skirt. Chloe tries to pull her head away, but she just can't, so she drops to the floor and breaks away from Tatyana before she can get a better hold.

"What are you doing! I don't like you like that!"

Chloe pushes Tatyana back on her shoulders, saying,

"What the hell was that! I was talking about Daniel!
Not you! We haven't seen Daniel or heard from him
in over six weeks! Where is he?!"

Tatyana takes a step back, realizing she's made a big
mistake. She puts her hand up to her forehead and says,

"What! Fuck I don't know! I've called that little shit
over and over. I've filed out a missing person's
report with the police and have heard nothing yet. I
was hoping he would show up here at one point!"

Tatyana looks closely at Chloe and says,

"But getting back to us, you do like me, don't you?"

"No! There is no us…I don't like you like that."
Says Chloe.

Tatyana licks her lower lip, then says,

"Yes, you do, you like me. I'm never wrong about
this stuff."

Chloe quickly walks to one of the upper cabinets in the
kitchen and pulls out a large envelope, walks over to
Tatyana, and hands it to her, saying,

"I don't like you. And I almost forgot, here!"

"What's this?" Tatyana says as she takes it.

"The truth." Says Chloe.

Tatyana opens the envelope and pulls out surveillance
pictures of herself. The first picture shows Tatyana letting
Mrs. June's cat into her house, and then another picture

shows her bringing out the cat in a bag. In another picture, Tatyana, in Mrs. June's front yard, is throwing a rock through her car window. The next picture shows Tatyana pouring lighter fluid into the back seat of Mrs. June's car, the next picture shows her throwing a match into the car, and the last one shows Tatyana running away, as the car goes up in flames.

Tatyana looks at Chloe without saying a word. Chloe takes the pictures from her hand and says,

> "I know it was you who stole my dad's checkbook; you gave it to your DJ buddy, didn't you. Police got him on video making all those crazy purchases. I know my dad, if you needed money, he would have helped you out; he was in love with you!"

Tatyana's face begins to turn red with anger, and she bites her lower lip as she begins to squint her eyes.

> "I just want to know why! We've only done you good, so why?" Asks Chloe.

Out of nowhere, Tatyana slaps Chloe on the face so hard that Chloe falls to the floor, hitting her mouth on the countertop as she falls.

> "I don't have to explain myself to you! Who the fuck do you think you are!! Yells Tatyana.

Chloe slowly stands up with a bloody lip, points to the door, and says,

> "GET OUT!"

Tatyana grabs Chloe's t-shirt and rips it from the collar.

"Make me." Tatyana challenges her.

Chloe looks down at her exposed sports bra, looks back up at Tatyana, and says,

"No, you need to leave!"

"No one tells me what to do." Says Tatyana.

Tatyana pushes Chloe really hard; she stumbles backwards and knocks over a scented candle, and it rolls to the window.

"I'm gonna get everything I want from you." Says Tatyana as the curtain catches fire from the candle that fell.

Tatyana slaps Chloe on the other cheek. Chloe falls to the floor again. Chloe looks up at Tatyana with fear, quickly gets up, runs to a kitchen drawer, and pulls out a steak knife.

"Get away from me!" Says Chloe.

Tatyana kicks it out of her hand and laughs out loud, amused at the measly attempt.

The fire spreads from the curtain to the upper kitchen cabinets.

Chloe tries to run out into the living room, but Tatyana quickly grabs her and throws her back into the kitchen, launching her into the air. Chloe lands on the opposite kitchen wall, hitting her head first on the wall, then the floor. Tatyana quickly makes her way to Chloe, saying,

"You think you can threaten me? Put me in a corner with some fucking pictures?"

Tatyana picks Chloe up by the neck, plants a long kiss on her mouth, then punches Chloe square in the jaw.

"Fuck you!" Says Tatyana as Chloe cries.

Tatyana punches Chloe right in the stomach again, Chloe spits out blood.

"Let her go! NOW!" Says Anthony from behind.

Tatyana turns around, still holding Chloe up in the air, and sees Anthony in his wheelchair in the living room, looking straight at her.

The fire spreads up the wall of the kitchen, and smoke begins to gather on the ceiling. The fire alarm suddenly goes off.

BEEP, BEEP, BEEP, BEEP

"Fuck you gonna do?" Says Tatyana condescendingly.

The fire begins to spread onto the ceiling of the kitchen.

"Tatyana, please let her go!" Says Anthony.

Tatyana takes Chloe from being up against the wall and dangles her in front of Anthony like a rag doll, shaking her profusely.

"AAAH, LET ME GOOO!" Chloe screams.

"Or what! Anthony…What the fuck can you do to me! WHAT?" Tatyana screams.

Anthony reaches under his lap, pulls out a gun, and holds it up to Tatyana.

"Just let her go!" Says Anthony.

Tatyana is completely enraged now. She walks into the living room, dragging Chloe, and then throws her down onto the living room floor. Anthony looks at the amount of smoke that's gathering as it begins to pour into the living room. The kitchen is now almost completely in flames.

"We need to get out of here!" Says Anthony.

Anthony looks over at Chloe as she lies on the floor unconscious, forgetting Tatyana for a moment.

"Chloe?" Says Anthony.

Flames begin to lick the threshold of the living room door that goes to the kitchen.

BANG!

Tatyana punches Anhtony right in the nose and catches him completely unawares. Anthony falls backwards, chair and all. Tatyana walks around the wheelchair, crouches down, and punches Anthony again, and again, saying,

> "No one is getting out of here! You thought you could drag me back to jail! I'm dragging you both to hell with me!" Says Tatyana.

Tatyana picks Anthony up over her head and body slams him on top of his coffee table. The glass table bursts into a million pieces, and Anthony screams in agony.

"I'm done with people ganging up on me! I just
wanted to live my life!" Says Tatyana as she picks
Anthony back up and body slams him again.

"I just wanted to wrestle, fuck, get high, and wrestle
some more!" Tatyana says as she leans down and
punches Anthony in the mouth, then continues to
say, "But NO!"

Anthony looks over at Chloe, and she's regaining
consciousness.

The wall of the living room facing the kitchen is beginning
to smoke, and large flames protrude out of the kitchen and
into the living room.

"So since I can't live my life the way I want, maybe
I'll have some say in how I die!" Says Tatyana.

Chloe stands up slowly, her face covered in blood. She sees
Tatyana standing over her father. She looks over at the
kitchen, it's engulfed in smoke and fire. At the threshold of
the doorway, she spots the knife she held up against
Tatyana resting under the door. Chloe runs to it and quickly
grabs it, avoiding the flames coming out of the kitchen.

Chloe runs towards Tatyana, and just as she leans down to
grab Anthony again, Chloe stabs Tatyana in the back.
Tatyana quickly jumps up and screams,

"AAAAAH, you bitch!"

Tatyana tries to reach for the knife, but she's so muscular,
she can't reach it. As Tatyana continues to try and get the

knife out, she stumbles around the room. Chloe goes to her dad and tries to pull him towards the front door.

"Go get help!" Says Anthony.

"I'm not leaving you!" Says Chloe as she falls to her knees, struggling to drag her dad.

Anthony reaches for Chloe's arm and says,

"Go get help, baby! GO, I'll be right behind you!"

Tatyana sees the exchange from across the room and runs towards them.

The living room wall opposite the kitchen is now on fire.

"GO NOW!" Says Anthony as he sees Tatyana coming towards them.

Chloe turns around, sees Tatyana coming, and runs out the front door, leaving it open. Tatyana reaches Anthony, who is still on the floor, and she sees Chloe running down the steps, then toward Mrs. June's house. Tatyana spits out the door, looks down at Anthony, smiles, and picks him up by his shirt. Anthony tries to pull away, but she's too strong for him.

The living room ceiling is now on fire, and it begins to reach another living room wall.

Anthony punches Tatyana in the face, but she just smiles and shakes her head.

"I always knew you had a pair of balls, Anthony, that's why I liked fucking you."

"But I got bigger balls than you!" Says Tatyana.

She punches Anthony really hard in the stomach, knocking his wind out. She head-buts him in the nose, causing him to bleed.

"Bring him outside! Get out of here now!" Says a police officer.

Tatyana looks outside the door and sees a cop calling out to her from the front yard.

"The whole place is going up in flames! Come on!" Says the officer.

Tatyana watches as more police cars begin to park in front of the house, and she gets more and more enraged. Fire from the ceiling licked the top of her head, and her hair goes up in flames.

"Get out of here now, or we're coming in and dragging you out!" Says one of the cops.

In the heat of the moment, one of the officers deploys his taser, but it does nothing to Tatyana. She looks down at the probes on her chest, drops Anthony on the living room floor, and runs out towards the cop, her head and blouse completely ablaze.

"AAAAAAAHHHH!" Tatyana screams as she runs out the door and lunges at the cop.

The officer is taken by surprise and falls backward as Tatyana straddles him and begins to punch him in the face, her head and back completely ablaze. Another officer deploys her taser, but it just ignites the fire on her head and back even more. As Tatyana continues to punch the cop underneath her, another officer comes up from behind, surprises her, and hits her on the side of her face with a baton, knocking her over on her side. Tatyana looks up at him for a second and tries to stand up, still on fire. More officers come, and they all begin to hit her with batons while another uses a fire extinguisher to put her out. They continue to hit her unmercifully until she is completely knocked out.

Chloe, standing beside Mrs. June, points to her front door and yells out,

"My dad's still in there!"

"Where, inside the house?" Asks one officer.

"I think I see him, maybe we can go get him real quick!" Says another officer.

Suddenly, Chloe runs past them and into the house. She walks into an unrecognizable burning room, and as she looks around, she finds her dad on the floor, trying to crawl to the door. The whole living room is up in flames. Chloe runs to her dad, reaches down, but struggles to move him. She keeps falling over as she coughs. Suddenly, two cops run up behind her, pick Anthony up quickly, and bring him outside with Chloe running behind them. They head over to Ms. June's yard, she puts some blankets down for them, and they lay Anthony on the ground.

"Thank God you got out of there!" Mrs. June says as she looks at their crumbling house.

The house is completely ablaze, a fire truck finally arrives, and firemen spring into action. Several ambulances begin to arrive at the scene as well. The medics come out, a few go and see Tatyana, now awake, but still on the ground, is surrounded by police. Several cops quickly come to see Chloe and Anthony.

As they put Anthony on a gurney, they all watch as the cops walk Tatyana, with a smoking, burnt head, being walked to the back of an ambulance, her hands and feet in steel restraints. Tatyana turns to look at Chloe and Anthony and gives them a furious glare of hatred. The roof of the house collapses, exposing a raging fire inside the shell of the house.

The next day, at the local jail, Tatyana is walked into the back of the jailhouse wearing pajamas. Part of her head is burnt, and her face is swollen and bruised from the beating the cops gave her the previous night. The four officers escort and push her along the long corridor. When they finally get to the last cell, they open the door and push her in. Tatyana looks around, and it's loaded with men; it looks like a gang of bikers, at least twenty of them. The cell door locks, and she quickly turns around and says to the officers,

> "Hey, I'm in the wrong cell, these are all men!"

> "Sorry, no room with the ladies right now. You'll have to hang out with the hounds of hell, at least that's what they call themselves," says one officer.

> "I don't think this is legal!" Says Tatyana.

"It's just a few hours until they come and take you to county. You're a big girl, I'm sure you'll be fine!" Says another officer.

Another officer looks at all of the men in there and says,

"This bitch likes to beat up men, thinks she can do whatever she wants to guys like you."

All of the bikers sitting down quickly stand up and begin to slowly walk towards Tatyana. The officers walk back up the hallway, open the large metal door, and walk out. Tatyana turns around and sees that the large men surround her; everyone's looking at her.

"Look, I had a bad night, I don't want to hurt anyone." Says Tatyana.

BAM!

Tatyana gets punched in the face. She tries to grab one of the men, but they grab her legs and she falls to the floor. They all pile up on her and begin to punch and kick her repeatedly. One of them takes his shirt off and says,

"Here, tie her up with this! Hold her down!"

"You're gonna learn some manners bitch! Says another.

The men repeatedly punch and kick her as she is held down.

"Help! HELP!" Tatyana screams.

One of the men kicks her in the head and completely confounds her. Tatyana tries to move, but there are too many guys holding her down. The man kicks her again in the head even harder, and she goes unconscious.

County jail, Tatyana is in the showers with a lot of other women. The place is big with multiple shower heads spread throughout the large room. Tatyana stands alone to the side, rinsing herself off; burn marks cover part of her back and shoulders. Her long blonde hair is gone, and she's bald with large sections of her head, back, and shoulders showing healing burn marks. Though her musculature has softened a bit, she is still very big and intimidating to approach, standing at least a foot higher than every other woman in there. A short Mexican woman covered in tattoos, dressed in an orange jumpsuit, walks up to her and stands behind her. Tatyana senses her. She wipes the suds off her face, turns around, and says,

"What! What do you want!"

The chola smiles and asks,

"You're the wrestler, right?"

"Yeah, what's it to ya?" Tatyana answers as she looks at the woman up and down.

Unsuspectingly, two of the women who were showering close to her quickly walk up behind Tatyana, and while she's being distracted, and shank her multiple times on her back and sides. Tatyana quickly turns to face them, her back now opened up with multiple stab wounds, blood

sprays outward and pours down her body onto the wet
shower floor. As the women step back, Tatyana gets
shanked in the upper back again by the woman dressed in
orange. Tatyana gets lightheaded and falls to the wet floor,
and they all jump on her and stab her repeatedly all over
her midsection, leaving Tatyana in a pool of blood. The
short woman leans forward, spits on Tatyana's face, and
says,

> "That's what you get for fucking my husband and
> son at the same time in Albuquerque bitch! I killed
> them, and now I killed you! I hope you go straight
> to hell!"

The attackers run away, and as they get to the door leading
out to the hallway, one of them hands a small bag of meth
to the guard at the door. The rest of the women in the
shower area begin to gather around Tatyana, as she lies in a
large pool of blood on the shower floor. Rivers of her blood
run into several drains. The girls call for help, but nobody
seems to be coming. The guard just stands there as if
nothing is happening; she just stares at the chaotic scene
from a distance.

At the same exact moment, on the other side of the state,
Chloe makes her way through one of the dorm lobbies at
Arizona State University. The place is packed with
students, parents, suitcases, and boxes; everyone seems to
be going somewhere. There are *Welcome Freshmen* signs
everywhere, with balloons and people handing out candy
and popcorn. Faculty and staff welcome students as they

enter the lobby and escort them to a welcoming center set up at the end of the grand entrance.

Chloe and Anthony smile and walk to the desk set up in the back of the large room.

"Hi, my name is Sandy, can I have your name, sweetie?" Says Sandy behind the desk.

"Chloe, Chloe Borgia." Says Chloe.

Sandy types the information into her computer and says,

"Ah, yes! Ms. Borgia, welcome to ASU! This is yours."

Sandy hands Chloe a welcoming bag with pamphlets and welcoming gifts.

"And here is your room key. Inside the bag, you'll find some great information about our campus, the eateries, facilities, etc., etc. ha, ha."

"Thank you so much! Says Chloe as she takes the bag and peeks inside.

"I think you are good to go upstairs, so feel free to reach out to me anytime. Again, I'm Sandy, my extension is 102, okay?" Says Sandy.

"I think I'm good, thank you, Sandy!" Says Chloe.

"You're welcome, honey!" Says Sandy with a smile.

Chloe and her father step away from the desk and make their way to the elevators with all of Chloe's luggage.

Chloe looks around, a bit nervous as she sees so many people coming and going, and the reality of what's happening is beginning to settle in. Anthony looks at her and says,

> "It's okay to be nervous, and even scared. I know it's a bit overwhelming right now, but you'll be okay. You got this!"

Chloe is about to say something to her dad when suddenly her mouth drops, her eyes widen, and she holds her hand up to her mouth. Anthony turns around to see what she's looking at and sees Mrs. June and Daniel walking in the door. Daniel sees Chloe wave and runs to her. Chloe drops her bags and runs towards Daniel. They meet halfway and hug in the middle of the room. They hold each other for a few minutes as Anthony and Mrs. June make their way towards them. Chloe finally pulls away with tears in her eyes and slaps Daniel's shoulder, saying,

> "I thought you were dead! Where have you been!"

> "Right after that night at the party, once I knew you were home safe, I walked all the way down to the Greyhound station in the city. I…I like I needed to just get away from everything. I called my grandmother and asked her to send me money to get a ticket to come see her. I'm sorry I didn't tell you, I just needed to get away from everyone, from everything. I needed to stay away from my mom, really. I just did not know how to deal with anything here." Daniel explains.

“I’m so glad you’re here.” Says Chloe as she reaches out and gives Daniel a hug, and continues, “ So you’re with your grandma?”

 “Yeah, I’ve been living with my grandma. I reached out to Mrs. June about a week ago, and she told me how concerned you were about me and how much you guys thought and talked about me. When she told me you were going to be going to college, I knew I wanted to be there. I figured this would be a nice surprise.” Says Daniel’s.

“You know what happened to your mom?” Asked Anthony.

“She’s dead to me, I don’t want to talk about her.” Says Daniel as he shakes his head.

“We understand, honey, just remember to forgive, ok?” Says Mrs. June as she pats him on the shoulder

Anthony opens his arms and gives Daniel a hug, saying,

“You’re welcome to stay with us anytime, Daniel, just glad you’re safe.”

“Oh, I’m getting some of this love!” Say Mrs.. June, as she hugs them both.

“I love you guys so much!” Says Chloe as she tears up and hugs them all.

After a few moments, Daniel says loudly,

“C’mon, let's get you situated, sis!”

They all let go of each other, and Daniel grabs some of
Chloe's luggage, Anthony grabs the rest, and says,

"You coming, Mrs. June?"

Mrs. June reaches for Chloe and gives her a kiss on the
cheek, saying,

"I'm going to stay here and wait for you guys. I just
need to rest for a bit. Chloe, I love you! You call me
if you need anything, okay?"

"I will, Mrs. June, I promise!" Says Chloe.

Chloe, Daniel, and Anthony walk away towards the
elevator area, away from the welcoming center. Mrs. June
sees a chair next to a large window facing the campus and
walks towards it and sits down. She watches as students
continue to enter the lobby, parents helping them bring
things in, and the staff guiding them. Mrs. June watches as
a few children chase each other and play as they run in and
out of the crowds, moving about. They make their way
towards her, and when they do, they all stop and look at
her. There are six of them, and they all stand in front of
Mrs. June in a half circle

"Hello." Says a little girl.

"Hi there." Says Mrs. June, smiling.

One of the boys pushes the little girl, and she falls to her
knees. Mrs. June extends her hand, and the little girl runs to
her and hugs her. Mrs. June looks at the children and says,

"Listen closely, ya'll have to be nice to each other,
love each other. Because this world is filled with

evil, it's all around you. This world is filled with plenty of people and things that want to hurt you. But there is good in this world. Jesus came to this world and gave us two commandments: love God, and love each other. And this is so you can have a chance at eternal life. He died on a cross for that reason. He is the good in this world, so believe in Him. What you do, the decisions you make, like pushing this little girl, for example, will determine where you will spend eternity, heaven or hell. So choose the good, not the evil. Choose to believe in Him, and trust Him, and live a good life. You need to be kind and forgiving."

One of the parents had walked up while Mrs. June was speaking, and while standing behind his son, says,

"This is the most still I've seen these kids today. Thank you… Are you a preacher or something?"

Mrs. June looks up at him and gives him a big smile.

The End

Want to Read More?